MW01676965

THE STORM WITHIN

GILL D. ANDERSON

The Storm Within © Gill D. Anderson 2025

ISBN: 978-1-923277-71-7 (paperback)

All rights reserved. No part of this publication may be reproduced, stored in a retrieval system, or transmitted in any form or by any means electronic, mechanical, photocopying, recording, or otherwise, without the prior written permission of the author.

Published in Australia by Gill D. Anderson and InHouse Publishing.
www.inhousepublishing.com.au

Printed in Australia by InHouse Print & Design.

IN HOUSE PTY LTD PUBLISHING

NATIONAL LIBRARY OF AUSTRALIA

A catalogue record for this book is available from the National Library of Australia

Dear readers

Please note that I write novels that often have confronting themes that tap into the psychology of deviant human behaviour. There are references to infidelity, domestic violence, childhood trauma, sex, betrayal, greed and envy. If these are themes that trigger or offend you, please do not read on. According to many of my book reviews, my strength is creating larger than life characters who are often not who they seem to be initially. I tend to peel back the layers of my characters until their true selves are revealed!

The Storm Within was inspired by a Mediterranean cruise we were on for my husband's 50th birthday. As usual my imagination went into overdrive as I observed other passengers and their interactions with each other. I began to cook up ideas about what might be going on behind their cabin doors!

I do hope you enjoy the book – I love hearing from readers and am endlessly grateful to those who leave reviews on Goodreads, Amazon, Bookbub and InHouse Bookstore (inhousebookstore.com.au). I also love receiving book photos from readers, particularly holiday snaps.

Reading a book while on a trip is one of my absolute favourite things to do. It's so indulgent to have nowhere to be and have endless time to read!

Happy reading,
Best wishes from Gill

This book is dedicated to Brent, my rock,
my true love and my travel partner.
May we experience many more cruises together.

Love always Gill x

Prologue

Golden light spilled across the balcony, illuminating the young woman as she leaned over the railing, her eyes lost in the rhythmic dance of the waves below. The sun glimmered on the water like a thousand scattered diamonds, and she inhaled deeply, savouring the intoxicating scent of the sea.

Floating in the middle of the ocean was magical; it gave one a sense of being completely carefree. She stood up tall and stretched her hands above her head, her chest puffed out as she thought smugly about her conquests on the cruise ship so far. She was in the prime of her life; she was young, beautiful, and well on her way to being stinking rich.

'Just a little longer,' she whispered to herself, envisioning the life that lay ahead, laced with luxury and ease. Hopefully, she could play the long game and create enough wealth to cease the immoral lifestyle she was currently embroiled in. Not that she had any remorse or any sign of a guilty conscience; it was more that she wanted to get to a point where she could choose men based on genuine attraction rather than merely focusing on what they could provide financially. She had no qualms about using and abusing others; after all, it was what her foster parents had role-modelled to her for many years. It shocked her how ridiculously easy it was to manipulate men to her advantage. The majority thought with their nether regions, and anyone who argued otherwise was a complete moron, as far as she was concerned.

As her thoughts swirled pleasurably, she became lost in the magic of her sea voyage. She was completely oblivious when the door to her cabin creaked open. The intruder was stealthy, slipping inside with a stolen cabin attendant's pass. The young woman absorbed in her daydreams, did not notice the figure until it was too late.

A strong arm wrapped around her waist and a hand covered her mouth. Panic gripped her. Her heart raced as a rag soaked in an overpowering chemical muffled her scream. She frantically lashed out. Adrenaline rushed through her veins as the metallic taste of fear filled her mouth. Everything she had done to hurt others replayed in a cruel montage, and an unexpected tide of guilt crashed over her. For some reason she thought of her foster father's words: *People are only sorry when their life is at stake…*

She struggled feebly against her captor, her mind racing, but her limbs quickly became uncooperative, as the chemical began slowing down her thoughts. In a fleeting moment, her assailant spun her around, so they were face to face. As their eyes locked, she felt a surge of recognition. Those amber eyes… familiar and fierce, were filled with a mixture of rage and determination. A chill seeped into her bones as realisation dawned on her. She saw a bronze statue bear down on her in slow motion as it struck her hard in the face. Her limbs became leaden and in her final moments of consciousness, she recognised her attacker despite the ill-fitting home-made balaclava. Then her world faded to black.

When she became semi-conscious, a sense of numbness had seeped into her body, chilling her to the bone. She tried to move, and realised her limbs were horribly twisted. Panic clawed at her throat as she realised she'd lost a lot of blood. Her hands and feet were bound tight, and a dull throb in her face and body were a painful reminder of the multiple blows she'd received. She knew in her heart that she was about to die in this cold, dark space. *It's true, your life really does flash before your eyes…*

The realisation that the end was near brought a fresh wave of despair crashing over her. Faces of the victims of her deceitful ways danced through her mind like phantoms; every lie, every deceitful sexual encounter, every man and woman affected by her irresistible charms. Hot tears sprang from her eyes, stinging the deep lacerations on her face. With each passing second, she felt her hands become stiff claws as her blood drained from them in a bid to flow towards her vital organs. She realised with sickening clarity that she was not merely a victim of circumstance, but the creator of her own demise.

As she lay on the balcony, she could hear a storm brewing. Distant thunder rumbled and she felt the storm within her more acutely. Was it a storm of guilt? Regret? She squirmed as she desperately tried to recall more about the intruder. As her body began to twitch, the icy grip of despair became her only focus as her breaths started to come out in shallow rasps.

As her eyelids fluttered, the thunder boomed, reaching a deafening crescendo. In her final moments, her heart felt crushed by the weight of realisation: the storm outside would pass, yet the storm within her had left her battered and broken, lost to the void forever. With one last shuddering breath, she succumbed to the inevitable. Desperation echoed in the silence, drowned out by the storm that buried her story along with the memories of her conquests.

Chapter 1

As the recently appointed Cruise Director of the luxury *Ocean Breeze* ship, Jake Bateman thrived in the high-energy environment. The expensive cut of his fitted navy suit was a testament to his meticulous attention to detail. Jake had been carefully selected for the Cruise Director position due his impressive resume. During his interview Jake had confidently showcased his various talents. Jake was a sought-after event planner and a semi famous radio presenter in London. His Bachelor of Business (Tourism, Events and Hospitality) had led him to places beyond his wildest dreams thanks to his personal drive and determination.

Jake's mum often teased him because he looked and sounded so smooth; he had a way of appearing unruffled even during the most stressful situations. Jake was aware he turned heads and gathered a rapt audience wherever he went. Due to his immaculate grooming, the female passengers often clucked over his appearance throughout the cruise. Naturally, it helped that Jake's well-tailored clothes hugged his body in all the right places.

Jake was duly warned about how much stamina the Cruise Director role required. He worked relentlessly from early morning when they docked in a new port through to after-hours parties that lasted close to dawn. Now on his second circuit of the Mediterranean cruise, Jake began to feel more like a pro.

The *Ocean Breeze* set sail in Barcelona and docked at Cannes, Florence, Pisa, Rome, Naples, Cagliari, Palma and Ibiza. A typical day for Jake while at sea meant working up to 16 hours, and he would be away from his family for months at a time. Thankfully the perk was that he could have a little down time at each of the stunning ports the ship docked at. He knew this was not a forever job, however as he was a 30-year-old single man, it meant he could give it his all for the time being. Jake sought perfection from himself and from his staff and was well respected for it. Or at least he hoped that was the case.

Jake ran a hand through his carefully styled dirty blonde hair, exuding the confidence of someone who had conquered many challenges before. Yet beneath the calm exterior, a storm brewed. The tension crackled in the air like static electricity when his gaze drifted to Vincent Laidlaw, the newly appointed Assistant Cruise Director (ACD).

Vincent had been openly sour about Jake winning the coveted Cruise Director position since they set sail. Instead of being happy to win the ACD position, which was also a great achievement, Vincent remained pissed off at not getting the role he believed to be rightfully his. Vincent's issues with Jake ran much deeper than that, however.

Vincent was not only jealous of Jake's career but also of his looks, his easy charm and his way with women. Even though Jake was fixated on his current lover Claire Davidson, Vincent still resented that the women onboard rarely gave *him* a second glance. Why would they when all eyes were firmly fixed on Jake? Even though Vincent had a wife back home, it clearly wasn't enough for him.

Jake leaned back in his chair, a stack of itineraries, cruise excursions and event fliers spread out like a colourful tapestry before him in the boardroom. The hum of the ship's engines vibrated beneath his feet, a constant reminder of the world outside this manic space. Around him, his staff busily typed on iPads, as they prepared for the whirlwind of activities planned for the day. He glanced at his watch; a long day stretched ahead, filled with a flurry of tasks that would keep him on the go from sunrise to sunset.

Later on, as the sun dipped beneath the horizon, soaking the ocean in hues of orange and pink, Jake found solace on the upper deck savouring a rare moment of solitude. It was finally the end of a long day. He glanced down at the bustling activities below and grinned. The cruise was going smoothly so far, and the passengers appeared excited about the excursions on offer, the fine dining options, and the theatre shows. The gentle lapping of waves certainly provided a stark contrast to the chaos of his office. He inhaled the salty air, hoping to wash away the remnants of the day's tension.

The grin suddenly fell from Jake's face, a sense of unease bubbled to the surface as he thought about Vincent's hostile jibe earlier. Jake looked out to the sea and sky which had merged into an inky black hue. He focused on being grateful that the formal dinner had gone well tonight despite the earlier tensions. As Jake walked back to his cabin to finally turn in for the night, he decided that after the gala later in the week, he would finally have the capacity to deal with Vincent's jealousy once and for all.

Jake reflected on the scene in the boardroom that morning. He had meticulously assigned roles and delegated tasks for the day's events to various staff members. He'd observed Vincent, slouched in his chair, arms crossed tightly over his chest. Vincent's expression was a mixture of disdain and forced submission. The atmosphere was thick with tension, and the rest of the staff felt it too as they glanced apprehensively between the pair. As he breathed in the salty night air, Jake went over the conversation in his head from that morning.

'Alright, team, let's make tonight's formal dinner night unforgettable!' Jake had announced, his voice brimming with enthusiasm. 'Vincent, I need you to manage the entertainment lineup.'

Vincent's lips had pursed in discontent as he retorted sulkily, 'Isn't that what I did last time? Maybe I could handle something more significant, like coordinating the themed decorations?'

Jake arched an eyebrow, a sure sign he was pissed off.

'You did a fantastic job of looking after the entertainment last time, and I know with you at the helm it will run smoothly without any hiccups. Trust me, Vincent. It's for the best that we stick with the current plan. Maisie is already sorting the decorations out remember?'

Vincent's knuckles whitened as he gripped the edge of the table, rage simmering beneath his polished facade. His lip curled as he sneered up at his boss.

'Right. Just keep tossing me the scraps while you and Maisie take centre stage.'

Jake grimaced, sensing that any further discussion would lead to an undesirable confrontation in front of the others. Jake promptly dismissed the staff with a wave, deciding it was best to attempt to retain their positive demeanour before tensions escalated further. Jake noticed Maisie's discomfort and was glad she had kept quiet; she knew how to play the game. Maisie was an extremely organised Events Manager and Jake was grateful to have her onboard. Vincent's posture had remained rigid, his arms crossed defensively as he slumped in his chair, an unsettling contrast to the vibrant enthusiasm of the rest of the team. Jake's jaw clenched involuntarily at the memory; he could still feel the weight of Vincent's disdain and was pondering on how best to handle it.

Against his better judgement, Jake decided not to confront Vincent at the time. His sole focus was to get the formal dinner over and then the coveted gala event out of the way without any feuding beforehand. He would deal with Vincent in his own good time.

It had taken him all his will power not to react to his second in charge's blatant display of disrespect, but he succeeded with gritted teeth. As Jake left the boardroom that morning, he noted the disappointment in Vincent's eyes. Jake had not taken the bait.

Jake shook his head as he entered his cabin to finally turn in for the night.

I'm damned if I do react and damned if I don't. With my schedule, I don't have the time or the energy for this shit. I will address Vincent when the time is right. This guy is turning out to be a prize arsehole!

Chapter 2

Tia Davidson strutted in front of the mirror as far as the constraints of her stateroom would allow. Her slinky blue mini dress left little to the imagination as it hugged her curves like a second skin. The fabric shimmered faintly under the soft glow of the cabin lights, enhancing the sun-kissed sheen of her skin. Tia loved the way she looked and, tonight, she felt unstoppable. She admired her slender toned legs once more, then slicked on a gooey red lip gloss with a satisfied smirk. Being a cock tease was great fun; she loved the power it gave her over the dumb unsuspecting men she conquered. Even the smartest of men could not seem to resist her once she massaged their over-inflated egos. She'd proven multiple times that men's hard-wired biological response to an attractive young woman was not something they could stop if they tried. This was the case even when they were highly intelligent, supposedly happily married and otherwise sensible. Tia was not quite old enough to legally order an alcoholic drink on board; not that it would stop her from drinking. She chuckled as she read the information pamphlet provided in the cabin. *Passengers must be 21 years of age or older to purchase or consume alcohol.*

Yet Tia believed she was already streets ahead of people three times her age. She knew what she was talking about as this was often the cohort she played around with. It was Tia's first time aboard a luxury cruise liner, and the air thrummed with excitement on the opulent *Ocean Breeze*. Underneath extravagant chandeliers, Tia pretended to be part of the elite as she mingled with various highfliers sailing the Mediterranean Sea. Tonight, Tia had a single mission: she was out to make her mark. As she applied a final touch of mascara, her phone buzzed on the vanity. It was a message from Tony, her partner in crime.

'So, are you ready for tonight? You'll knock him dead whoever he is!'

Tia smiled at the screen yet felt a flutter of nerves in her stomach. It wasn't that she had any insecurities about her appearance; rather, the job at hand represented a leap into the world of making copious amounts of money. Wealth was the one thing in life she so desperately wanted. Tia's role was to target unsuspecting wealthy men, and succeeding was crucial in order to keep Tony happy. With one last glance in the mirror, Tia sprayed herself in Chanel No 5 then grabbed her small clutch bag as she stepped out of her stateroom. The corridor was bustling with well-dressed passengers in evening attire. Tia caught snippets of conversations from open areas as she strode along. As Tia made her way to the atrium, the jazz music grew louder, filling her with anticipation of the night to come.

Entering the central bar, Tia was immediately struck by the sheer opulence of the ship. Crystal glasses clinked like delicate chimes as wait staff glided past with trays of canapés and champagne. Tia took a deep breath, reminding herself to own the moment. As Tia stepped further inside, she was aware of many pairs of eyes turning in her direction. A group of young men nudged each other and pointed, and Tia couldn't help but smile inwardly at the attention.

The evening carried on as Tia worked the room, mingling with the other passengers, sharing laughs, and exchanging contact information with those she thought might be relevant in her world. Tia felt like she was a part of something much bigger than herself, and every moment intensified her passion for the mission at hand.

It irked Tia that she'd made a point of introducing herself to Jake the sexy Cruise Director and he'd barely given her a second glance. While Jake had been charming and friendly, he had not succumbed to her advances. At first Tia thought he was being professional and merely following the code of conduct associated with his job. Then a girl she recognised as one of the theatre performers put a possessive hand on Jake's arm while giving Tia a look that could kill.

Instead of taking the hint, Tia immediately saw it as a challenge. Highly used to having any man she wanted, she had a sudden urge to have Jake in every sexual position imaginable. Tia gave Jake's love interest a fake smile.

'You must be the lovely Claire Davidson, I read about you in the ship's newsletter. It must be a blast performing live on a cruise ship. I bet there are a lot of after-hours antics, eh?'

Claire regarded Tia cooly before remembering she was expected to be pleasant to the passengers whether she felt like it or not. The performers had it drummed into them that their performance offstage was just as important as onstage as far as keeping the passengers happy was concerned. Any complaints were likely to get you booted off at the next port. There were no shortage of performers waiting to take her place. Claire put on her best sickly-sweet smile as her eyes regarded Tia with contempt. Claire hoped her disdain was written all over her face.

Claire smirked. 'Yes, there is certainly a lot of after-hours fun, isn't there Jake?'

Claire flicked her chestnut hair, licking her enhanced lips provocatively while winking at Jake who watched the whole exchange between the two young women with a bemused expression. Jake was glad to be interrupted by a loud male American passenger who had several questions about the dining options and after-hours entertainment. As Jake turned away to assist the man, the two women locked eyes. Both were challenging the other with unspoken words. Claire openly glared at Tia.

Don't even think about it. Jake is mine and I will scratch your eyes out if you come near him.

Tia stared back. *I always get what I want and that includes Jake. Challenge accepted.*

The silent stand-off was broken unknowingly by the appearance of a waiter who stood between them with a tray of champagne. As Claire looked up to thank him after accepting a glass, she noted Tia darting off in the other direction.

Good riddance you slut. I hope you don't come to watch the show tonight!

When Claire finally had two minutes with Jake to herself, she accused him of flirting with the girl in the sparkly blue dress.

Jake hissed under his breath. 'For god's sake Claire, I don't have time for this crap. I was just being friendly towards a passenger. I gave her nothing, I certainly didn't flirt with her. You don't know me all that well if you think I did. Quite frankly, this is a stressful enough job without you on my back every two minutes. Maybe we should cool things off for a while huh?'

Jake was quickly realising that becoming involved with one of the performers after hours was a recipe for disaster. He enjoyed a few drinks with the staff, but he should have resisted Claire's hot dancer's body and was kicking himself for being so irresponsible.

Claire's eyes instantly filled with tears. 'Sorry Jake, you're right, I overreacted. I'm just really into you. I know I shouldn't admit that as we both know this is probably only a cruise fling, right?'

Jake knew that to be the truth but could tell it wouldn't go down well if he admitted it right now. His eyes skimmed lazily over Claire's cleavage, and he remembered why resisting her was futile.

'You are still the hottest girl on the ship. Does that make you feel better?'

Claire's face brightened at the compliment and Jake realised she was only a girl, barely into her 20s. He must tread carefully with Claire as she was erring on the clingy side. He was mindful that he was still fairly new to his role and was quickly learning the dos and don'ts while cruising. As Claire walked off to prepare for tonight's show, his eyes followed her high rounded buttocks and toned dancers legs, and he let out a loud groan.

I already know I'm going to have a piece of that arse again later. Who am I kidding?

As Claire approached the theatre dressing room, the smile suddenly slipped from her face. She realised with a jolt that Jake had avoided answering her question and simply boosted her ego instead.

Tia deliberately sat in the front row of the theatre and caught Claire's eye as she strutted out onto the stage in a gold catsuit. As Claire and the other performers broke out into their song and dance routine, Tia sat looking bored and did not clap after the final act. As Claire smiled and bowed with the cast during the encore, she glanced Tia's way. A shiver ran down her spine. Something was not right about the girl in the sparkly blue dress. That girl had eyes that could pierce your soul. Claire tried to tell herself it was down to the theatre's lighting but deep down she had a sixth sense the girl had more to her than merely a competitive edge. She was danger personified.

Following on from the lacklustre theatre performance, Tia knew she had a job to do, so for now conquering Jake could wait. As the night wore on, a handsome older man named Graeme Wilkinson handed Tia a business card after chatting to her at the bar about his company and the vacancies he had.

'Let's continue this conversation another time, eh? I see a lot of potential in you,' he said, his smile warm and inviting.

Tia took the card and winked, 'I will definitely be in touch, you can count on that.'

As she sashayed off, her inner dialogue made her chuckle softly.

You think you are it and a bit mister; your ego is bigger than King Kong's cock, but you are just another challenge for me to tuck away and win over later.

Graeme hoped the bulge in his trousers was not too obvious as he repositioned himself on the barstool. Business cards were a great cover up for giving out your number to hot young women. He had a feeling this one intended to call too.

Tia's next job for tonight was to align herself with other 'single' girls on the ship to go on the prowl with her. A meet up had been arranged for such girls in the bar near the atrium in approximately 15 minutes; just enough time to fluff up her hair and reapply her lip gloss.

The girls meet up was a success, and after a night of laughter, connections and a few unexpected surprises, Tia returned to her stateroom feeling electrified. She caught a glimpse of herself in the mirror and realised that in the sparkly blue mini dress, she'd not only turned heads, but she'd also opened more doors, going by the company she had Googled. The man Graeme from earlier in the evening was a legitimate business owner and obviously had copious amounts of money. It was a good start. In the gentle sway of the ship, Tia stood on her balcony and envisioned her future unfolding like the waters before her: a vast, exciting expanse waiting for her to chart her course. Tia closed her piercing blue eyes, and tossed back her blonde mane, breathing in the scent of salty air. She considered all of the possibilities on this ship, safe in the knowledge that her adventure had only begun.

Chapter 3

Richard Henderson looked at his wife Belinda with disdain. As predicted, she'd insisted they head straight for the buffet as soon as they'd returned to the ship after a long day ashore. To be fair, it was what most passengers did given it was possible to access food and drinks twenty-four hours a day. Richard wasn't interested in being fair or logical though, he was simply at the stage in his marriage where he felt bored with his wife of 30 years. They had booked this cruise in an attempt to rekindle the lost spark between them, however as he watched Belinda wolf down an extra-large serving of fish and chips, he felt a mounting sense of dread. He wished he was back in Sydney where he could at least hide from her constant guzzling in his study. Richard suddenly felt trapped. He was longing for a bit of excitement in his life again. Perhaps he was having a midlife crisis. He stared at the other passengers as they bustled past, a gloomy expression on his face.

Maybe I'm struggling to accept my age and stage of life. Is this it now? The only thing my wife has an appetite for is food, not sex.

Richard went as far as fantasising about being a free agent again, although he knew deep down it was his misspent youth that he missed. He also knew that his adult son and daughter were likely to side with their mother if they ever separated. Richard knew he'd probably see much less of them, and he'd be a sad old man. He let out a dramatic sigh. Richard did love Belinda, he just wasn't sure if he was in love with her anymore.

He merely felt indifferent towards her these days. Deep down he knew he had no right to have scornful thoughts about her bodily changes and unhealthy food choices as he was not much better himself. They were two of a kind, however he was not prepared to face that reality, so he pushed the thought aside.

Belinda nudged him, 'I'm going up to suss out the dessert counter, do you want me to get you something on the way back?'

Richard glared at his wife as she wiped a trickle of tomato ketchup from her chin with a paper napkin and retorted, 'We don't all need to eat like gluttons the minute we get onboard you know!'

Belinda snorted loudly, 'You honestly are hilarious Richard. I'd love to take you seriously, but I know you ate a couple of pastries when I was at the loo just before! You think I don't know, however there are flakes of pastry stuck to your face and I saw a staff member whip your empty plate away as I was walking back to the table. Practice what you preach you hypocrite!'

Richard's expression changed from scornful to sheepish as it sunk in that he'd been busted. Instead of responding, he folded his arms across the top of his rounded belly and looked the other way; a defeated expression on his sulky face. Belinda rolled her eyes and strolled off to check out the endless counters with every type of sweet and savoury food one could possibly imagine. The truth was they were both feeling much the same way about each other. The difference was Belinda thought their marriage was worth fighting for. Sadly, she wasn't so sure that Richard was still as invested. Maybe this cruise would be make or break for them. Belinda shuddered at the thought.

That evening, Richard reluctantly began dressing for dinner. His beige chinos were already feeling too tight on his protruding belly and that was *before* dinner. He'd prefer to slob out in their stateroom and watch TV, but Belinda would never have let him hear the end of it. His wife appeared at his side dressed up to the nines and reeking of a sickly-sweet perfume that made his eyes water. Belinda tried to twirl her dress in the confines of their cabin and fell back on the bed laughing. Richard noticed his wife had not shaved her legs for a while and was disgusted to note the long ginger stubble on her milky white shins. His other half definitely did not resemble the slim pretty red head in their wedding photos. He grimaced; it was going to be a long time onboard in a confined space together.

He spoke on autopilot, 'You look nice love, new dress?'

Belinda smiled, 'Yeah it is, you were with me when I bought it at David Jones, don't you remember?'

Richard narrowed his eyes. *I remember all right, you struggled into the next size up because you grow larger every year.*

He gave a weak smile and nodded dutifully as he patted his pockets to make sure he hadn't forgotten anything before they explored their restaurant of choice on the vast *Ocean Breeze*. As they closed the cabin door behind them, he let out a muffled guffaw.

The drinks package is what will get me through this trip!

Richard's inflated ego did not allow him to consider that he looked nothing like his wedding photo either. Little did he know that his double standards would eventually be his downfall. Dinner was pleasant enough and Richard was impressed with the French Bistro they picked; the choice of delicious dishes on the menu was extensive. Once they'd ordered their food, the conversation inevitably revolved around their adult offspring; the only safe topic they were both equally interested in these days.

The waiter came back with their entrées and Belinda began talking with her mouth full of French onion soup. She crunched a crouton noisily, much to Richard's annoyance.

'Do you reckon Emma and Leon will get engaged soon? I do hope so, he is definitely son-in-law material, don't you think?'

Richard nodded as he shovelled in a spoonful of clam chowder, unaware of his own slurping noises that Belinda was choosing to ignore.

'Yeah, Leon is a good lad, our Emma could do a lot worse. Hard working and loyal, that's what we want for our daughter, eh?'

Belinda nodded enthusiastically while wiping a dribble of soup from her bosom with a crisp white napkin. She began to drone on about her hopes that a wedding was on the horizon and Richard zoned out. He was discreetly checking out a stunning blonde girl wearing a slinky blue dress. The girl strutted confidently past their table ensuring that her wiggling bottom was in his line of vision. Richard almost choked on his next spoonful of soup as his eyes followed the girl to a table full of giggling girls in similar outfits.

I need to pull my head in! The girl is likely younger than my Emma!

Belinda was looking at him expectantly. She'd obviously said something, and he'd missed it due to having dirty thoughts about that girl. Richard squirmed in his seat feeling inwardly ashamed. He turned his focus back to his wife.

'Sorry love, I think I'm still a bit weary from all the traveling. What were you saying?'

Belinda sighed however she made a snap decision not to have a go at her husband. She wanted their trip to be a fun one.

'I was only saying that we should try and put a bit of money aside in case Emma and Leon do make an announcement soon. Just in case we need to put on an engagement party at our place. You know what they are like nowadays, they put all their events on Instagram to show off how perfect the setting is.'

Richard sighed, 'Yes, I know only bloody too well how it works now. It's all about the public show. Well maybe Leon's parents will put in a fair bit of money too? All this expectation that the bride side of the family pays for everything, that's surely all-old hat now. Anyway, let's worry about it if it happens, eh?'

Richard did not hear his wife's reply, her whiney voice was getting on his nerves, and he'd zoned out again. Miss Slinky Dress was definitely staring at him from across the room in a provocative way. The girl was winking and pouting at him and even though Richard guessed she was probably taking the piss in front of her friends, he became a little hot around the collar as he felt a stirring in his pants. The girl was leaning forward now, her pert little breasts on show. Richard felt his sparse hairline become damp and he began to unbutton the top of his shirt. Belinda was oblivious and still rabbiting on about engagement parties and the cost involved. She stopped talking abruptly.

'Richard, are you alright? You look awfully hot and bothered. Do you reckon you got too much sun when we were queuing to get back on the ship? Do you want to go back to the cabin?'

Richard nodded; he was glad he wasn't required to pay the bill, just a quick signature and off you could go. Everything was either pre-paid or added to your account at the end of the cruise. As Belinda led him out of the bistro, he hoped the effect the girl had on him was not evident to any onlookers.

Back at the cabin, Belinda lay on the bed, her head firmly stuck in the latest spicy novel her book club had chosen, and Richard felt restless. He went out to the balcony and marvelled at how the sea stretched endlessly, reflecting the glimmering stars above, as the ship swayed gently in the warm night breeze. He felt a moment of gratitude as he breathed in the salty night air. It honestly was a floating paradise; an oasis of luxury and indulgence. Richard reminded himself once again that this cruise was a chance to escape the mundane routine of his daily life. He decided to stop being so lazy and explore the ship instead of wasting the rest of the evening slobbing around with Belinda. He knew his wife would rarely glance up from her book, so she'd be unlikely to want to join him. Richard mumbled something about burning off some calories on the walking track and promptly left before his wife could object.

As he strolled along the upper deck, the rowdiness of younger passengers filled the air, mingling with the bass of the live band playing. Richard felt a pang of nostalgia, recalling the vibrancy of his youth. His eyes widened as he recognised the striking young woman with the slinky blue dress from dinner. She was standing by the railing, gazing out at the moonlit horizon. He hesitated as he was aware it could appear creepy if he approached her. The girl felt his presence however and turned to face him, a wide smile lighting up her pretty features. Richard was mesmerised by her blonde hair flowing in the evening sea breeze, and the intensity of her piercing sapphire eyes which were somehow both stunning and terrifying at the same time.

Her eyes swept over him appreciatively. 'Well, hello again, have you come out to play after dinner?'

Richard blinked rapidly, unsure whether to go with the devil or angel part of his conscience. He knew the minx was coming onto him and questioned her motives. He was certainly no Brad Pitt. Richard's sensible side was saying *don't be ridiculous, she is far too young and gorgeous to be interested,* and his wild side was saying, *I'm not getting any younger, if there is a hot chick on offer here, I should take it!*

His eyes darted guiltily around him; he was half expecting to see Belinda standing there with her arms folded. He decided to engage with the girl but stick to safe topics. Deep down he knew he was on dangerous territory, however his feet remained glued to the spot.

'Uh hi, I'm just stretching my legs and walking off my dinner. Where are your friends?' Richard thought he'd done a good job of sounding casual.

Tia pouted coquettishly, brazenly moving closer to Richard.

'My friends went to the 90s dance party after dinner, and I wasn't fussy about joining them. I like to do my own thing, a bit like you it'd seem?'

Richard nodded as he met her direct gaze; he was already under her spell.

The girl put out a dainty hand, 'I'm Tia, nice to meet you.'

Richard returned the handshake, feeling somewhat awkward. 'Richard,' he mumbled.

He fully intended to keep walking but found himself captivated by her wit and enthusiasm for life. Tia laughed inwardly at how quickly he was taken with her free spirit and alluring charm.

I am such a pro at this!

They were standing near an outdoor bar with inviting sunken lounges that were miraculously not occupied. Richard waved a hand towards the bar, shocked at the words coming out of his own mouth.

'Can I get you a drink Tia?'

As soon as he spoke, he knew he was making a big mistake, but the throb in his groin did not care one iota.

Tia hid her smirk and put on her best innocent face as she purred with a jaunty wink,

'I'd love a drink, can I have the Hanky Panky cocktail please?'

As the evening progressed, they shared stories over several more cocktails, their laughter echoing across the waves, bridging the gap between their ages. Richard's eyes skimmed hungrily over Tia's body. The way she sat with one leg crossed over the other made her short dress ride even higher. He was practically panting at the possibility of seeing her naked.

Richard glanced at his watch. He knew it was best to call it a night and return to his wife, however he was also certain she'd be fast asleep by now. Belinda had a habit of zonking out while reading and a herd of wild elephants would fail to wake her up. In any case if she wasn't texting to ask where he was then it was a sure sign she was out for the count.

As if reading his thoughts Tia said her standard line, her eyes rounded with her best angelic look.

'Look I will be upfront with you Richard. Here is the deal. I've always wanted to have sex with an older man, no strings attached, it's purely a bucket list thing. I honestly get off on the wisdom and experience vibe that older men bring. Boys my age are so immature…' Tia averted her eyes, her voice trailing off.

Tia stood up abruptly, 'Oh my god, I'm so sorry Richard, I've had too much to drink, I shouldn't have said that I'm so embarrassed, I…'

Richard leapt up and held Tia by the shoulders, his voice was low and husky.

'I'm super flattered and, don't get me wrong, I want you so much I could explode with desire right now. But I'm an old married man and you are awfully young, so let's not get carried away here. I think we should leave it at that and call it a night, okay?'

Tia looked searchingly into Richard eyes while standing close enough to kiss him. She placed a hand on his bulging crotch and whispered in his ear,

'Don't you want to do something about this?'

Richard's eyes protruded as his mouth opened and closed, as he fought to resist the magnetic pull she exerted. He inhaled the fragrance of her perfume mingled with a wild, enticing smell that was uniquely hers; a blend of musk and something earthy and untamed. It sent shivers through him, each whiff enticing his primal instincts. He knew he must have his wicked way with her.

'I have my own cabin,' Tia said, her voice soft yet playful, dangling possibilities in the air that made Richard's pulse race.

The way Tia spoke the words ignited something in him, a powerful urge to venture into her world, to shed the mundane constraints of his everyday life and dive into the unknown, wild and free. It was animal magnetism pure and simple.

As her words trailed off, he felt her breath brush against the nape of his neck, sending a tingling sensation down his spine. It was intimate and electrifying, and it reeked of promise. Richard was caught, ensnared in her allure, and he found himself not thinking, but merely reacting.

Tia grinned at him, a playful challenge in her gaze, and without a second thought, he surrendered to the sensation of her hand gliding dangerously up his leg.

'Tia your perfume makes you smell so sexy…'

Richard was dismayed to hear himself slurring his words, he was talking crap in a bid to stall and connect with the rational part of his brain; the part that was meant to make him walk away from this wicked temptress.

Tia spoke in her best breathy Marilyn Monroe voice, 'Richard, fragrance doesn't make a girl sexy. It's the girl who makes the fragrance sexy. Now follow me.'

Tia led the way, her backside wiggling enticingly as she moved. It was as if she were weaving a spell, and Richard was more than willing to be ensnared. Richard was acutely aware of the thrills and fears coursing through him as he followed Tia to her stateroom.

As the cabin door closed, Tia turned to him, her eyes sparkling with mischief and in that moment Richard felt convinced an undeniable connection existed between them, it was electric and raw. His heart raced as he stepped inside, the primal urge to claim what he desired overpowering all rational thought.

The air in Tia's cabin felt like it was charged with a magnetic energy, and while completely lost in the moment, Richard surrendered to his primal urge. Tia stripped off revealing an impressive figure with prominent nipples and curves in all the right places. As Richard sucked hungrily on her breasts, all rational thoughts disappeared from his mind. The sex was passionate, a whirlwind of sensations that drew him back into a world he thought he had long left behind. Richard had not felt so alive for a long time. He shivered with anticipation as he guided his manhood towards her open legs. When he plunged into her wetness, he thought he might explode with desire. The deed was quick and dirty, and he soon found himself panting in a pool of sweat wondering if he was dreaming about what had taken place only minutes before.

As soon as he came down from the high, Richard was immediately filled with remorse and guilt. He dressed quickly as though doing so would somehow make the deed seem less real. He had never cheated on Belinda in 30 years, despite many temptations along the way. He noticed Tia's demeanour had immediately shifted, which was making him feel uncomfortable. She turned to him, her expression unreadable, the playful charm from earlier in the night now faded into a steely gaze. Richard hoped to God she was not in fact underage, and some father figure was about to appear and beat him to a pulp.

'Richard,' she began, her voice devoid of the warmth it held earlier. 'There's something we need to talk about.' The stark shift in her tone sent a chill down his spine.

Richard stopped midway through buttoning his shirt, suddenly uneasy. He turned to face her, his expression grave.

'We shouldn't have done that. I'm a married man, my daughter is close in age to you. I feel so ashamed. I....'

Tia cut him off with a raised hand as she leaned in closer, her voice low and steady.

'Cut the crap, I've heard it so many times and it gets old. I don't care about your infidelity shame or about your age for that matter, but there's something you should know pronto. I now have video evidence of us having sex together.'

Richard felt his stomach drop. His heart began to race as he turned to her, his eyes wide with fear. It was the oldest trick in the book and his stupid inflated ego had fallen for it. 'What do you mean?'

Richard looked frantically around the cabin for evidence of a camera. He was aware that they were so miniscule these days that he may never spot it.

Tia stretched nonchalantly, allowing her nipples to strain against the cream satin negligee she had slipped on post sex.

'Let's just say, if things don't go the way I want them to, the video could find its way to your wife, your family, your friends... even your employer.'

Her words rang in Richard's ears, thick with implications. He struggled to compute the competing emotions that surfaced as shame, guilt, and fear engulfed him. He felt the weight of the betrayal settle in his chest, his fear suddenly turning into rage.

'You can't be serious; you are nothing but a conniving little bitch!'

Tia regarded Richard's reddening face with contempt.

'Oh, I am perfectly serious,' she replied coldly. 'I know you're a well-respected man with a reputation to protect. From what I understand you are even on TV with your job sometimes, aren't you? I don't think you'd want anyone to know about your little adventure on this cruise now, would you?'

The gravity of her threat hit him like a tidal wave. His mind raced to his wife, Belinda, who had trusted him implicitly throughout their three decades together. The shock of being blackmailed by a girl who was barely an adult left him reeling. This was ridiculous. Who the hell used blackmail in this day and age? How could he trust that she'd destroy the evidence even if he paid her? Richard was on the verge of shaking sense into Tia when a man suddenly entered the cabin.

The man sauntered cockily up to Richard, 'What a sucker you are mate, you fell for it hook, line and sinker! It never fails to surprise me how easy it is to bait old married geezers like yourself.'

The man shook his head in disgust, doing his best to appear patronising. Tia walked over to stand next to her guest.

'Meet Tony, my accomplice. Now there's a big word!'

As Tia smirked up at Tony, Richard realised he'd fallen for a scam these two scumbags obviously used regularly. They were a modern-day version of a prostitute and her pimp. Richard felt a thick slick of sweat run down his back as he ran his hands through his unkempt salt and pepper hair.

'What do you want exactly?' Richard's voice was hoarse, barely above a whisper.

Tony folded his arms across his chest as he tapped his chin with his index finger pretending to ponder. He reminded Richard of a stereotypical bouncer stationed outside a night club.

'I want money mate. A hefty sum.'

Tony pulled out a piece of paper from his pocket and handed it to Richard.

'This is the sum I expect, and these are the bank details to transfer it to. No negotiations.'

Richard stared at the figure, feeling the walls close in on him. It was an amount that could threaten his financial stability, and all for one night stand that he'd foolishly thought would be forgotten with the passing of the waves.

Richard tried to hide the tremor in his voice.

'This is ridiculous. I can't just conjure this amount out of thin air and how do I know you won't come back for more? This is like a bad TV show, this shit doesn't happen in real life! You two need to grow the hell up!'

Richard was annoyed to hear the fear in his voice as he grappled with the reality of the situation. He looked at the young woman, trying to appeal to her conscience. Tia suddenly seemed ugly as her true colours shone through.

'This isn't right, Tia, and you know it.'

'Neither was fucking a girl young enough to be your daughter,' Tia countered coolly. 'But here we are. Here is what's gonna happen. You have until the last day of this cruise to come up with the money. I will stay in touch throughout. Rest assured we know everything about you and will have eyes on you. Let's just say I have friends at the Guest Services desk on deck six and there is nothing I don't know about you, including your passport number and mobile phone number. Be on your way. I will text you, so you will have my contact number. Save my name as Frank and tell your wife it's one of your employees if she sees a call or text from me.'

Richard gaped at Tia in shock. 'How do you know I have an employee called Frank?'

Tia laughed. 'Would that be Frank who you recently overlooked for a promotion? Who do you think schooled us up on you being an easy target?'

Tony shoved Richard in the small of the back towards the exit and promptly pushed him out, slamming the cabin door. On quaking legs, Richard walked miserably back to his cabin and prayed for mercy. He knew that each consequent moment of the cruise would be overshadowed by Tia's ultimatum. He'd feel her presence like a shadow. He imagined her eyes lingering on him from across the deck. The knot in his stomach tightened as he wondered how sleep could possibly come.

Chapter 4

Jake was eager to make the most of his fleeting stop in Cannes. He had prepared well for tonight's gala event and was ready to enjoy a little down time during the day. The sun was high in the azure sky, casting a warm glow over the vibrant streets. Jake adjusted his Gucci sunglasses and the scent of fresh pastries wafting from a nearby boulangerie made his mouth water. The Mediterranean Sea sparkled in the distance, dotted with luxury yachts, mere toys in a grand playground for the affluent. As the Cruise Director, he'd mastered the art of completing his duties while at sea, and while on land he was determined to let loose; at least for a couple of hours.

Claire joining him had been a last-minute decision, one he might live to regret. Claire was obsessed with celebrity spotting; she had practically begged him to let her tag along with him in the hope that she might spot a few Hollywood stars. At first, he'd thought her enthusiasm would be a welcome distraction, but now, as they waded through a group of tourists, he felt his patience wearing thin. Apparently, all she cared about was glitz and glamour.

'Jake, look at that dress!' Claire pointed excitedly toward a boutique showcasing high-end gowns. The display contained silk garments and jewellery that called to the wealthy elite. Claire was merely a cruise fling, so if she thought he was willing to treat her to the dress, she was sadly mistaken.

'Yeah, that looks nice,' he muttered, forcing a smile while shifting his weight from foot to foot.

'We should probably move on though. I want to get a feel for the place and only have a couple of hours until I gotta be back onboard. The sponsors for tonight's gala are counting on me to make sure everything goes smoothly.'

Ignoring his subtle hint, Claire was already gliding towards the shop entrance, entranced by the cut of the dress.

'I just want to see if it's as gorgeous in person,' she chirped, bounding inside with an energy that made Jake crave a second coffee to stave off his rising frustration.

As he waited outside, Jake scanned the street, half-heartedly loitering while he felt the sun's rays beating down. Several luxury cars zoomed by, as well as a group of women in designer outfits. Jake was not adverse to nice things himself, but as his time was limited, he itched to explore. Shopping could be done anytime. He peered through the shop window and when Claire spotted him, he pointed at his watch. After what felt like an eternity, Claire emerged, a dress bag flung over her shoulder, her face radiant.

'Jake!' she gushed.' You should see it! It's absolutely breathtaking. Thank God I had my Visa card on me, it cost a small fortune.'

'Glad you are happy with it,' he muttered, doing his best to feign enthusiasm. 'But we should think about checking out the beach now.'

Jake started to walk toward the sea, a subtle cue for her to follow. He gritted his teeth when he realised Claire was still distracted.

'Look!' she pointed, practically bouncing on her toes. 'Isn't that the actor Chris Hemsworth?'

Jake squinted but couldn't make the star out due to a flock of minders around him.

'Oh good, you've spotted a star. Can we move away from the mayhem of these parts now?'

Jake tried to focus on moving on from the bustling street.

'Look over there!' Claire persisted while pointing at a glamorous woman. 'She looks like Selena Gomez. Wasn't she in that movie about …'

'Claire,' he interrupted, finally losing his patience. 'Just because we're in Cannes doesn't mean every passerby is a movie star. We need to move on, there's more to the place than the glitz and glamour!' His voice was sharper than intended, catching Claire off guard.

'I—I'm sorry,' she stuttered, taking a half-step back, her eyes wide. 'I didn't mean to…'

Jake sighed, realising he probably seemed like a prize dickhead.

'No, I'm sorry, I didn't mean to snap.'

He waved his arms around. 'It's because this area is too busy, it does nothing for me. Cannes is beautiful, I'm just reminding you there's more to it.'

Noting her sulky pout, he softened his tone, 'I appreciate you wanting to enjoy the day with me, and I want to enjoy it too, although my idea of downtime is a bit different to yours. I've never been great at the whole shopping with girls thing, and I don't give a shit about famous people.'

Claire bit her lip, nodding slowly. 'I get it Jake, I honestly do. I just thought it might be fun to spot the celebs.'

Jake smiled, 'Let's have a look at the beach, grab some gelato, check out a few of those cool looking market stalls and then we can head back to the ship, okay?'

Her face brightened at the suggestion. 'Gelato sounds heavenly!'

As they walked side by side towards a quieter area, the resplendent escapade of Cannes became more enjoyable for Jake. He couldn't deny the allure of the French city. He grinned at the thought of ravishing Claire's sexy body later on. All in all, Cannes was promising to be a rather pleasurable day.

Later that evening Jake dressed in a sharp fitted black suit, and prepared for an enchanting night filled with music, dancing and exquisite cuisine. Guests began to mingle outside on the grand deck, and he moved through the crowd smoothly, exchanging polite conversation, ensuring his charm was on full display. As the hours passed, he couldn't shake the feeling of being watched. It was more than the usual admirers. He felt a lurking presence, a shadow that gnawed at his resolve.

The evening went on without a hitch, and once the music became louder and the guests lost themselves in the festivities, Jake finally made his way to his office to check that his staff had organised the raffle prizes to be given out. He was greeted by an eerie silence, the type that prickled his skin. As he entered his office, the air instantly thickened with an unmistakable sense of doom. The only illumination came from the faint glow of the desk lamp where papers were strewn haphazardly. It was in that moment he heard it, a sob, coming from across the room. Treading cautiously, Jake braced himself against the door frame and peered in. There, to his shock, was Vincent, hunched over in a chair, his head buried in his hands. The sight startled Jake, his stomach lurched with a mixture of wariness, compassion and confusion.

'Vincent?'

Before he could get any closer, Vincent leapt up, his eyes blazing with an intensity that sent a jolt down Jake's spine.

'What do you want, Jake? Here to gloat? To show me how perfect everything is for you?'

Jake stepped back in shock. 'Whoa Vincent, it's not like that. You're my mate. We can work through…'

'Mate?' Vincent scoffed, contempt dripping from his voice. 'You're everything I'm not, Mr Fucking Perfect!'

A flash of rage crossed Vincent's face as he grabbed a heavy object from the nearby desk and raised it threateningly.

Jake was shocked to see the sleek bronze statue; the unexpected gift Claire had bought for him in Cannes. Jake instinctively blocked Vincent's raised hand with his forearm and roared at his second in command.

'What the fuck are you doing Vincent? Put it down!'

In a heated moment, their eyes locked, and Vincent's face twisted with fury. Jake had never seen this side of the man he had thought he knew, the man who was supposed to step in for him when required. Vincent's grip tightened, but within a split second, his expression changed from furious to shocked and he slowly placed the statue back down on the desk with shaking hands. He couldn't look Jake in the eyes. Jake willed Vincent to look at him, his own face a mixture of anger and pity. He knelt down next to Vincent, hoping his voice wasn't shaky.

'Do you want to tell me what the hell is going on?'

Vincent spoke in a flat voice, 'Jane and I are getting divorced. I haven't mentioned it as I still don't want to believe it's true. I'm not getting into it right now, but apparently, I am not who she thought I was. It came totally out of the blue and I'm fucking devastated. I'm not only dealing with a broken heart, it's also the stress of splitting our assets. It's going to put me in a seriously shit financial position. I guess I felt the world owed me something and that included the Director position. When you won it over me, it was another nail in the coffin. I know I've taken it out on you ever since and I know I'm being an arsehole. I'm clearly not in a great head space...'

Jake softened after hearing his colleague's sorry tale. It certainly explained the bizarre behaviour and obvious decline in Vincent's mental health recently. He regarded his assistant warily, 'I'm sorry to hear that, Vincent. I know you guys haven't been married for long... and your son, he is still a baby, right? Do you want to talk about it?'

Vincent shook his head vehemently, his dark curls flying around his head. 'No, I don't!'

Jake put up a hand in defeat. 'It's okay, I'm not going to pry … if you don't want to talk to me, then you need to find another confidante. You shouldn't go through this on your own. How about we get through the rest of this cruise and then you take a bit of time off to sort yourself out?'

Vincent nodded, his expression that of a petulant child.

'Can we keep what happened tonight between us Jake?'

Vincent's eyes were wide and moist as he looked at Jake pleadingly.

'By all intents and purposes, I know I should be stood down as your second in command. I know how this works; my outburst gives you grounds to have me taken off the ship. But I think I can keep it together for a few more days until we disembark. Can you please not add to my stress by making all of this known right now? I know you probably think I should see a counsellor, but if you take me out the picture at this point, I think it will finish me off and it will be counterproductive.'

Jake hesitated. He knew the correct protocol was to have Vincent attend a mental health assessment with immediate effect. After all his state of mind could directly affect the crew and passengers. If any further incidents happened, then Jake would be held responsible. On the other hand, he felt that Vincent had a point about the further mental decline he'd face if he was told to do the walk of shame off the ship.

The selfish part of Jake was calculating how much labour and working knowledge would be lost without his second in command onboard. He'd probably never find time to sleep if he tried to cover Vincent's duties as well as his own. His staff were all under the pump as it was. Delegating any more work to them at this point was unfair, particularly when many of the tasks were well above their pay grade. Jake made a snap decision.

'Okay, this stays between us for now. While I'm sorry about your situation, you have got to get your shit together and do your job until this cruise is over, do you understand? You also quit with the condescending act towards me, got it? And if you so much as step a toe out of line or attempt to attack me like that again, you will be off this ship quicker than you can say 'Ahoy Captain', comprende?'

Vincent gave a curt nod, and Jake could only pray that he had made the right decision.

Chapter 5

Kayla was floating on air. This was going to be her year and she was embracing every second of it. She'd finally met her soul mate Alex after a few disastrous relationships. She felt sure they were heading towards moving in together, even though it was still early days. As Kayla boarded the *Ocean Breeze* cruise ship, she walked behind her handsome boyfriend and admired his broad muscular frame as he strode ahead. The cruise was expensive, and Kayla was still pinching herself that Alex could afford to pay for them both. Alex's friends felt that the relationship was moving too fast, and thought they'd become serious way too soon, but what would they know?

That evening, Kayla sang softly to herself as she dressed for dinner and put the finishing touches to her outfit. She was inserting small gold hoops into her ears when Alex appeared behind her in the mirror. Kayla's smile fell short as she noted his stony expression. She spun around to meet his gaze.

'Are you okay?'

Alex held up a business card in his hand and waved it around.

'No, I'm not fucking okay. I've been stewing about this since you flirted with that guy at the shore excursions desk earlier.'

Confusion crossed Kayla's face at the sting of his words. She had not been aware of Alex having a jealous streak and it came out of nowhere. Kayla let out a nervous giggle.

'What the hell are you talking about? I spoke to him about a few excursions we might be interested in, and he gave me his business card just the same way he did to every other passenger who made enquiries! Come on you can't be serious?'

Alex stared at her, his mouth set in a grim line, his steely grey eyes boring into her.

'But it wasn't only a card exchange, was it? I saw a bit of chemistry happening there between you two. Don't deny you were being pretty suggestive towards him!'

Kayla's mouth dropped open. 'You're genuinely serious about this? This is so unreasonable. I did not flirt with him! I can barely recall what he even looks like!'

Alex charged towards her, his eyes bulging, veins protruding from his neck.

He slapped Kayla hard across the face.

'Liar! You tarts are all the fucking same, every one of you!'

Before Kayla could react, Alex stormed out of the cabin slamming the door behind him. He thundered past the older couple next door who'd stepped out to see what the commotion was all about. He heard the man yell something after him, but he'd already entered the lobby that led to the lifts. His breathing became shallow as he broke out into a cold sweat.

What the fuck have I just done? I gotta go somewhere and be alone to calm down and think how to fix this. I gotta get my jealousy under control before I lose her like all the others. I'll sweat it out in the gym, that usually does the trick.

Kayla was rooted to the spot with shock. Her hands shook as she touched the red welt across her left cheek. Tears slid silently down her face as she looked at the hand imprint across her face in the mirror. How the hell had this happened? Alex had shown zero signs of being possessive or aggressive until now. Had she truly teased the guy at the shore excursions desk?

Maybe I did…

Kayla sat on the cabin floor unable to move. She lost all track of time as she wrapped her arms around her knees, hugging herself tight. She became aware of the tightness in her stomach, the sour taste in her mouth and the pounding of her heart. No matter how hard she tried to calm herself down and think rationally, these sensations kept her in an uncomfortable state of awareness. After an hour she slowly stood up and looked into the mirror. Her face was still swollen and red, her mascara ran in two dark rivers and her eyelids were puffed up.

I look like something out of a horror film. I must have truly wound him up.

Kayla observed her ever changing expressions in the mirror as she oscillated between rage and feeling as though she deserved it. She jumped as she heard the cabin door open then slam closed. Alex stood in front of her, his shoulders hunched, a defeated and forlorn expression on his face. His face was blotchy and his eyes damp. Kayla felt some of her anger dissipate as feelings of apprehension took over. Alex looked genuinely distraught.

'Kayla, I'm so sorry, I can't believe I hurt you, I had no right, I was totally out of line. I've acted like an utter bastard, and I know I've probably lost you as a result.'

Alex began to cry as he sat on the edge of the bed with his head in his hands. Kayla sat next to him and rubbed his back.

He sure knows how to turn on the water works.

'I appreciate the apology, but I don't think I can come back from this and be the same with you again. I've never seen this side of you and its pretty damn ugly to be honest. I'm gutted Alex. I thought you were the one. Every guy I've been with has let me down in some way and now you have proved to be no different. Since we started this holiday, a possessive side has come out that I didn't know existed. We have literally just got on this ship and now I want to get the fuck off. Not a great start to the trip, is it?'

Alex looked up, his face pained, his remorse evident. He wiped his eyes with his sleeve.

'The truth is that I find it difficult to control my temper. I know I don't deserve a second chance. I'm scared of ending up alone. It's as if a part of me wants to get the break-up over with because it will happen anyway.'

Alex couldn't read Kayla's expression. For a moment she looked spiteful and she seemed insincere somehow. Although he couldn't exactly blame her for being wary of him after he'd hit her. Kayla cocked her head to one side.

'That's really sad, Alex. It sounds as though you feel you don't deserve to be in a loving relationship. Believe me I know only too well what that feels like.'

Kayla noted with dismay that he didn't ask her to elaborate, instead he launched straight into his story which was all about *him*. She balled her fists at her sides, but he was too self-centred to notice. Alex cleared his throat, ready to launch into his sorry tale.

'Let me explain where my blatant distrust of women comes from, I've never told you much about my past…'

'Okay,' Kayla said slowly, 'I want to hear all about it.'

Alex's shoulders sagged as he took himself back in time. 'When I was around 8 years old, my dad used to go away on business a lot and one time he was away for longer than usual. My mum was in a permanent bad mood whenever he left. Anyway, one night I got up in the middle of the night to get a drink and I saw a man leaving my parents' bedroom. I saw him tiptoe to the front door, and I felt a prickle on the back of my neck. I still get that sensation even now when I think about it. I knew there and then that my mum was doing the dirty on my dad. I got pretty upset.'

Alex paused and Kayla rubbed his arm, nodding at him to continue his story. Alex exhaled loudly.

'I went to my parents' bedroom and my mum was whispering quietly on the phone. I stood in the doorway listening and she didn't see me until it was too late. I knew she was talking to the man that had just left. My mum was saying something about hating the fact he had to sneak off. Then my mum told him she'd be getting rid of me soon as I'd be staying with my grandparents at the weekend. She was making plans for him to come over again.'

Kayla noted the pain on Alex's face as he relived the story. She looked at him with damp eyes.

'That's a really sad story Alex. For what it's worth my dad worked away too, and one time he…uh, he left and never came back. So, I know it's hard…I don't want you to feel as though you must tell me the rest of what happened. I can see you are struggling with it.'

Alex stared ahead moodily.

'Nah I want to tell you. Once my mum noticed me, she looked fearful; obviously she was wondering what I'd seen or heard. I was honest with her and told her I'd seen the man and heard what she'd said on the phone. I wanted her to explain I was wrong and tell me I'd made a mistake, even though I knew it'd be a lie. After all, what you don't know can't hurt you, right? Then my mum sat me down and gripped my arm tightly as she was talking. I remember staring at her nail marks on my skin for ages afterwards. Anyway, she looked ferocious. I'd never seen that side of her. My mum basically told me in no uncertain terms that if I breathed a word of this to anyone then I'd be responsible for breaking my parents' marriage up, we'd lose the house and be moved to a terrible area by the housing trust. She thought of everything under the sun that could go wrong as the result of the truth being out there. She made me swear not to tell a soul and said I'd be cursed for the rest of my life if I did. I was 8 years old, for fuck's sake. Why couldn't she see what she was putting on me?'

Kayla wasn't sure what to say so she merely nodded for him to continue. Alex's face was white as he finished telling his story, and she had no doubt that he was telling the truth. He wiped his nose with the back of his hand and Kayla noticed he had a slight tremor.

'So, Kayla, as you can imagine, that night changed my life forever. Not only was I expected to play happy families when my dad came back and watch mum fawn all over him when she had a secret lover, but I also carried an ugly truth around with me for the rest of my childhood. Unfortunately, what it taught me was you can't trust anyone, not even your own parents. It was ingrained in me that women cannot be trusted because they lie and cheat. From that moment onwards, my mum didn't even hide her lover when he came over. They'd have sex where I could see and hear them. It was so messed up. No matter what I do, I can't seem to shake the belief off that women are all lying whores. You aren't the first girlfriend this has happened with; I'm not going to lie. I get so paranoid about cheating that I start to invent scenarios that don't exist. I know its irrational, I just can't seem to help it. It's as if I'm possessed. Then when I perceive that the woman is lying which in my mind she must be, the red mist comes over me and I lash out. It's messed up and I know it's not okay. So, to give you the long story in short, my dad did eventually catch my mum in the act, and he beat her up. I heard all of that too. Mum expected sympathy from me, but she never got it because I felt she deserved it. They separated and I went to live with my dad. I see my mum now and then, although I still resent her big time. I've never told my dad I knew all along because he'd think I betrayed him too. How fucked up is that?'

Kayla looked suitably shocked as she processed Alex's sorry tale.

'I'm so sorry this happened to you as a child, that is truly awful. It explains why you don't go interstate to see your parents much. I can see it's taken its toll on you. But you can't just assume I'm cheating as a result of that. I'm not responsible for your past. You need to get help to change your thought patterns.'

Feelings of confusion flooded through Kayla as she became torn between her feelings for Alex and the raw sense of betrayal she felt. Her initial urge was to retreat, however she found herself being drawn back to him, unable to dismiss his pleas for forgiveness.

Alex looked at her earnestly. 'I did see a counsellor once. She said my betrayal trauma has continued to impact me and make me have crazy jealous thoughts that are unfounded. The terror of these thoughts becoming a reality makes me lash out. I'm a fucking dickhead.'

Fresh tears spilled down his face and Kayla willingly took him into her arms. The room was charged with emotion as the vulnerability in Alex's voice softened Kayla's resolve. Torn between anger and love, she recalled the tender moments that defined their relationship: the laughter, the dreams, the undeniable chemistry that had drawn her to him. Kayla never spoke of her own childhood experiences and now her throat felt raw, she was too depleted to talk anymore. Their conversation had triggered memories of her own upbringing, yet she felt his needs were more important than hers right now, so she pushed them down. Kayla sat quietly reflecting about the damage Alex had caused and the fear that now surrounded her.

I have my own demons dammit. I don't need to be dealing with his too.

Sensing her unease, Alex gently tilted her chin upwards, and they shared a tentative, lingering kiss; a symbol of their connection which swiftly turned into a moment fraught with emotion. The kiss carried the weight of their struggles, filled with both hope and uncertainty. Kayla was shocked to find she was aching to feel him inside of her. Their chemistry was undeniable, and taking control, she pushed him onto the bed, straddling him as she hitched up her dress. Alex tore off her lace thong in one swift movement and as Kayla lowered herself on to him, she convinced herself she was back in charge. Once spent, they made a pact. Kayla sat up, propped up on one elbow; her cheeks flushed with pleasure as she looked deep into Alex's grey eyes.

'I'll agree to give you another chance to put things right, but only if you commit to getting help. Your one-off counselling session was clearly not enough Alex.'

Alex smiled and nodded at her, appearing to wholeheartedly agree. Kayla relaxed, feeling sure she had gained the upper hand. By the end of the evening, Kayla believed that Alex's actions stemmed wholly from his pain, and not from a place of malice. They both slept fitfully as Alex spooned Kayla and she conveniently forgot about the fading mark on her face.

Chapter 6

Belinda could not bear listening to the wails of distress coming from the cabin next door any longer. It had been evident since the first day of the cruise that all was not well with the couple next door. Belinda knew a domestic violence situation when she heard one.

She was aware that the male had stormed out *again* and his poor young girlfriend was trapped in the confines of their stateroom all alone. Richard was off on walkabout again and she was not sure what he was up to, however that was a separate issue altogether. For now, she must do something about the situation with her neighbours. Belinda thought about scribbling a note for Richard then thought better of it. Let him wonder where she was for a change. He never answered any of her calls or text messages, so it was pointless communicating with him that way.

Belinda let out a loud sigh as she placed the novel she was reading on the nightstand and braced herself. It was time to see what she could do to help. Belinda approached the cabin next-door and knocked softly. The wailing stopped abruptly, and she sensed that the young woman was afraid. Belinda raised her voice, 'It's okay love, I just want to make sure you are alright. I'm not here to make things worse.'

Kayla stiffened; she could faintly make out a women's voice behind the solid door. She strained to hear better, it was difficult to understand what she was saying. Belinda looked around the passageway nervously. The childish part of her wanted to be out when Richard came back however, she also didn't want to come face to face with the perpetrator. She knocked again, still no reply. She repeated knocking a few more times to no avail. Belinda had no choice but to return to her cabin. She wondered if she should slip a note under the door as a way to get the girl's attention. *Before I do, I wonder if she might be on her balcony.* Belinda unlocked the sliding door to her balcony and stepped outside. Tentatively she leaned over the left-hand side and poked her head over to next door.

Kayla was leaning on the balustrade, her face buried in her forearms.

'Excuse me love.' Belinda said softly. Kayla's head snapped up; her eyes wild as they connected with hazel eyes of the curly red-haired lady from next door. Kayla began to scurry towards the sliding doors leading to her stateroom to hide her mortification. She was sporting a black eye and did not want anyone to see it.

'Please wait, I want to help you!' Belinda yelled out.

Kayla stopped in her tracks, torn between wanting to hide away and the ache for some moral support. Belinda called out again, 'Come to my cabin love, there's no one here except me, you will be safe I promise.' Kayla did not reply, and Belinda heard her go back inside and click the sliding door shut.

That will be that then, she obviously won't accept my help.

Feeling exasperated Belinda checked her phone. A text message popped up from Richard.

You won't believe this! I bumped into Frank from work – what are the chances? He booked a last-minute trip on the same cruise. Going to have a couple of beers together, be back in a bit x

Belinda placed her phone down on the vanity. Her neck prickled with unease.

There's something very odd going on with Richard and I must get to the bottom of it.

Belinda didn't believe a word of his text. Although what was the point in trying to find him amongst over 4000 other passengers? She noted he hadn't said which bar he was in, and she decided not to ask him for fear of receiving further vagueness from him or worse still, no reply at all.

Belinda's thoughts were interrupted by a faint knock on the door. She quickly jumped up in case it was the girl from next door as she knew if she didn't answer her straight away, she might change her mind. Belinda pulled the door open and tried not to gasp at the state of Kayla's swollen eye as she swiftly ushered her in. The girl was a nervous wreck, her eyes darting from left to right rapidly. Belinda held Kayla by the shoulders and looked into her face.

'You are okay love; you are safe here. My husband will be away for a while so it's only us two here, okay? Now take a deep breath and explain to me what is going on so I can figure out how to help you.'

Kayla was shivering so Belinda took down the spare blanket from the closet and wrapped it around the girl's shoulders while guiding her to sit on the bed. She then called room service to request someone bring her a cold compress.

'I'm Belinda by the way, what's your name love?' she asked gently. Kayla looked up, her expression blank.

'My name's Kayla.'

Belinda's kind face was etched with concern. She could see the hurt in the girl's eyes, and it made her sad.

'Do you need a hug right now?'

Kayla nodded in a childlike fashion and fell into Belinda's ample bosom. The two women hugged as Belinda rubbed Kayla's back as though she was an infant needing to burp.

Belinda spoke softly, 'I'm worried about your safety love. I know your partner has hit you and you don't deserve it no matter what his excuse is.'

Kayla stared ahead as she spoke. 'Alex was the perfect guy at first; we fell hard for each other, and he was literally Mr Perfect. We are both 25 this year, so I thought we were mature enough to become serious with each other, you know? As soon as we got on this cruise, he began acting in an irrational way. First, he said I flirted with a staff member at Guest Services and this time he said I was getting too chummy with the barman making our drinks. Tonight, he has hit me for the second time, and I'm so confused. We spoke about it for ages after the first time and I honestly believed that the thought of losing me meant he'd never do it again. I don't understand how I got myself into this situation. Now I'm trapped on this fucking ship. I rang reception to ask if there are any free cabins and was told the ship is at capacity. I couldn't afford my own cabin anyhow. So, I'm stuck in this nightmare until we get off. It's not like I can escape at one of the ports. All my things are onboard, and he won't tell me what the combination is for the safe; it has our passports in there. I really don't know what to do at this point.'

Kayla began to cry, and Belinda placed an arm around her shoulders.

'Kayla, listen to me honey. As soon as you accept the unacceptable, you can be damn sure you are giving the green light for it to happen again. I've seen this pattern with so many women, it's not funny. No matter what his sob story is, you are not his punching bag. You deserve so much better than that, okay?'

Kayla nodded sadly with a jolt of realisation that this lady was spot on with her advice. An unwelcome flashback from her childhood flitted through her mind, and she quickly dismissed the thought.

'Kayla, let me ask you something. Do you feel confused because the kissing and making up was so damn good after he hit you?'

Kayla's head snapped up in surprise.

'Funny you should say that. I think there is something wrong with me because after he hit me, we had the best sex I've ever had.

I've heard of bastards turning women on but I'm not some stupid bimbo. I can't understand how I can be up for it after he has been violent! I mean what kind of girl does that make me?'

Belinda gave the younger woman a wise smile.

'Listen love, I used to work at a women's domestic violence shelter and one of them shared with me what her psychologist explained to her. What happens is that when you feel strong emotions such as passion or anger, your logical brain can't tell one emotion from another. What I'm saying is that passion and anger are closely linked. When you are angry, you release adrenaline, your heart rate increases, and you become flushed, right?'

Kayla nodded, unsure where this conversation was going. Belinda sat up straighter.

'Well, all of those things are identical feelings to what happens when you are horny, so your brain can confuse the two. Therefore, a fight can lead to amazing sex. It's simply a transfer of emotions – do you see where I'm coming from?'

Kayla ran a hand through her thick chestnut hair. 'Bloody hell I think you have a point. I was shocked at how aroused I was, and we did have mind blowing sex afterwards. I couldn't think straight the next day. I was so ashamed that I allowed the intimacy because being that close indicates complete forgiveness and I don't forgive him deep down. I resent the bastard so much…'

'But the kissing and making up made you ridiculously horny all the same,' Belinda finished knowingly.

Kayla nodded wearily in response to Belinda's words of wisdom as her eyes filled with tears yet again.

'Thank you for reaching out in my time of need. You are a lovely lady.'

Belinda smiled and clasped Kayla's hand in-between hers.

'You are welcome love, my heart breaks for you. No woman deserves this. Now we need to figure out how to keep you safe and how to handle him until you get off the ship. I wish you could stay here with me.'

Kayla nodded sombrely. 'I'm sure your husband wouldn't be over the moon with that idea.'

Belinda's eyes narrowed as she thought about her errant spouse. 'Well, if you must know I think there is something untoward going on with my Richard. I'm not sure what exactly … he is acting super shady, you know all secretive, sneaking off and telling me a pack of lies about where he is. So, I understand what it's like to want to pretend something isn't happening when it's clear that it is. If I had my way, I'd move you in here and shove the two pricks in with each other next door!'

Kayla managed a small giggle at that comment. Belinda had such a sweet face that her anger seemed out of place. She kind of wished Belinda was her mum. They both jumped in unison as someone knocked sharply on the cabin door. The two women looked at each other in fear.

'Do you think that's Alex?' Kayla whispered.

The caller knocked again. Belinda recognised the muffled voice on the other side as Ricardo, the sweet Filipino cabin steward. She sagged with relief and opened the door, although only slightly.

Ricardo smiled from ear to ear. 'Here is the cold compress you asked for ma'am.'

Belinda smiled. 'Thank you so much Ricardo, have a lovely day.' She closed the door as relief flooded through her. Belinda knew Alex wouldn't be too far away though. Men like him always went to cool off then come back with their tail between their legs, ready to bat their sad puppy dog eyes.

She turned to Kayla. 'Gosh we got so caught up in our chat, we forgot I'd asked for this!'

Belinda waved the cold compress in the air. 'Do you want to lie down and hold this over your eye for a bit? Then we can figure out what to do next. I'm sure Alex will be back soon and won't take too kindly to you being in here. Should we agree to keep our little friendship quiet?'

Kayla nodded her agreement and winced as the freezing cold face towel connected with the hot swollen skin around her eye.

Kayla sighed. 'I was thinking the same thing. Let's swap numbers and at least I know I can reach out to someone on the ship if I need to.'

Belinda was deep in thought again. 'We need to think of the best way to play this to maximise your safety. I seriously don't want you going anywhere near him. I also know from experience that keeping perpetrators onside until you have a clear exit plan is sadly sometimes the safest way.'

Kayla sat up. 'I think you are right, and I also think that I need to get back to my cabin pronto. I have a sixth sense that he is on his way back. He tends to do a gym workout and then come back once he has worked off his anger. I feel a lot better knowing you are looking out for me though … your help today means more than you will ever know.'

The two women exchanged a fierce hug and after exchanging mobile phone numbers, Kayla returned to her cabin. Belinda suddenly felt the urge to go after her, to get her the hell out of there.

Why on earth did I send the lamb back to the slaughter? The poor girl could sleep on our sofa if she needs to. To hell with what Richard thinks!

Belinda paced back and forth as she thought about the advice she had given the girl. She knew deep down that she couldn't get involved to the extent that she wanted to. Richard would go nuts if she harboured an unknown girl in their cabin. This Alex guy was likely to find out and then all hell would break loose. Then they might all end up in danger. Belinda reflected that perhaps the girl should have gone straight to the Security Personnel on the ship, but what would happen to her then? She had already been told the ship was at capacity with no vacant cabins. Where would they make her stay and was it wise to involve foreign police?

Belinda had heard that cruise ships were subject to the law of the country they were in a 200-mile limit of, although another friend reckoned the ship was bound by the country it was registered in. It all sounded too messy to figure out who the responsible jurisdiction was. Surely this Alex guy was better off being dealt with by the police on his home turf if he was to get what he deserved? Belinda's left eye began to twitch, a sure sign she was agitated.

She sent an angry text:

Where the hell are you, Richard? We need to talk, you better get your bloody arse back to the cabin pronto.

Richard did not reply despite the read receipt message. Belinda felt another prickle of unease wash over her as she noted the tell-tale tightness in her belly that was her body's signal when all was not well.

Chapter 7

Richard knew that avoiding Belinda was not the answer. He ignored the vibration of his mobile phone in his jacket pocket. It was a sure sign his wife had sent another text message demanding to know where he was. Right now, he needed alone time to think things through. The salty air, usually a symbol of freedom, was now a suffocating weight on his chest. The luxury cruise ship that yesterday seemed like a haven of indulgence, had quickly become his personal purgatory. All because of a stupid decision, a fleeting moment of weakness. His dalliance with the vivacious Tia due to his lapse in judgment threatened to shatter his carefully constructed life.

Richard's face was scrunched up in fury as he marched along the ship's walking track. He needed to outsmart this stupid little bitch and her partner in crime. Tia was nothing more than a viper, poised to strike on unsuspecting male prey. He'd received a cryptic text message, delivered shortly after their sexual encounter, that had plunged him into an icy terror. It was a short video clip, a snippet of his indiscretion with Tia was the chilling evidence. The message was simple:

Pay up and it disappears.

Panic seized Richard. The thought of Belinda discovering his infidelity was unbearable. He suddenly saw with great clarity that she was the rock of his life and the thought of his grown-up children finding out he was a cheat made him bow his head in shame.

He had built a genuine reputation as an honest family man and businessman. He'd lived a life of respectability, and this one foolish night threatened to tear it all down. Richard realised with clarity that he'd taken Belinda for granted and had no right to be scornful about her fading looks. She was one in a million and ten times the woman that Tia could ever be.

I'm a bloody moron having a midlife crisis. Why the hell did I let my stupid ego believe that girl truly fancied me when I've got more chins than a Chinese phone book?

What a dickhead!

Richard tried to think straight but it was becoming increasingly difficult to focus. He realised that Tia's blackmail was no more than a calculated game of fear and manipulation. She knew he'd be paralysed by fear and guilt, and he realised with shame that he had found himself trapped in a web of his own making. As he marched on, the luxurious surroundings of the ship continued to mock him. They served as a constant reminder of his predicament. The care-free vibe and the laughter of other passengers amplified his despair as he passed by them with a glum expression. The weight of his secret was crushing him. Richard felt the fear begin to gnaw at his sanity. He was a prisoner on this floating palace, trapped in a nightmare of his own creation. Richard's desperation reached a fever pitch as he thundered on.

I must find a way out of this mess, to reclaim my life. But how can I when the evidence is on that manipulative little bitch's recording device?

As Richard finally slowed down to look out to sea, he realised his only hope was to outsmart Tia and her pimp before she could ruin him. Suddenly a semblance of a plan started to formulate in Richard's mind and it made him feel a little better.

Every problem has a solution, right?

As he slowly made his way back to his cabin to face his wife, he shuddered at the dark thoughts he was having. Who knew that revenge could make you consider taking such extreme action...

As Richard suspected, Belinda leapt up in a rage when he finally entered their cabin. She jabbed a stubby bejewelled finger in his face.

'Where the hell have you been and why are you not answering your phone? I've been out of my mind Richard. I've been worried sick, you selfish bastard!'

Richard put up a hand to defend himself. Belinda had taken on the appearance of a wild banshee, her hair stuck out at odd angles and her eyeliner was smeared, which only added to her look of derangement.

'If you'd calm down, I will explain it to you.' Richard used what he thought was his best contrite voice.

'Okay well I'm waiting so let's bloody hear it!' Belinda spat, her eyes glittering with fury. She was up on her tiptoes trying to match his height; a sure sign she was enraged.

Richard sighed. 'Sit down love and please simmer down, it's hard to talk when you are so worked up.'

Belinda narrowed her eyes, wanting to retaliate to his patronising comment yet at the same time wanting to hear what he would say for himself more. Somehow, she bit her tongue. Belinda wasn't stupid. She observed Richard's tight jaw and his rigid defensive posture, and had a gut feeling he was about to tell her a pack of lies. She was dismayed to find that her main concern was that a part of her wanted to shelve whatever the hell was going on so they could enjoy their hard-earned trip given the cruise had been so expensive. Couldn't she simply enjoy the holiday she'd been counting down to for so long and then deal with whatever the hell was going on later? Why did the stupid prick go and rain on her parade?

Richard sat on the small sofa that was strewn with various items, including several straw hats and bottles of sunscreen. He knew Belinda must be livid because when she was calm, everything was put away in its place. He sighed wistfully and looked down at his hands. His fingers were laced together, and he was twirling his thumbs nervously. Belinda looked on scornfully; she knew he did this with his hands when he was either extremely nervous or lying. In this case, she felt sure it was both. After 30 years together she had her husband's body language down pat. Richard wiped his sweating brow with the back of his hand as he spoke quickly, his words tumbling over each other.

'Look love I'm just going to come right out with it. The other night when I went out myself after our dinner at the French Bistro, I went to the casino. I had a few drinks and got caught up in the excitement of some guy's win. I've been so sensible all my life that I thought why the hell not? Why not have a bit of fun for a change? I stupidly thought maybe I'd win enough to pay for our Emma's wedding.'

Richard glanced up nervously, he knew from Belinda's arched eyebrows and lack of outrage that this indicated she didn't believe a word of it. Belinda interjected, 'So what you are going to tell me next is that you did not in fact win any money and that you lost it instead?'

Richard nodded sheepishly. 'I'd rather not worry you about the amount because I promise I'm going to fix this mess, okay?'

Belinda stared at him thoughtfully. She knew she should be livid at what he'd told her but every fibre of her being told her the story was a bid to cover something even bigger up, therefore it was difficult to react accordingly. Richard was definitely not the gambling type; he was far too risk adverse.

So, what on earth had made him go to the extremes of fabricating this story? What the hell has he done?

Belinda swallowed down the scream that threatened to leave her throat and stood up.

'I'm not sure what to say Richard. This honestly doesn't sound like you at all. You have been acting shady ever since we set sail to be honest, and what is all this bullshit about bumping into Frank as well? Do you expect me to believe that?'

Richard's eyes were fixated on a blemish on the carpet, 'Yeah that was a cover up. The guy who won the jackpot felt sorry for me and we met up again so he could teach me how to win it back. As it turned out, I didn't have the guts to go through with trying to win the money back though. I will sort it out love; I promise. I've already got my secretary looking into selling my vintage car so that will take care of most of the debt. I know I've messed up and I'm so sorry. Can we please just try to enjoy this cruise that we have worked so hard for in the meantime?'

Belinda was torn between exploding with anger at his stupidity and confronting him about what was truly going on. She was utterly shocked to find that it was easier to go along with his narrative because it was too painful to consider any alternatives for his story. She sat down on the bed with a thud as the realisation hit her.

I'm no better than the girl putting up with the domestic violence, am I? I'm going along with lies that are easier to swallow because the truth is too scary to face. What have I become? I am determined to enjoy this cruise, and then I will face the music when we go home. He is a lying bastard and we both know it.

That night Richard and Belinda slept facing away from each other, both staring into space as sleep evaded them. Richard knew Belinda didn't believe him and the fact she had not challenged him unnerved him more than if she'd gone ballistic as expected. For now, though, his priority was dealing with Tia and her scumbag side kick Tony. Sorting out his marriage would be his next priority once he'd eliminated the problem. Richard thought hard about the best way to handle his dilemma. He surely couldn't give into never ending blackmail, he wasn't that stupid. Richard knew he must act quickly and decisively; he was determined to be the one in control. He considered his options, his mind racing with possibilities. He could go to the ship's security personnel to report the extortion but that meant admitting his mistake and risking public embarrassment. No, that wasn't an option. He'd find a way to handle the situation himself.

He decided he'd confront Tia and show her he wasn't afraid of her. As a grown man, he must not allow himself to be pushed around. With a steely resolve, he set out to find the little madam responsible for this mess so he could put an end to it once and for all. As he racked his brains for ideas, a sense of unease grew within him. Tia had obtained intel on him. She was obviously trying to anticipate his actions. It was as if she and Tony were always one step ahead. Richard was determined to find a solution, so he pushed the niggling doubt out of his mind. He must stay sharp and alert. Richard knew he must be careful; one wrong move could lead to disaster. He needed to plan his next steps meticulously, ensuring he had the upper hand. With a cunning strategy forming in his mind, he prepared for the necessary confrontation, ready to put an end to the nightmare.

The culmination of his plan was a risky manoeuvre. A confrontation needed to occur with Tia, that much was certain. In bed Richard tossed and turned, a mixture of fear and determination swirling within him. Finally, he decided on his counter move: he'd place a hidden camera strategically positioned in the breast pocket of his blazer. The silly little cow hadn't considered that the ship had a shop that sold state of the art micro cameras, had she? Tia would be caught in her own web of lies and hopefully when he gained the upper hand it would leave her speechless.

Chapter 8

Jake's gaze drifted out of focus, as his thoughts took him a thousand miles away. He inhaled deeply and rolled the cool beer bottle between his palms. The bar was dimly lit, a sanctuary from the whirlwind of guests needing his attention; a brief escape where he could catch a breath. As he took a long sip, the crisp taste washed over him, momentarily drowning out his never-ending obligations. He was making the most of his small window of downtime and ignoring his mobile phone as the screen lit up with a flurry of missed calls. His parents and sister kept leaving irate voice mail messages. They could not seem to comprehend how busy he was due to being responsible for the smooth-running of the entire ship. They were always in a huff when he was too tied up to call them back. Jake sighed. His mother wanted to marry him off and see him settle down with a mundane 9-5 job. Jake doubted she'd have her wish any time soon. He was the black sheep of the family and had his sights set on living life to the full by sampling as many countries and women as he could. Jake was still in his prime and was not ready for a predictable life. The thought of returning to his bachelor pad in London bored him. It had been a dream come true to win the coveted Cruise Director position. He was the youngest to ever win the title and he was going to make the most of it, even if the work was non-stop.

Each day brought an endless supply of passenger queries, mishaps and requests. Jake knew this was all part and parcel of being the Cruise Director, but he couldn't deny that the job was relentless. Still, this was the part of the evening that was all his and he was going to make the most of it. Claire had finished her theatre performance for the night and was rather pleased with the wolf whistles she'd received from the men in the audience. She'd headed straight to the bar to find Jake and unknowingly shattered his peace. Jake snapped back to the present as he became aware of Claire's high-pitched voice.

'Jake are you even listening to me?'

He turned to face Claire noting her narrowed eyes and curled lip. That was all he needed. She'd be stamping her foot like an irate toddler next. Couldn't a guy simply have a beer in peace?

Jake sighed. 'It's been a big couple of days Claire. I'm exhausted and frankly not in the mood for any crap. I honestly don't have the energy.'

A flurry of expressions crossed Claire's face. Jake guessed in all his wisdom that she wanted to respond angrily, then thought better of it. Jake noted that the female passenger who'd come on strong to him the other night had suddenly appeared at the other side of the bar. Claire stiffened as she followed Jake's gaze which landed on Tia's cleavage. Tia's dress featured a plunging neckline that almost reached her waist; her pert breasts threatening to spill out of the skimpy fabric at any moment.

Recognising the flirty girl from the other night, Claire immediately snuggled into Jake, placing a possessive arm around his waist. She noted that this time Tia's sparkly dress was silver rather than blue. She hated her on sight.

Jake did his best to pretend he hadn't noticed Tia, turning the bar stool so that his back faced her. A cat fight was the last thing he needed. Feeling a sense of triumph at Jake's move, Claire made a point of standing in between Jake's open legs as he sat on the stool, and she kissed him softly on the lips while wrapping her arms around his neck.

Jake wriggled on the stool. 'Claire!' he hissed. 'You know damn well that even when I'm having down time, I'm still expected to behave in a professional way in front of the passengers. Let's save the ear lobe nibbling for later on in my cabin, okay?'

Claire pouted and untangled herself from Jake, using the pretence of moving away from him to lift her drink from the bar. She snuck a glance at Tia who was staring smugly at her. Claire gave her a dirty look and turned back to Jake.

An hour later, Jake and Claire were both surprised to see Vincent in a deep conversation with Tia. They appeared rather merry together as they clinked glasses in a toast while laughing loudly.

Jake ruffled Claire's hair playfully. 'Looks as though Vincent may have scored.'

Claire chuckled, 'If it keeps her occupied and stops her throwing herself at you then I'm all for it.'

Jake ignored the comment and glanced over at Vincent and Tia. Wasn't Vincent meant to be gutted about separating from his wife? Something about his little charade with Tia was off, staged even. He put the thought to one side, too tired to give it much consideration. Claire was momentarily distracted; she clapped her hands with glee as the rest of her dance troupe trickled into the bar. She ambled over to Joel, a tall Jamaican male dancer. Joel went through boyfriends at an alarming rate and Claire found his stories hilarious. As the other dancers gravitated towards Joel, she knew they were in for a treat as he began regaling them with tales of his colourful love life.

A few of Jake's team members dropped in for drinks. Most of the team had turned in for the night due to the inevitable early rise the following day, but there were a handful who liked to wind down with a nightcap or two. Jake felt blessed as he observed their weary faces. He was grateful to have such a hard-working group around him. Jake was still concerned about Vincent's behaviour but kept telling himself the cruise would be over before they knew it. He would get to the bottom of his melt down then. As if reading his thoughts, the Events Manager Maisie approached Jake. Her cheeks were flushed, and she appeared anxious. Jake gave her a reassuring smile; she worked extremely hard and deserved the praise he often lavished on her.

Maisie's smile was more of a grimace. 'Jake, I hate stirring things up and I wasn't going to say anything, but I think you should know I overheard Vincent talking disrespectfully about you earlier. To be honest he has been pretty rude about you winning the Director position since we set sail. He keeps saying you shouldn't have got the job. I'm so sorry to be the one to tell you that. I just can't listen to his vitriol anymore. Just for the record no one agrees with him, and he only causes awkward silences. I'm telling you simply because I want you to be aware that I think he is a nasty piece of work.' Maisie tightened her pony tail nervously as she watched Jake's expression. Her uniform suddenly felt uncomfortable, and she wished she could undo a couple of buttons on her cream blouse.

Jake's stomach churned. It appeared that despite the support and olive branch he'd offered Vincent, he was still carrying on like a dickhead behind his back. He decided it was time to issue him with a verbal warning.

'Thanks for making me aware Maisie. I know how hard it is for you to get involved in such things. I appreciate you looking out for me and giving me the heads up. I know how he feels about me and can assure you that I'm dealing with it. Do let me know if you hear anymore though, okay? I won't mention my source. I know the hierarchy don't appreciate snitches.'

A dull flush crept up Maisie's neck. Jake quickly back pedalled. 'Oh, Maisie I'm not implying that I personally think you are a snitch, I simply meant that the team generally don't appreciate things being repeated back to the boss so I'm protecting you if that makes sense?'

Maisie relaxed a little and sipped her wine. As she glanced across the bar, she caught Vincent's eye and her blood ran cold as he stared at her, his beady eyes fuelled with venomous rage. Feeling panic rise within her, she turned back to Jake to seek his support, however a female passenger in a sparkly silver dress had blocked the way and Jake was being his usual professional self, answering the girl's query about the ship's activities for the night, rather than getting into having a confrontation with his swine of an assistant.

Maisie muttered something about turning in for the night and promptly headed back to her cabin feeling sick to her stomach. Vincent noted her demeanour as she slunk out the door and Maisie felt his eyes bore into her back. She knew without a doubt that Vincent was on to her. Maisie shrugged and told herself that she'd done the right thing, even if it caused waves. She had been observing Vincent for some time, and while she had liked him at first, she now saw a man perpetually shrouded in a thin veneer of politeness who was in reality a ticking time bomb. He tried and failed to convince anyone who'd listen that he was the rightful Cruise Director, believing his experience and meticulous planning far exceeded Jake's skills. Maisie also noted that every compliment Jake received and every appreciative glance from female passengers made Vincent's permanent scowl deepen even more.

Claire was giggling at something Joel said when she spotted Jake and Tia intimately chatting together from across the room. The smile fell from her face as a whirlwind of rage consumed her. She stormed away from her dancer friends and was about to barge in-between them when Joel grabbed Claire by the arm and stopped her in her tracks.

Joel towered over her, his chocolate skin glistening under the light. He pointed a long-manicured finger in her face.

'Girl, you gotta stop with this jealously crap! Aint nobody on this cruise gonna marry who they are shagging right now and that includes you. That girl talking to Jake; she'd love to see you lose control and Jake will be pissed off with you because the wellbeing of the precious passengers always comes first, and you know it. My advice to you is to play it cool and stop walking into her trap. As for Jake girl, you gotta know he aint a one-woman man! He aint gonna enjoy you being all possessive.'

Claire skidded to a halt her eyes wide as Joel's words sunk in. Deep down she knew her jealousy was flaring at every interaction Jake had with other women, particularly the slut with the sparkly dress collection. She used every ounce of will power to turn towards the open deck instead of where Jake and Tia were standing. The fresh air might calm her down and clear her mind. She turned to Joel.

'You are wrong about Jake, what we have, its… it's becoming something more serious.'

Joel looked incredulous. 'You are a very naïve little girl.' He waved a hand at the other dancers. 'We can all see you are getting all demanding with him. Girl you just don't wanna accept it's a casual fling with Jake. Now I'm gonna leave you to think about that.'

Claire watched the dark amazon flounce off. She liked Joel, however he was the last person she'd take advice from. He chewed up men and spat them out at a scary rate.

Claire watched Jake and Tia from outside, staring intently at the alluringly bubbly girl, who clearly found Jake irresistible. The girl with the bright smile and infectious laughter was a reminder of everything Claire lacked; she was a lightness of being, a carefree spirit. All Claire could see was a potential threat to her fragile claim on Jake. She needed to eliminate her somehow.

Claire reminded herself she must do her best to remain professional. As one of the ship's main performers, she understood the importance of maintaining a dignified demeanour, even when she felt turbulent on the inside. After watching Tia drape herself over Jake, throwing her head back in laughter at what appeared to be a private joke, Claire felt her mask slipping away.

Jake had warned her about the challenges of managing her feelings towards him onboard, lecturing her incessantly about conducting herself properly. It was hard to remember those words while Tia toyed with everything Claire was clinging on to.

The final straw was watching Tia brush against Jake's arm in a move that Claire knew was designed to provoke her. Claire scanned the room, her heart pounding with the weight of jealousy and the sting of betrayal. When Tia finally sashayed toward the ladies' room, Claire promptly followed, her heels clicking against the polished floor.

'Excuse me,' Claire said as she stepped into the intimate space of the powder room, her tone crisp and laced with barely concealed anger.

Tia turned, her eyes wide with surprise before quickly shifting to a sly smirk. 'Oh, hello! I didn't expect to see you here. Don't you need to be on stage again for the late performance?' Tia taunted the other girl, her voice dripping with mock sweetness.

'You need to stop trying to get your claws into my boyfriend,' Claire snapped. She stepped towards Tia, her hands balled into fists at her sides. 'This constant flirting with Jake... it's pretty pathetic.'

Tia laughed, a tinkling noise that only fuelled Claire's frustration. 'Pathetic? What's pathetic is thinking you can keep him all to yourself. He's a man, Claire. They all crave excitement; the sooner you realise that the better. There is no such thing as a man who can't be snared and, believe me, I've tested this theory out many times.'

The realisation struck Claire then. Tia was using Jake. He was a pawn in a sick game and she must be prepared to fight to protect her territory.

'One day you are gonna mess with the wrong couple you know! I hope you get your eyes gouged out in the process!'

Claire snapped back. 'This isn't a game. Jake isn't some trophy to win. He's my partner on and off the ship. If you can't respect that, I will take matters into my own hands.'

Tia rolled her eyes, holding up her hands in mock surrender. 'Oh please, as if anyone can take you seriously on this ship. You're just a crappy singer and dancer who couldn't make it on land, so you perform on cruise ships instead.'

Something about Tia's sneering face made Claire snap and she lunged at her, grabbing at a fistful of her blonde hair as her blood pounded in her ears.

'Oi that's enough of that you pair of animals!' A large African American lady prised the girls apart, her huge bosom heaving with indignation.

Claire and Tia noted a little crowd had formed around them and both mumbled their apologies, stepping away from each other so that the drama seeking passengers would disperse. Claire turned on her heel and stomped out.

A few minutes later, Tia stepped out of the ladies to find Claire waiting for her outside. She hissed in Tia's ear, 'If you think you can get away with this, you're sadly mistaken. Jake is taken by me, and I'm not going to let you manipulate him simply for your own amusement.'

For a moment, the air crackled with tension. Tia's bravado began to falter, then she promptly straightened herself up.

'You seriously think he's that into you?' Tia mocked, looking incredulous, her voice low.

'I know he is,' Claire shot back, although her words were laced with doubt. 'If you think your little games can come between us, then you are sadly mistaken and dumber than you look.'

Claire marched back towards the bar, leaving Tia staring after her with a wicked grin on her face. Claire burst back into the bustling lounge, the warmth of the evening air and the buzz of voices calming her racing thoughts. She caught sight of Jake across the room, his smile fading as he noticed her ferocious expression.

With the weight of the confrontation with Tia lingering in her mind, Claire approached him. 'Jake,' she called softly.

Jake gave her the once over with those sexy eyes that made her stomach flutter. She took a deep breath, ready to confront him about what had been troubling her.

'Can we talk?'

Jake glanced at Claire's nipples, clearly visible through the flimsy material of her dress and replied with a wink.

'I had other things in mind…'

Claire gave a seductive smile as she took his hand and led him back to her cabin. She hoped the slut was watching them leave together. Claire intended to give Jake the ride of his life and then she'd lay down the law about Tia. Perhaps the evening wasn't over yet, and the real performance was yet to begin.

Chapter 9

The following day, Tia felt the steady thrum of the treadmill beneath her feet as she jogged absentmindedly. The gym aboard the *Ocean Breeze* boasted a dazzling array of modern equipment, but today it felt like a gilded cage. Taylor Swift sang about heartbreak and freedom, and the bittersweet lyrics were all too resonant with her current situation. She felt trapped between the lure of an easy fortune and the chains of loyalty to Tony.

Richard's early morning phone call had stirred something inside her; a mix of intrigue and apprehension. She knew that Tony was using her to make easy money, but the allure of hard cash was hard to ignore, especially now that they were at sea, living in a bubble without the prying eyes of the rest of world. Even though Tia was the one with the goods, Tony was the brains behind the outfit. He knew how to gather intel on their victims and how to extort money from them. Also, their victims tended to be afraid of his stature, whereas if Tia was doing the scams on her own, she was more likely to end up being beaten up. Tia's mind drifted back to Richard's call, how he spoke so easily about her creating a future without Tony, one where she could make legitimate money for herself if she were free of his clutches. Maybe Richard had a better offer for her? She was certainly curious to hear what the sucker would say.

In the back of Tia's mind, a nagging doubt remained. Richard was the type of man who was careful. He had a dirty secret, yet he had jumped straight into the fire, taking the risk to reach out to her directly. That unsettled her. Was he truly looking out for her, or was he merely playing a dangerous game, seeing how far he could manipulate her?

With each step she took, she envisioned a potential confrontation with Tony, how he'd react if she made a deal directly with Richard. He'd track her down and become violent. Tony definitely had a nasty streak, and she did not want to get on the wrong side of him. Tia bit her lip, her heart rate increasing not from the exercise, rather it was from the possibilities spinning in her mind. The treadmill's electronic screen flickered before her, showing the logged distance she'd covered, however the workout had not given her the usual high, nor had she gained any clarity about her situation.

As the song shifted to a more upbeat tempo, she decided that a cold shower might clear her head. She wiped the sweat from her brow, pulled her earbuds out, and walked over to the massive glass windows that looked out over the endless ocean. The waves lapped rhythmically against the hull, and for a moment, she felt a pang of envy for the freedom they represented. In her peripheral vision, she became aware of the presence of Alex, the hunk she'd become acquainted with earlier. He'd begun to show up in the gym whenever she was there. She gave him an appreciative once over, her desire evident in her sparkling blue eyes.

There will be time to appreciate that sexy specimen in all his entirety later, but for now, I have things to do…

Later that afternoon, Tia found herself standing outside the library on deck eight. She gave a wary glance around her surroundings. The library was surprisingly quiet, the smell of old leather and paper took her back to her school days. Standing there, she felt small and uncertain beneath the imposing wooden archways. Richard arrived moments later, a dishevelled casually dressed figure.

To onlookers he appeared to carry the weight of the world on his shoulders. His eyes narrowed slightly as he took in Tia's expression; he could tell she had conflicting emotions.

'I'm glad you came,' he said, his voice low and conspiratorial. 'We need to talk.'

Tia took a deep breath, her mind racing. 'You know it's dangerous to meet like this,' she said, trying to mask the apprehension in her voice. 'What if Tony finds out?'

Richard leaned closer, and hissed, 'This is the only way we can get you out of his grip. You're too smart to let this go on. Look at the life you could have, Tia. No more being controlled, no more living under his shadow. He is nothing more than a pimp taking his cut while you do all the dirty work. I could help you get a well-paid job, a dignified one at that.'

When Tia didn't reply, Richard's voice rose slightly. 'Tia, I know Tony won't let you walk away from your agreement with him without putting up a fight. Look I'm going to take an educated guess here. Maybe I'm way off the mark but my worldly experience tells me I'm probably spot on. For Tony to be using you the way he is, and for you to be going along with it so willingly, it makes me think that you must be a rather vulnerable young woman who doesn't have much in the way of family or older role models to guide you. Am I right?'

Tia's bravado suddenly disappeared, and her face crumpled as a huge lump formed in her throat. She turned away from Richard and began blindly browsing a shelf of books, anything to avoid eye contact. Behind her Richard nodded knowingly, a triumphant look on his face. He'd hit the nail on the head and now he could use her weakness to his advantage. He continued talking to her in a low voice.

'Tia let's look at the facts. Tony uses you to lure men, you let them do the deed and then he goes in with the hard man act to scare them into paying up. Be truthful, how much of that money will you even receive for yourself?'

Tia glanced up at him, he could see the turmoil playing out on her pretty face, her previous brittle façade faded, giving a glimpse of the lost young girl in its place.

Tia silently motioned to a table and chairs in the far corner of the library where they wouldn't be heard. She swallowed hard, uncertainty coiling tightly in her stomach. Richard was obviously trying to get out of paying and yet something made her hopeful about his certainty that he could help her find a way out.

I have daddy issues.

She tossed back her hair in a bid to shake the thought away.

'What are you getting at?' she asked, realising this was no longer simply about the expected transaction; it felt more about the chance to start a new life.

The corners of Richard's mouth twitched into a gentle smile, but his eyes remained serious.

'I want to talk sense into you so that you can take control of your future.'

As the waves gently undulated against the ship, Tia felt time slow down. She looked at Richard, his expression earnest, and felt the weight of the choices before her. The money, the future, the fear that had held her captive, it all surged around her as she contemplated her next move.

Richard's intention to uncover the truth behind Tia's act of blackmail sharpened his focus. He thought carefully about the best way to address her.

'Why is a girl like you choosing to set men up to extort money from them? You could be doing so much more with your life! One day you will pick the wrong guy and come off extremely badly, I can assure you of that! You know the way you are going about it is pretty amateur too, right? I've done my own digging and note that you and this Tony fella are dumb enough to use your real names, really? It's a bit amateur.'

Richard spoke quietly and clearly, fully aware that the mini camera in his blazer pocket was recording every word and hopefully her confession in the coming minutes. Tia managed to compose herself and wore an air of defiance, her striking features hardened by life's injustices. Richard grimaced. He didn't want her to retreat behind a façade; he needed the truth.

Tia crossed her arms defensively, shaking her head slightly.

'We use our real names while on this ship dumbo. Are you forgetting our photo flashes up to match our passports every time we disembark at each port? Why are you so interested in my life choices anyway Richard? I do what I must to get by in life.'

Richard shook his head, he could find no logic in what she was saying, and he realised Tia and Tony were not as smart as they thought they were. Sighing, he tried to appeal to any shred of decency she might possess.

'Do you think it's right to exploit men after your sexual encounters with them?'

He pressed the point, holding his breath for her response. To his surprise, she didn't scoff or deflect. Instead, her eyes glistened, and a shadow passed over her features.

'You think I care about right or wrong?' she snapped. Richard noted a tremor in her voice and sensed he'd hit a deep nerve that ran along the edge of her carefully constructed façade. He leaned in closer, intrigued.

'What happened to you, Tia? No one enters this sort of life without a good reason.'

The blonde girl looked vulnerable for a fleeting moment before she let out a brittle laugh, tinged with pain. Her voice was thick with bitterness as she reflected back to that time.

'You truly want to know? Fine. I grew up in care from a young age. You'd think that'd mean I was safe, right? But I was passed around like a broken toy. My foster father was a monster who used and abused me in every vile way you can imagine. When I finally found the courage to tell my social worker, I ended up in a residential care unit as I obviously couldn't live in the same house as him anymore. My foster mum chose him over me, so I not only lost my birth parents, but I also lost my foster parents. I'm not worth holding onto it'd seem....'

Richard was caught off guard and momentarily speechless, 'Tia, I'm sorry to hear that, I ...'

'So, do you think I chose this life because I enjoy it?' Tia interrupted, her voice hardening.

'What I do is not about pleasure. It's survival. There's a difference.'

Richard shifted slightly, his expression softening. He could see the little girl she had once been.

'You've had to fight to feel wanted, haven't you?'

Richard realised it was more of a statement than a question.

'Every single day,' Tia replied, an edge of pride amidst her sorrow. 'I didn't have the luxury of playing the helpless child card. There was no other choice than to grow up fast. I learned to use my body in exchange for the big bucks. It's the only thing I have that anyone has ever wanted. So, I guess that makes it addictive. I'd be lying if I said I didn't enjoy the thrill of the chase.'

She paused, as she thought of all the nights spent giving herself to men.

'Maybe one day, when I'm in a better position, I'll stop. Find something real. But for now? This is what I've got, and you are only young and hot once.'

Tia blew her nose then threw the tissue into a nearby trash can. The act made her appear childlike somehow. Richard's heart sank as her voice cracked with pent up emotion.

'Tony was supposed to help me. He was one of the few youth workers who made out he gave a shit. For a while there, I thought he was someone who truly cared about me, but it was all bullshit. I was just another project for him, an easy target to exploit when I turned eighteen. But we are as bad as each other and I dunno… I'd be lying if I said I was here against my will…what we do, it just works… it paid for this cruise, something a girl like me could never afford.'

The camera silently chronicled the shift in Tia. Her exterior started to crack under Richard's penetrating stare.

Tia ran her tongue over her dry lips. 'I didn't have anyone to look up to in life, Richard. No adult role models to guide me. The only thing I learned was how to survive, and that meant becoming cold and hard. I use others before they use me. If I can't find happiness, then why should anyone else?'

Her lip curled, her feelings of contempt evident on her pretty face. Richard's breath quickened. This wasn't the confession he had anticipated. Instead of being solely focused on blackmailing men, Tia's part in this sorry mess was nested in a web of trauma and survival instinct.

'Tia, you need to understand that hurting others won't heal your pain,' he urged gently, leaning forward. 'You can make different choices, put things right you know?'

Tia paused, the fight within her flickering. 'As I said it's easier to pull others down with me.'

Her eyes held both the rage of a wounded girl and the yearning for understanding.

'The idea of true happiness seems to be a cruel joke, Richard. I just want to feel something, anything at all, after all the shit I've been through.'

Once again Richard caught a glimpse of the little child beneath the hardened shell, someone who had only ever yearned for love, understanding and connection. As the camera continued to capture her vulnerability, he felt a stirring of guilt. He was starting to feel genuinely sorry for her.

'Surely you don't feel good about stealing from men and wrecking their families and their livelihoods in the process?' Richard prompted her weakly.

'Give me a break!' Tia scoffed. 'You made your own choice about following your wandering dick's desires. You can't put this all on me!'

Tia's face hardened, the mask was back in place. "Now then, Richard, you apparently wanted to meet me to offer me a deal that doesn't involve Tony, so let's quit with the small talk and get down to business… one way or another, you are still paying me that money! Unless you want wifey to get the low down?'

Chapter 10

Kayla sat on the edge of the bed, the gentle sway of the ship beneath her making her heart flutter; not from excitement, rather from a growing sense of dread. She walked out to the balcony and tried to focus on the waves lapping rhythmically against the side. All she could think about was Alex. He'd gone to the gym to work off his latest mood. *Again.* She knew he'd be gone for at least two hours. She envisaged his face during their last fight and the way his intense grey eyes pierced through her only moments before he exposed his ugly side once more. Kayla sighed, she knew deep down she was far from perfect herself. She'd had her own destructive patterns in her past relationships that so far she'd managed to keep concealed from Alex.

Maybe we are not so different after all.

Kayla understood that Alex's childhood experiences had created a sense of mistrust and fear that he couldn't seem to shrug off. She had seen the glimpses of vulnerability, of the boy who'd needed nurturing instead of a mother who behaved like a whore. He definitely had mummy issues.

But I have my own issues and baggage from childhood – who doesn't?

How could she want to help him so badly and at the same time feel so trapped? Regardless of that, what was wrong with her that she was willing to put up with what he'd done? Why was she making excuses for him?

Kayla picked up her mobile phone, her fingers hovering over the screen as she thought about Belinda, the kind-hearted woman in the adjoining cabin. Belinda had offered advice that had rung true. There had been sincerity in her laughter and an authenticity in her words that made Kayla feel understood. Taking a deep breath, her thumbs moved rapidly over the keyboard:

Hey Belinda, it's Kayla from next door. I could do with your advice again.

She paused, the weight of her emotions swirling within her, adding to her hesitation. Could she articulate the chaos she was experiencing? Could she explain the way she still felt a pull towards Alex despite everything? Kayla continued typing, mindful of each word.

I'm feeling pretty overwhelmed. Alex and I had another fight, and I'm scared. There's a lot happening, and I don't know who to turn to. I feel so lost. Can we chat when you have a minute?

Kayla hit send, as she thought of Belinda's comforting presence. The woman had a way of making life's problems seem less daunting, and she hoped this time would be no different. A few minutes later, her phone buzzed, and she quickly skimmed Belinda's reply:

Of course, love. I'm here for you. Let's meet in the lounge in the atrium in 10 minutes. You're not going to deal with this alone, okay?

Relief washed over her, but anxiety soon took its place. She thought about the last time she and Alex had kissed and made up, the intoxicating heat of that moment clouding her mind. She remembered his touch, which ignited something deep within her, a deep desire intertwined with the fear of his violence. It didn't make sense and the confusion gnawed at her.

She flopped back onto the bed, a sense of foreboding in her heart. Was she betraying her own safety by thinking she could help him? Was she simply being naïve? She hoped Belinda might offer more words of wisdom. With a quick glance at the time, Kayla sprang to her feet, determined to pull herself together before facing Belinda. She took a moment to gather her thoughts, recalling the warmth in Belinda's eyes and the understanding in her smile. Maybe she could help her navigate this whirlwind of emotions, this chaotic dance between love and fear. As she stepped out of the cabin, the ship rocked gently and Kayla felt a flicker of hope ignite within her. Each step towards the lounge brought her closer to the opportunity to hear another perspective. Maybe with Belinda's help she'd find a way to make sense of the storm within her and, more importantly, a way to reclaim her life.

Belinda was perched on the edge of a plush, green velvet armchair in the atrium, her eyes darting as she scanned the bustling crowd to find Kayla. The elegant ship, with its shimmering chandeliers and vibrant atmosphere, was a strange juxtaposition to the gravity of her thoughts. The Mediterranean sun filtered through the grand glass windows, casting warm light on the floors, but at that moment all she felt was the weight of Kayla's situation. A few feet away, she could see couples laughing and children running around, their carefree joy a stark contrast to what was going on in the cabin next door to her and Richard. It was hard to believe that a young woman like Kayla was trapped in a cycle of fear and violence. Belinda's face took on a sad expression as she thought of the hesitant way Kayla spoke and the prickly tension she herself experienced when she'd heard their raised voices next-door.

Her mind drifted momentarily to Richard, who had become a ghost of the man she'd known before this cruise. She still couldn't believe he'd claimed to have been gambling at the ship's casino, a past time she knew him to be indifferent to. He'd been taking long walks, disappearing for hours, always returning with a smile that seemed more practiced than genuine. It unnerved her. Though she'd tried to brush it off as him needing space to sort out whatever was truly going on, something gut-wrenching gnawed at her, whispering that his excuses were nothing more than a smoke screen hiding a darker truth. If she was honest, she was glad for the distraction that Kayla caused.

'Belinda!'

She looked up, her breath catching in her throat as Kayla bustled toward her. The girl's cheeks were flushed and her eyes wide. She looked as if she was the carefree young woman she should have been. But even from a distance, Belinda could see the signs, the slight tremor in her hands, the traces of unease in her smile.

'Hey!'

Belinda stood and gestured to an empty table, hoping to convey a sense of safety, a sanctuary where they could unearth the truth without fear of prying ears.

'I'm glad you made it Kayla. How are you doing?'

Kayla hesitated, brushing her hair back anxiously and, for a brief moment, Belinda caught a glimpse of desperation behind her eyes.

'I… I'm okay. Just a little… overwhelmed.'

Belinda's heart sank.

'Overwhelmed with Alex's latest outburst or just in general about the situation?'

Kayla bit her lip, shifting her gaze to the floor.

'Alex… he can be pretty intense and to be honest I think a part of me is addicted to the danger despite knowing we can't stay together. I don't know what I've got myself into. If the truth be known Belinda, we all have a dark side, you know like our shadow self…even me.'

Before Kayla could elaborate on what she meant by such a comment, a figure appeared behind her, his dark shadows lengthening off the edge of the table. Belinda immediately recognised Alex from the few times they'd passed in the corridor. She stiffened as the disdain in his eyes sent a chill down her spine.

'There you are, Kayla!'

He clapped a hand possessively on her shoulder, grinning in a way that set off alarm bells in Belinda's mind.

'I was wondering where you were. I wasn't up to doing my usual workout today. Let's go grab a coffee instead.'

Kayla looked trapped, glancing back at Belinda, who tried to communicate a silent message of support with her eyes.

Kayla stuttered, 'I'm not sure if you know, um this is Belinda, she is staying in the cabin next to ours. We got chatting and both fancied trying the trivia quiz questions…'

'Yeah, well I think we should have a bit of time alone,' Alex insisted, the undertone of his voice sharp as a knife.

Belinda's pulse quickened, now wasn't the time to confront him, even though every fibre of her being wanted to. She had no doubt he'd hit Kayla again. She forced a smile that was more of a grimace. She needed a bit of time to work out her next move.

'Before you go Alex, I'd love to hear your thoughts on the various excursions on offer? Kayla and I were talking about the destinations at each port, and she was telling me about all the research you'd done. There are so many choices. My husband and I can't quite decide! We should have had this all sorted and prebooked like most people, we just never got around to it.'

Belinda knew she was babbling and she tried to avoid looking directly at Kayla as she feigned interest in Alex's expertise. For a tense moment, Alex's expression darkened as he weighed his options. Finally, he relented, rolling his eyes as he dragged a chair towards the table. His ego had been duly massaged. He enjoyed giving other passengers advice, it made him feel important. Kayla's shoulders sagged in relief knowing that it bought her a little more time with Belinda.

Tia watched them from the other side of the atrium, her eyes greedily skimming the outline of Alex's muscular physique. She licked her lips, turned on her heel and walked away.

So many men, so little time…

As the trio spoke, Belinda's mind churned. She gripped the handle of her coffee cup tightly, trying to put on a brave face while Alex regaled them with the information he'd sourced about each port. Belinda nodded politely, trying to look suitably impressed, although it was difficult to ignore the simmering anger bubbling beneath his charming façade.

A knot tightened in Belinda's chest, the same knot that formed whenever she thought about Richard's increasingly erratic behaviour. If she didn't act soon, both she and Kayla might slip further into their problems, lost at sea among the waves of pretence.

Finally, after several agonising moments, Belinda excused herself, the need to gather her thoughts suddenly overwhelming her. As she stood up from the table, she leaned close to Kayla, her voice low and steady.

'We can maybe do the quiz another day, okay? You know where to find me if you are at a loose end when the next one is scheduled.'

Kayla's eyes spoke to her with a mixture of gratitude and fear as she nodded her agreement. Belinda made her way out of the atrium into the corridor, where the atmosphere seemed less intense. With resolve, Belinda decided she couldn't expect Kayla to be strong if she couldn't even role model this herself. It was time to unearth all the hidden truths about Richard, and come what may, she'd also find a way to support Kayla to escape from her nightmare. Belinda's mouth set in a determined line. The Mediterranean sun blazed brightly as she stepped onto the deck. She'd spent her career telling women that life was full of endless possibilities. Now it was time for both her and Kayla to reclaim their lives.

Practice what you preach, old girl.

Chapter 11

Alex steered Kayla by the elbow towards the upper deck, where fewer prying eyes and ears would be around the place. He felt uncomfortable about the way the lady from cabin next door had made him feel. Clearly the old bag looked straight into his soul and didn't like what she saw. Earlier at the gym, Alex had thought about the violence he'd inflicted on Kayla and was mad with himself. He'd managed to remain the perfect gent until they had boarded this ship. Something about being confined onboard the *Ocean Breeze* was driving him mad.

It's not all down to me though. Kayla has definitely been goading me…

All the same, he must show her he was sorry. Alex felt ashamed about the fact his true colours had been revealed. The childhood issues he'd shared with Kayla were true, yet he didn't comprehend that he remained stuck in the past, perpetually stuck in victim mode, blaming everyone except himself for his own actions. Alex was completely unaware that he was having a never-ending pity party.

He glanced sideways at Kayla, noting her face was pale and tense. A ripple of guilt washed over him, which was quickly replaced with the self-righteousness that had become a part of his inflated sense of self. Finally, they reached a quiet area and Alex motioned for her to join him on two deserted lounge chairs. It was windy today, hence less people were milling around outside.

Kayla was in a trance; she was recalling a comment made by Belinda that stuck in her mind and was playing on a loop. It was as if the universe was trying to give her a message. Belinda knew her stuff; she'd shared stories about women she'd worked with in the domestic violence shelter. Although on another level Kayla was still trying to convince herself that her situation in no way compared to those women. Belinda's words appeared in her mind once more.

'Kayla, what you need to realise is that past behaviour tends to be the biggest predictor for future behaviour....'

Alex broke her train of thought, his expression reminiscent of a petulant child.

'Kayla, I need to know that you can accept me for who I am, faults and all. I know I've done the wrong thing by hitting you but if you were honest, you'd admit that you enjoy winding me up at times... As I said, I will get help, I just need to know you still see a future for us. I can't do this without you. I can't be all bad, can I? Look at how much I spoil you for starters, this trip cost me a small fortune.'

Alex failed to reveal his involvement in drug dealing, which greatly supplemented his income.

Kayla blinked up at him, shielding her eyes from the sun. She was trying to buy herself a bit of time so she could respond with careful words. Again, all she could hear was Belinda's voice in her head.

'Listen love, it doesn't matter if he has spent a fortune on you, that doesn't give him the right to raise his hands. In fact, if he continually mentions how he has given you the earth, the moon and the stars, then that is called love bombing, which is a manipulative tactic often used by violent men to gain control and a sense of ownership over their partners.'

Kayla was smart enough to know that she needed to remain respectful towards Alex, despite the urge to scream and lash out at him. She needed to get through this cruise first and foremost, and then decide on her next course of action. Her head told her that she needed to leave him as soon as possible. She was shocked to find her heart was listing his good points instead. From what Belinda had said, allowing Alex to feel heard and validated was more likely to keep her safe in the meantime.

Kayla spoke in a cracked voice, 'I feel upset and confused Alex. I think that's the best way to describe it. I hate what happened to you while growing up, but I don't think it's fair to assume that all women must be the same. You are essentially punishing me for your mum's mistakes.'

Kayla bit her lip, worried that she'd said too much. A flash of anger danced across Alex's face which was quickly replaced with a wolfish smile. He took Kayla's hands in his as he looked earnestly into her eyes.

'That's a fair comment Kayla, I can't argue with that. I just want you to know that I love you more than life itself and no one could ever take your place. I'm so sorry for hurting you, I will do anything to make it up to you.'

A single tear dripped down his nose, his vulnerability making Kayla's heart constrict with confusion.

'Come here you,' she whispered.

As they embraced, Kayla closed her eyes and inhaled his aftershave, feeling his toned body against the softness of hers. His scent intoxicated her as she felt the stirrings of desire and then a flicker of shame sweep over her. She knew deep down he was a nasty piece of work and did not deserve the time of day. Yet the throbbing ache inside her made her want him with a passion that overpowered her senses. Without a word they walked briskly back to their cabin and once inside they began tearing at each other's clothes.

Alex lowered his mouth to Kayla's, and they both felt the heat of their bodies sear through them. As he devoured her mouth, he found her as eager for him as he was for her. His tongue plunged between her lips, tasted her, and found her tongue as it twined around his. His hands drove into her hair, as he playfully grabbed a fistful. Kayla felt her body melt into his.

He swivelled them around throwing her back against the wall, pressing his hardness against her. Every nerve ending was alert as his hunger for her reached a crescendo. Kayla ached. She strained against his body, feeling the weight of his broad chest, tasting the salt on his muscled shoulders that glistened with sweat. The touch of his hands on her bare skin sent a burst of warmth straight through Kayla's core and a whimper escaped her lips. He hooked his fingers under her panties and slipped the lace garment down her thighs.

Kayla twitched as his hand slipped between her thighs and she gave a cry of pleasure as he touched her delicate, aching moist flesh. Kayla opened her legs wide for Alex, her desperation mounting. As he thrust into her wetness she orgasmed within seconds.

What the hell is wrong with me?

Kayla pushed the thought aside as she held his face, soaking in the masculinity of his square jawline and stubbly chin. He took her quickly against the wall and then at a more leisurely pace on the bed. Finally, as his hot seed spurted into her, she bucked upwards to meet his rhythm, while fresh spasms rocked her body. All feelings of ill will towards him were forgotten in that moment. As their breathing returned to normal, they fell asleep in each other's arms, a tangle of sweaty salty limbs.

When Kayla woke up early the next morning, her mind was in turmoil. A part of her wanted to repair her relationship with Alex and give him another chance; another part of her knew she'd only be giving him the green light to repeat the toxic cycle of violence and forgiveness. In order to maintain the peace and ensure her current safety, she saw no reason why she couldn't go along with the façade of kissing and making up so they could enjoy the remaining beautiful ports along the Mediterranean. This cruise was not to be wasted. Today they had sailed into Livorno, and she couldn't wait to see the Renaissance architecture and distinguished cultural heritage in Florence. She sighed as she watched Alex sleeping; he looked angelic with his long dark lashes and rosy cheeks.

How can I have such a love-hate relationship with him? I could kill him for ruining things! But look at that face…

Later that morning, the pair of them stood in front of the Cathedral of Santa Maria del Fiore, furiously snapping photos of its magnificence from every angle. The cathedral's intricate façade, composed of stunning white, green and pink marble, glinted in the bright sun and, for a brief moment, Kayla felt a glimmer of happiness as she conveniently forgot about her tumultuous relationship with Alex.

'Wow, I can't believe there are people staying on the ship and not getting off at this stop. You'd be mad to miss it, even if you'd been here before!' Kayla exclaimed, taking a step back to capture the cathedral in perfect focus.

Alex nodded, his eyes bright with excitement. 'I know! Florence has such a medieval vibe, but it feels modern, too. It's one of the most beautiful places in the world; it's like taking a step back in time. It's so steeped in history, it's just beautiful!'

Kayla grinned, caught up in the magic of the moment. 'I know it's simply stunning! I love the smell of leather everywhere too. It's meant to be amazing quality here. How about we browse the markets afterwards? I might treat myself to a new handbag!'

Alex looked happy as he considered her plan. 'Sure, we can go to the markets, but first,' he said loudly enough to gather a curious crowd, 'I have a surprise for you!'

Alex puffed out his chest, a grin stretching from ear to ear. Instead of feeling buoyed by his enthusiasm, an uneasy sensation niggled at Kayla. Even in the midst of the beauty surrounding them, something felt off. Before she could register what was going on, he had dropped to one knee. The vibrant colours of Florence suddenly blurred into darkness in her peripheral vision. The stunning scenery that only seconds ago had been so fascinating now seemed sinister; the looming cathedral suddenly began closing in on her. Alex reached into his jacket pocket and produced a small blue velvet box. Kayla's stomach lurched horribly. She was glad she was wearing her oversized sunglasses, which shielded him from seeing the horror in her eyes. The world paused as tourists gawked, phones appeared out of thin air to capture the moment, and time twisted around her. She likened it to a tightening noose. With a flourish, Alex opened the box to reveal a dazzling pear-shaped diamond ring.

'Kayla, will you marry me?' he boomed, his voice echoing through the piazza.

Gasps erupted from the crowd; two girls exchanged 'naw's,' and an elderly Italian lady pressed a hand to her heart, clearly enjoying the romantic spectacle. All Kayla could do was stare, her mouth agape. Shock rushed through her.

'Oh my god,' she stuttered, 'Alex…I…I wasn't expecting this!'

Alex's smile faltered, his embarrassment thick in the air between them. Wasn't this the part where she was meant to scream with joy and bolt towards him with her left hand outstretched? This was not the response he had anticipated. In his mind, their passionate night had been a confirmation that everything was moving along perfectly. To him it was a sure sign they were back on track. It had not occurred to him that she might not want to get engaged following his recent displays of violence. Yet Kayla definitely had given him signs she wanted a ring so what was she playing at? For a brief moment, Kayla considered playing along to spare his feelings, then she quickly shook off the thought, knowing that the fallout from that might be even worse. No, she couldn't be fake.

Taking a step toward him, she whispered, 'I'm so sorry, Alex. I'm not ready for this.'

Gasps rippled throughout the onlookers, and faced with suffocating mortification, she turned and fled. She dashed down the nearest side street until her breath came in gasps. She eventually stopped outside a quaint boutique, her palms slick with sweat, her heart racing.

'Kayla!'

The fury in Alex's voice pierced through the air, reverberating off the cobblestones as he appeared puffing and panting at the street corner.

'You nasty fucking bitch!' he seethed. 'How the hell could you embarrass me like that? You have been hinting for ages that this is what you wanted! Are you playing with me right now? Another passenger from the ship was filming it for me! How mortified do you think I feel?'

The coldness in her gut deepened as she stared at him, lost for words. Confusion danced across her features.

'Alex, can we go somewhere private and talk about this?'

His wild eyes flared with a mix of anger, hurt and confusion, frustration contorting his features. He abruptly pointed toward a deserted narrow cobbled street, and without waiting for her, he marched ahead. Kayla followed, calling out for a rational conversation.

'Alex, we haven't been together that long…I hoped we were heading in that way, but since you hit me, I can't get over it... I'm not sure you are who I thought you were…and I need to know you're serious about therapy.'

As they reached the narrow alley, Alex's fury reached a crescendo. Kayla was overcome by familiar feelings of disassociation, and she simply lost time. With one swift motion, Alex turned and punched her in the stomach. As Kayla crumpled to the ground, the world spun, and shock mingled with agony.

Lying there in the gutter, gasping for breath, Kayla felt utterly defeated. She stared at the cobblestones, tears spilling from her eyes.

Unable to comprehend what had happened, she stalled, unsure of her next move. The grave reality of their relationship hit her harder than the blow. She was trapped, yet she knew she could no longer allow herself to be. She slowly pushed herself into a sitting position, despair mingling with determination. Kayla decided to get up, she'd fight back, not only against him, but for what she deserved. The sun above glinted sharply, a reminder of the beauty that still existed beyond the darkness that encroached upon her. She took a deep breath, steeling herself for whatever came next.

Kayla winced in pain as she stood up slowly and brushed herself down. She must get back on the ship and get help. The holiday of a lifetime was quickly turning into a nightmare of epic proportions. The once exciting Mediterranean cruise had been overshadowed by the sickening realisation that her boyfriend was nothing more than a violent bully. Kayla felt shame wash over her as she thought about how she'd allowed the passionate sex with Alex to reel her back in each time he'd hit her. She had led him to believe all was well and somehow it had led to a proposal. If she'd been strong enough to resist his charms and tell him it was over the first time he'd hit her, he may not have asked her to marry him. Or would he? She knew he was being manipulative using this calculated move. Alex was relying on her being too weak to refuse him. But she *had* refused his proposal, and rightly so. She'd always be proud of that fact. She was stronger than she thought. Even though this whole thing was such a mess, it'd be far worse if she was now wearing his ring. Kayla shook her head sadly as she thought back to the start of the trip and how she had been dreaming of a ring in the near future at that point. It already seemed like a lifetime ago.

I had hoped he'd propose, he was right about that, but not since he showed me his true colours.

After managing to flag down a taxi, Kayla was relieved when the driver understood her hurried instructions and sped off towards the port which was a considerable distance away. The fare would be a fortune, but the upside was it would give her time to think. Each jolt of the car sent waves of anxiety crashing through her. She replayed the morning in her mind. She'd been enjoying herself until he proposed. Why did he go and ruin everything?

When Kayla finally walked back onto the ship, the familiar scent of sea salt and sunscreen no longer appealed due to the heaviness in her chest. The corridor leading to the main dining room felt impossibly long. With each step, her heart felt heavier, the thrumming bass of music reverberating as she walked through the pool area where a DJ entertained a group of hyperactive teenagers. It was a jarring reminder that other guests were having a great time. Kayla felt herself dissociate again; she was so in her own head that she could not recall getting from A to B. She felt surprised to find herself at the main dining room, in her dream like state, her legs had somehow taken her there.

As Kayla entered the expansive buffet, the sights and smells coupled with joyous laughter only heightened the surreal sensation of her situation. As people milled about, plates piled high, she realised she had no appetite. The thought of kicking back and relishing the ambiance felt impossible. Suddenly, the world around her spun, and she staggered forward, colliding with a group of women walking towards her.

'Whoa! Are you okay?' One of the women gasped, reaching out to steady her. Kayla lowered her eyes.

'I…yeah, I'm fine. Just a bit dizzy, I've just had too much sun today,' she managed to reply, trying to feign normalcy.

The woman shrugged and walked on. As Kayla glanced around the dining room, her palms sweaty, she suddenly wasn't so sure that it was such a good idea to be here…

Chapter 12

Tia took a sip of her cappuccino, the frothy milk swirling in the warm cup as she laughed while watching footage on her phone. The salty sea breeze from the open deck of the ship ruffled her hair, giving her the wild look of someone who had found unexpected joy in a rather mundane moment. Tony leaned back in his seat as he studied her face.

'Check this out, Tony!'

Tia's eyes sparkled with mischief as she scrolled through her phone with glee, a huge grin on her face as she revealed the footage she'd captured in Florence. As Tony peered at the screen, the beautiful backdrop of the Italian city faded and the screen filled with the image of a young man on one knee; he held up a ring, his face full of hope. Instead of whoops of joy, the video showed his girlfriend stepping back, her obvious horror turning into overwhelming discomfort as the man's face radiated with embarrassment. The scene was one of major awkwardness and Tia cackled uncontrollably again, nearly spilling her coffee.

'God, you are a real bitch, Tia,' Tony laughed, shaking his head as he watched, half-amused and half-appalled. 'Even I feel sorry for the guy.'

Tia's giggles faded as she placed her phone down with a frown.

'Wow, you are such a fucking hypocrite, Tony. We film men in bed with me to blackmail them, and you're acting like you care about this guy? Really?'

Caught off guard, he raised his hands in mock surrender. 'Okay, fair point…'

Tia rolled her eyes, knowing that their antics involved capturing moments that could demolish men's reputations in a matter of minutes. She paused, her tone serious for a moment.

'Maybe I truly am cruel and heartless, Tony. But let's be honest, marriage proposals are a joke, there is no such thing as true love.'

Tia omitted the fact that to all intents and purposes she'd taken a fancy to the man in the video and had been actively pursuing him on the ship. Tony sighed, he set his cup of black coffee down and leaned in closer. He wasn't about to agree or disagree.

Tony's dark eyes narrowed. 'So back to business. That Richard guy is taking his time with his payment, isn't he? What's happening there?'

Tia groaned, feigning frustration. She was still weighing up Richard's advice that she should free herself from Tony. She wondered idly what kind of job Richard could help her get and how much the salary might be. But in her bid to get the money out of Richard, she'd lost the opportunity to hear any more about it. As usual, greed had overcome her and she was regretting it now. Tia avoided Tony's eyes, thankfully he was too busy scraping out the froth from the bottom of his cup with a teaspoon.

'He's just stalling, Tony. I mean, it's all fun and games until you need to come up with the money. He's looking for sympathy, but he isn't getting any from me.'

Tony glanced at his Apple watch and groaned. 'We don't have time for this discussion right now. We're supposed to be heading off to the midday Hawaiian party!'

Tia smiled, the idea of the party and the possible conquests rekindled her earlier glee.

'Okay, Tony. Let's have a little talk with Richard soon. If he wants to play games, he is gonna regret it.'

Tia's statement was full of bravado. She was damned if she went along with Richard's idea and damned if she didn't. As Tia and Tony plotted their next move, the ship rocked gently beneath them. Tia stood up, her eyes glittering as she planned her provocative outfit for her next unsuspecting culprit.

She felt a rush of excitement course through her veins. The Hawaiian party was the kind of event she lived for, and she savoured the thrill of potential that awaited her. Tony watched her with a mix of admiration and bewilderment, recognising the vibrant energy that always surrounded her.

'Alright, my little heartbreaker,' he mocked. 'What's the outfit plan? You can't show up to a Hawaiian party without wearing something provocative.'

Tia smirked, her mind already racing through her wardrobe full of tropical prints and low-cut tops.

'Naturally it needs to be something daring. Maybe a bikini top and a sheer cover-up, something that leaves just enough to the imagination,' Tia replied, her eyes gleaming wickedly. 'For a touch of innocence, maybe a flower in my hair. Gotta look the part, right?'

Tony chuckled, shaking his head in mock disbelief. 'You're going to give some poor man a heart attack.'

'I will be a vision,' she said, already seeing herself sashaying through the crowd, commanding attention as usual. 'Who knows, maybe Richard will finally step up and pay today...'

They both knew the stakes of what they were doing were high, but the thrill of it all made Tia feel invincible. It wasn't only about the money or the game they played; it was about being unapologetically herself in a world that often tried to box her in.

Once dressed, Tia stood in front of the mirror as she adjusted the flower in her hair. She caught a glimpse of herself: a wild figure infused with confidence and mischief. She muttered under her breath.

'Let's see how this works out for Richard.'

Under all the bravado, a sliver of doubt crept in. Was this honestly the game she wanted to play? Was Richard right about her being better off without Tony? Despite the knowledge that Tony used her, in some warped way she still enjoyed spending time with him.

Because I don't have anyone else, and I need to feel needed…

With a quick flick of her hair, she shook the thoughts away.

'Enough of that,' she boldly told her reflection. 'I'm here to have fun. I'm not going to stop being me.'

As they walked into the fray of the Hawaiian party, vibrant music was pumping through the air and chatter filled every corner. Tia lost herself in the crowd, dancing and flirting with abandon. She spotted a group of men who looked both intrigued and intimidated, and she devoured their attention, pouting, winking and shimmying at the best contenders.

She spotted Richard across the deck, his face reddened from too much sun or maybe it was anxiety. He had his game face on while clumsily trying to navigate a conversation with another passenger, his discomfort visible. A smirk crept across Tia's lips; this was her moment.

'Hey, Tony!' she shouted, pulling him close to conspiratorially whisper in his ear. 'Look who is here!'

As she glided over to Richard, she could practically smell his fear, he'd obviously been dragged to the party by his wife who was chatting to another woman at the bar.

'Richard!' she called out. 'Living it up, I, see?'

Richard scowled while glancing nervously at the bar. 'It's not the time or the place!' he hissed.

Tia laughed, 'You're stalling on that payment. Want to talk about it?'

He faltered, and for a brief moment, she relished his unease. Then she suddenly recognised the vulnerability hidden behind his bravado, and deep down she knew he wasn't the only one struggling to keep up appearances. Tony watched from the sidelines; he was enjoying the show.

'Please Tia, not now.' Richard hated hearing the desperation that crept into his voice. Tia studied him for a moment before replying.

'I will let you be for now, Richard, but later we will talk business, alright?'

Richard's shoulders relaxed slightly, and then immediately tensed again as he saw Belinda approaching.

'Deal,' he muttered, as he willed her to walk away.

Tia slunk off with a little wave and stole a glance at Tony, who grinned back at her.

'Good move. You're not such a heartless bitch after all.'

Tia laughed, playfully nudging him. Yet as she danced, her laughter intermingling with the music, she couldn't help but wonder once more if Richard truly *could* lead her to new opportunities, new connections, and perhaps even a new life entirely. Tony watched Tia, he was intrigued at the way her moods could swing from high to low so quickly. So far, he'd seen her expression go from elated to defeated in a matter of seconds. He'd love to know what went on in her head at times. As her youth worker, Tony knew that she had undiagnosed mental health issues related to her childhood. Tia had always refused point blank to engage in any mental health assessments, however.

As predicted, Tia stood up abruptly and announced she was going to her cabin to have a late lunch delivered by room service. The activities on the *Ocean Breeze* were non-stop and, if you tried to do it all, eventually you'd become worn out. The afternoon parties took it out of her more than the evening ones did for some reason. Tony frowned as he watched her leave. He had an ominous feeling of doom that he simply couldn't shake off.

Chapter 13

As the lift doors slid open with a soft chime, Belinda stepped into the bustling buffet area, her gaze drifting over the sprawling spread of food beneath the twinkling lights. The air was thick with the aroma of grilled fish and tropical fruits, and she began to salivate. Richard was off on one of his solo walks again and she was becoming increasingly pissed off. She was startled to see the Cruise Director Jake standing beside her, gazing at the never-ending choices on display. She'd assumed he'd eat in private to get away from everyone.

Jake's chirpy demeanour did a poor job of concealing his weariness. Belinda caught him casting furtive glances around, his brow occasionally furrowing. The cruise had been a whirlwind of activities, and while Jake handled it all with an infectious enthusiasm, Belinda sensed he was both tired and troubled.

'Your job must be incredibly demanding,' Belinda said, setting her plate down and leaning against the buffet railing. 'You're constantly having to make sure everyone has a good time while keeping an eye on everything. It must be so full on!'

Jake chuckled softly, the corners of his mouth curling up. Belinda noticed his smile failed to reach his eyes.

'You could say that there are those who think I'm the fun police around here. Even fun has its regulations, right?'

'Sure,' Belinda nodded, her tone serious now. 'But what if something more serious happens? For example, if someone feels threatened while onboard?'

Jake paused, the question bringing a shadow to his face as Vincent popped into his mind. His laughter faded, and he looked into her eyes with a sudden intensity.

'If anyone ever feels uncomfortable or unsafe, they need to find one of the crew members, immediately. We have protocols in place which are discreet, yet effective. No one should feel as though they're in danger while at sea. Why do you ask? Is someone in trouble?'

Belinda hesitated; she didn't want to say too much for fear of what Alex might do if he was approached. It wasn't her place to mention Kayla's predicament. She'd felt the weight of his words, and despite the bustling surroundings, the atmosphere suddenly felt loaded. She changed tack, a tone of concern lacing her words.

'Do you feel safe doing this job?' Belinda stared up at the handsome young man, curious for his reply.

Jake nodded. 'Most days, yes…but…'

'But?'

Belinda's instinct urged her to pry a bit deeper. Jake sighed, rubbing the back of his neck as if carrying an unseen burden.

'It's only that, sometimes, the environment and the people can become a bit…'

'Intimidating?' Belinda offered.

'Exactly', Jake sighed. 'You'd be surprised how some guests act when they're on holiday and think the rules don't apply to them. I've been required to intervene more times than I can count, and not all of those situations end well.'

Belinda nodded thoughtfully; she didn't envy his job at all.

'That must be exhausting. Do you get a lot of help?'

Jake thought about Vincent's betrayal and a flicker of vulnerability crossed his features. He gave a deliberately vague response.

'I get help if I need to... however the buck still stops with me. It can be tough to know where to draw the line when there is an incident. I don't often ask for help as I don't want to appear weak in front of my team or the passengers.'

Jake tried to appear as upbeat as possible. Belinda directly met his gaze, her voice firm.

'Jake, asking for help is not a sign of weakness; it's a strength. No one can do it all alone. You're human, after all. Even superheroes need a break. Maybe you need to delegate more.'

His lips quirked into a more genuine smile.

'Thanks, that means a lot. I guess I've been too caught up in sorting everything out myself.'

The two shared a moment of understanding as voices mingled around them amidst the clinking of crockery and chatter. Suddenly, a commotion ensued by the entrance.

A young woman was standing there with wide eyes, looking lost amidst the jubilant crowd. As Belinda edged closer, she gasped as she realised who the girl was.

She clapped a hand over her mouth.

'Oh my god, it's Kayla.'

The momentary panic in Kayla's expression sent a rush of protective instinct through Belinda.

'Not sure who Kayla is,' Jake replied. 'But she looks as though she might need my help.'

Without hesitation, Jake crossed the room, Belinda at his heels. As they reached Kayla, Belinda felt saddened by the fear and confusion in her eyes. The girl looked slightly deranged.

'Hey, are you okay?'

Kayla took a shaky breath and nodded. Belinda wasn't convinced.

'Has Alex been up to his old tricks?'

'Yes', she whispered, glancing furtively around as if wary of prying eyes.

Belinda took a step closer, lowering her voice.

'You're safe here, Jake can help you.'

Jake stepped forward, offering Kayla a reassuring smile.

'Hey, I'm sure you know I'm your friendly cruise director, after all I'm on the TV in your cabin every day! Let me take you somewhere more private, you can tell me anything. I promise I will do my best to help.'

Belinda felt a sense of relief as she watched Jake ushering Kayla out of the dining room, swiftly steering her away from the other guests. Belinda knew it was no coincidence that the meeting between the two of them had taken place. It was serendipity at its best. She felt a weight lifting from her shoulders knowing that she was no longer solely responsible for Kayla while on the ship. Jake had the vibe of a genuine young man, and he'd know how to keep Kayla safe. As she walked towards the starboard end of the ship, her euphoria was short lived as she realised that once again, she had no idea where her husband was.

Chapter 14

Vincent leaned against the cold steel of the refrigerator, feeling the hum reverberate against his chest, taking deep breaths until his anger subsided. The fluorescent lights above flickered with an irritating buzz, like they were mocking him as he reflected on his earlier unexpected meeting with Jake. The reprimand from his senior echoed in his mind, sharp and stinging, it may as well have been a slap across the face.

'A fucking verbal warning! Really?'

Vincent muttered under his breath, scoffing at the injustice of it all. He replayed the exchange over and over, every word a dagger. He recalled Jake leaning back in his chair, a scowl evident on his overly tanned face, as if he had every right to command respect while Vincent sat there, feeling smaller than ever. It turned out that a snake on the team had been telling tales and Vincent was more furious about this than the actual telling off from Mr High and Mighty himself. He highly suspected it was Maisie who'd been telling tales, although Jake refused point blank to deny or confirm his source at this point.

The kitchen was buzzing as the staff bustled about hurriedly while avoiding his gaze. Vincent's paranoia intensified and he couldn't shake off the suffocating belief that they were all in on it, colluding with Jake, feeding him poison. A familiar darkness crept into his heart, and he grinned bitterly to himself.

'Let them think what they want.'

Although he muttered the words convincingly, Vincent knew that deep down, he craved feeling respected, maybe even liked. The more he fumed, the more isolated he felt.

'Maybe I should give Jake a taste of his own medicine.'

Vincent began picturing Jake swaggering through the halls, attempting to dodge the fallout of his poor decisions. Vincent's mind ran wild with scenarios, each one darker than the last. Could he plant seeds of doubt and turn the team against Jake? Then they'd all see how incompetent he truly was! Vincent tore himself away from the refrigerator, wiping his clammy palms on the front of his trousers.

His eyes swept over the kitchen, locking onto Miranda, a young waitress who accidentally dropped a tray of dishes that morning and broke two plates. She was currently huddled near the sink, whispering with the others. Her eyes rested on him before she darted off to speak with the head chef. If they were all avoiding him, how was he meant to remedy the situation?

He stepped outside into the crisp air on the deck, and once he was away from the heat, the tension began to lift, at least temporarily. He inhaled deeply, letting the smell of the sea wash over him. Every breath reminded him of what he enjoyed about cruising. It allowed him to pretend his home life wasn't a train wreck.

As he thundered up and down, contemplating his next move, he wondered how the team truly viewed him. Did they see a man trapped in his own anger, telling tales about Jake that they didn't think were true? He touched the railing, feeling the cool metal beneath his fingertips, and thought about how he could plot his vengeance. Perhaps he'd spread a few more tales amongst the staff about their precious Jake.

Vincent thought back to the other night. He'd heard the gossip about Jake's love interest Claire having a heated argument with that hot young passenger Tia, the one who continually got other women's heckles up. Coincidently, he'd been chatting with Tia himself that night and ascertained that they were two kindred spirits. Tia had tried chatting Vincent up and he'd seen right through her act, even guessing she was simply after men for their money. Naturally Tia denied it, however, she couldn't do so with a straight face, and they'd ended up having a real laugh about it. Vincent couldn't truly be disgusted with her as they were so similar in nature. Vincent didn't stop to consider that this meant they were both malicious, devious and out to take from others. As he thought about Tia and Claire's obvious dislike of her, he wondered if this could be used to his advantage. He'd encourage Tia to continue pursuing Jake! If Jake fell into Tia's trap, his fall from grace would be glorious to watch. It'd also put the snivelling Claire in her place. Vincent would never admit that he had tried it on with Claire before she'd got together with Jake, but she'd only had eyes for the suave looking Cruise Director.

What Jake wants, Jake gets! Well not anymore!

With a deep breath, Vincent turned back towards the kitchen, determination replacing his simmering resentment. As he entered, the chatter in the kitchen quietened down momentarily before it resumed. Vincent didn't care. He was too focused on the plan formulating in his sick mind.

Vincent's resolve deepened as he stepped deeper into the fray, the familiar clatter of pans and the aroma of sizzling spices enveloping him; a welcome distraction in the heat of his brewing vengeance. The stench of betrayal lingered in the air, and he revelled in the thought of turning the tables on Jake. His gaze swept across the busy kitchen staff. Miranda, still nursing the embarrassment from her clumsiness earlier, shot him a furtive glance before disappearing behind a row of pots. She was an easy target, always dithering under the shadows of more dominant personalities such as his own. Perhaps he could find a way to draw her into his plan, make her his loyal little bird who might spread a few rumours.

'Hey, Miranda!'

Vincent called out, forcing a casual tone that belied the rush of adrenaline coursing through him. Miranda blinked and cautiously approached, wiping her hands on a kitchen towel as she noted Vincent's ill-fitting suit. She realised with an inward chuckle that money couldn't buy you style.

'Can I have a word?'

Miranda noted Vincent's attempt at a friendly tone, and she frowned at him with uncertainty. Vincent was one of these superiors who talked to you one minute and blanked you the next. The staff detested this about him. All the same, curiosity got the better of her, and she stepped closer, her voice low.

'What's up, sir?'

With a conspiratorial air, he leaned closer, ensuring no one else could overhear.

'Heard anything juicy about Jake and Claire lately?' he asked nonchalantly, his voice dripping with false innocence.

Miranda hesitated, her eyes darting to the others, who were too preoccupied to care.

'Not really,' she stammered, though her natural nosiness had piqued her interest.

Vincent pressed on, a sly smile creeping across his face.

'Come on, even you've seen how Jake can be, right? It's crazy how he struts around as though he owns the entire ship. I heard something interesting about him and his precious Claire, something about a certain passenger coming between them.'

A flicker of interest lit up Miranda's features, and Vincent knew he had her hooked.

'That Tia girl, she's always sniffing around Jake, making sure everyone knows she's the centre of attention. I hate to say it, but I hope Jake isn't breaking the code of conduct, if you get my drift?'

Miranda's expression shifted, a bare hint of excitement breaking through her initial hesitance to get involved.

'What do you mean? Do you think Jake is giving Tia one?' she asked, her true gossiping nature coming to the forefront.

Vincent leaned back, adopting a more relaxed stance as if all he was doing was making casual conversation.

'Oh, I've seen the way that Tia acts around him, and I'd put money on it that she's had her wicked way with him. Can you imagine the fallout if he gets caught? Claire wouldn't know what hit her and Mr Perfect would be fired for breaching the "no intimate relationships with passengers" rule. How funny would that be?'

Miranda's imagination went into overdrive, her eyes sparkling with appreciation for the potential drama unfolding.

'That sounds like a show worth watching,' she said, a mixture of intrigue and bitchiness evident in her voice.

Vincent allowed his feigned innocence to slip a little more, feeding her crumbs of enticement. He gave her a sly conspiratorial wink.

'Maybe you should let it slip to the rest of the team – they deserve to know Jake isn't so perfect after all! Between you and me, there are rumours that Tia was seen leaving Jake's cabin, but hey I didn't see it for myself, so who knows?' He threw his hands up in the air in mock innocence.

Vincent guessed that Miranda would enjoy spreading rumours about Tia's slutty ways, of Jake's womanising reputation and of Claire's insecurities. He left her with those thoughts. He'd loaded the metaphorical gun, it was up to Miranda to shoot it. Most of the staff were loyal to Jake, although Vincent had seen Miranda roll her eyes at him at times, so he'd correctly assessed her to be the best staff member to gossip with.

Over the course of the cruise Vincent felt a perverse satisfaction each time he noticed jealousy flickering in Claire's eyes, and he watched Jake, who was torn between indulging in Tia's provocative charm and maintaining his fling with Claire. Vincent knew that at this point his anger had transformed into something else entirely. It was no longer about seeking justice or having a say in the hierarchy; it was about establishing domination through manipulation. Vincent grinned in dark satisfaction. It was fun being unhinged.

Chapter 15

Claire stood under the steaming hot shower, lathering her taut body furiously. It had been a long night of performing on the ship, and she felt the weight of Miranda's words pressing on her chest.

Jake is flirting with Tia behind your back...is it possible that there is more to it?

Miranda mentioned the way Jake laughed at Tia's jokes, and his lingering glances when Claire wasn't around. Apparently, Vincent had noticed Jake and Tia exchanging intimate looks too; not that she'd trust Vincent as far as she could throw him.

Claire pressed her lips together, trying to contain her anger. She'd already had an altercation with Tia and if it wasn't for the fact she was Jake's current love interest, she'd probably have been thrown off the ship at the last port as a result. The crew turned a blind eye because no one wanted to challenge the current lover of the Cruise Director. Claire let out a shaky sigh.

I need to keep my jealousy under control! Joel reckons Jake is simply a fling, and maybe he is. I think I'm falling for him. Am I truly a laughing stock when I'm performing and not around to see what's going on?

As she stepped out of the cubicle, steam swirling around her, she wrapped herself in a plush towel and caught a glimpse of her reflection in the fogged-up mirror. Wiping away a large circle in the steam, she gazed at her naked body and, for a moment, she smirked. There she was, radiant and sculpted, evidence of tireless hours spent perfecting her physique while rehearsing dance routines each day. She'd also caught the sun during the recent excursion to Pisa with the other theatre performers and was glowing as a result.

Claire chuckled as she thought of the fun she'd had with the other performers while in Pisa. She had taken part in the obligatory 'hold it up' pose when she had her photo taken near the leaning tower of Pisa. She knew she looked great in the photo and had immediately sent it to Jake. It was taken in exactly the right light, the sun's golden rays lighting up her pretty features. Her tan accentuated the curves of her muscles, a testament to her disciplined lifestyle. Claire flexed a bicep in the mirror, a fierce scowl on her face as she fantasised about punching Tia's smug face.

What was standing in her way wasn't Tia, it was the voice of insecurity in her head reminding her that she wasn't good enough, a narrative that mummy dearest had led her to believe all of her life. With renewed determination, she reached for her makeup bag, needing to create an armour of confidence. She reached for her favourite bold red lipstick and applied it to her generous lips.

I'm not going to shy away from my feelings! I'm gonna confront Jake and sort this out once and for all. He must have feelings for me too, right? Surely, he wouldn't go for a girl like Tia? No way! Jake obviously prefers brown-eyed brunettes over blue eyed blondes. He is with me and not her after all…

Claire smacked her red lips together then practiced her lines aloud.

'Jake, can we talk about us? Because I can't pretend this is just a fling anymore.'

As she fantasised about his response, her voice became stronger with each repetition. Tonight, was going to be a turning point. No more second-guessing herself. Claire was ready to stake her claim.

She was more than simply a performer; she was a girl who knew what she wanted, and she'd damn well fight to get it.

With one last look in the mirror, Claire stepped into a stunning cream coloured dress that clung to her body in all the right places; no underwear was required underneath this little number. She was ready to face the night, to confront her fears, and tonight, she'd be bold and not let jealousy dictate anymore. She intended to eliminate the problem….

Claire stepped out of her cabin, the door clicking shut behind her with an unsettling finality. The soft, ambient music echoed through the narrow corridors of the ship, mingling with the chatter from huddles of passengers. As she moved through the vibrant lounge, her eyes darted across the crowds of people, seeking the familiar face that stirred both longing and trepidation within her… Jake.

The lounge was filled with the scent of mixed drinks, laughter and the occasional outburst of song that came from the karaoke stage. Claire's heart rate increased as she spotted Jake, a broad smile lighting up his face as he playfully bantered with Tia across the room.

Miranda and Vincent were right, Tia isn't going to give up until she wins Jake over. Even though I've already had a fight with her she is still game, unbelievable…

Claire clenched her fists at her sides, this was the moment she had been preparing for, the moment she was meant to declare her feelings to Jake, but as she observed him with Tia, a pang of self-doubt flickered in her chest.

'You've got this,' she whispered to herself, the words drowned out by the music. Claire took a deep breath and made her way through the crowd, moving closer until she was a few steps away from them.

'Hey, Jake!' she called out, injecting a confident edge into her voice.

As he turned to her, a flicker of surprise crossed his face, quickly replaced by that warm smile that always made her heart flutter.

'Claire! You look amazing!' he said, glancing at her accentuated curves with a hungry look in his eyes.

'Thanks,' she replied coolly, feeling a flutter of nerves rippling through her.

Tia smirked bitchily as she eyed Claire up and down. Jake sighed. This Tia girl always talked to him at the wrong moment. It had already resulted in her having an altercation with Claire. He hoped there wouldn't be a repeat performance tonight; he was tired of defending himself to a chick who had no claims on him. He needed to do his utmost to keep them apart at all costs.

Jake pulled Claire gently into their circle giving her a reassuring smile.

'We were just talking about the next port and what's on the itinerary.'

Claire's eyes narrowed. Tia was looking at Jake with a knowing look, obviously designed to cause trouble. Claire decided not to fall for it.

'I think I need a drink,' Claire declared, forcing a smile as the tension in the air prickled her skin.

Jake took the hint and gave Tia a dismissive wave.

'I need a top up too. Nice chatting to you, Tia.'

Tia pursed her lips, silently fuming as Jake followed his bimbo to the bar like an obedient sheep. Claire handed Jake a beer and sipped at an Aperol spritz.

'Jake, can we talk?' she blurted out, an urgency in her tone that surprised even her.

'In private?'

Jake frowned at the intensity of Claire's words, and nodded, leading her towards a quieter corner of the lounge. With each step away from Tia, Claire felt lighter somehow.

Once they were secluded behind the rows of plush seating, Claire leaned against the wall.

Jake looked at her, his eyes intense in the dim light. 'What's up?'

'Listen, Jake,' Claire began, her voice surprisingly steady. 'I need to be honest. This…us…it's becoming more than a fling to me.' Claire hesitated, scared of his response.

'Jake I can't ignore it anymore. When I see you with Tia, I feel…'

'Jealous?' he interrupted, anger clouding his face.

'Claire, it feels as though we keep having the same conversation over and over again. I keep telling you that I'm obligated to speak to the passengers, even the pretty ones. I'm not going to deny that Tia seems to turn up everywhere I am. Let's face it, it's not hard to work out where the Cruise Director will be when you get an itinerary under your cabin door every night, is it? I like you Claire; you're strong, fierce, talented and beautiful. But at no point have I implied that we are exclusive. I haven't even known you that long! I'm a commitment-phobe and have never hidden the fact!'

Claire blinked back tears, swallowing the lump in her throat. She knew she looked stunning. Why wasn't that enough for him?

It must be because Tia has already slept with him and now has him under her spell. Well boy, is she is going to pay for this!

Jake saw the venomous look in her eyes and put a hand on her arm.

'Claire, I know you have a habit of jumping to conclusions. Whatever you are thinking right now, it's not true.'

The tension between them increased, and as Claire was about to respond, she caught a movement from the corner of her eye. Tia had moved position so she could see them in her line of vision. She stood at the edge of the crowd, an ominous figure with her arms crossed, watching them with an expression that was anything but friendly. Claire felt a surge of rage course through her.

I'm going to put an end to this, once and for all.

Chapter 16

Belinda was struggling to keep burying her head in the sand. Her initial plan of confronting Richard after they returned home was not going to work. So that night, once she was sure Richard was fast asleep, she went through his mobile phone and finally plucked up the courage to read through his texts. Her breathing started to come in short shallow breaths when she came across the sickening video clip of him with Tia. She tried to steady her hands as she read the follow up threatening messages allegedly from 'Frank.'

Belinda swallowed down the bile in her throat as she squeezed her eyes shut. Once her heartbeat slowed down a bit, she placed a hand on her chest, the pain of her husband's betrayal felt physical more than mental at this point. Richard must have thought he was so clever changing his mobile phone PIN. With shaking hands she'd worked it out on the second attempt. She'd also found the hidden camera in his blazer pocket and was finally able to piece all of the events together. Her stomach churned horribly as she oscillated between rage and fear. It was 2.00am and she doubted she'd sleep one wink. Unwanted images of the girl's sexual liaison with her husband were playing on a loop in her racing mind. It had taken all of her will power not to wake Richard up and smash his stupid face to smithereens. Instead, she walked across the carpet in a daze as she replaced his phone back on the charging dock. As feelings of devastation consumed her, she realised the violent fantasies she was having could get her jailed.

I need to calm down and be smart about this. I'm determined to take matters into my own hands. In the meantime, it's time to keep my wits about me and play dumb.

The next day, Belinda played Richard at his own game and disappeared without telling him her whereabouts. She didn't want to look at him or be anywhere near him for that matter. At least not until she'd figured out her next move.

Belinda decided to approach the cabin attendant Ricardo to find out Tia's cabin number with the information she had. Belinda found the girl on social media using the ship's hashtag #oceanbreeze and was able to show her images to Ricardo. The girl obviously wasn't the sharpest tool in the shed given she was so easily identified, or maybe the little tart was simply too brazen to care. She guessed it was probably the latter.

Wide eyed with shock, Ricardo told Belinda he could do no such thing, as it was a sackable offence to share information about passengers. When Belinda waved a wad of $50 notes at him. She saw him hesitate. Belinda smiled at Ricardo innocently.

Even good honest people have their price...

The cabin attendant thought Belinda was nuts, but in the end, greed won him over. Ricardo managed to convince himself she had merely forgotten her friend's cabin number, so no harm would occur in him sharing it with her.

She is a sweet lady who means no harm, right?

Coincidentally, it so happened that Ricardo was rostered to clean the young woman's section also. Ordinarily, he'd be unable to access the information Belinda was asking for. It was too good to be true that he happened to know the answer off the top of his head. Ricardo glanced around making sure they were not about to be captured on one of the ship's many cameras. The coast appeared clear, so he made a snap decision. It was easy money that he could send back to his family in the Philippines.

'The young lady is in cabin 12812,' he whispered hesitantly, 'but you should probably….'

'Thank you,' Belinda interrupted, as she stormed off, already dismissing his advice.

As Belinda thundered along the passageway, she figured she'd try to reason with the girl who'd obviously had a hard life according to the footage she'd watched on the mini camera. With a semblance of a plan in her head, she tried with all her might to mask her fury. The ship was a bustling hive of passengers and crew. Belinda struggled to shut out the sounds of incessant chatter echoing in every corner. As Belinda lurked close to Tia's cabin, she reflected that she was edging towards the precipice of insanity. She was meant to be having fun alongside everyone else onboard.

Am I truly about to confront the girl who invaded my marriage in such a vulgar way? The little bitch has it coming, karma will prevail!

Finally, she caught a glimpse of Tia as she emerged from her cabin. Belinda fell into step behind her. Tia headed towards Starbucks in the atrium.

It's now or never.

Gathering her courage, Belinda kept her eyes glued to Tia as she entered the café. Belinda watched Tia flick her long blonde hair while exchanging smiles with the barista, her laughter bubbling over the hum of the crowd. Belinda began to tremble as she gained traction on the girl she had seen on the footage. No one else realised that behind Tia's tinkly laughter, there lurked deception. Belinda felt the inside of her mouth turn into sandpaper as her mouth formed a grim line.

'Excuse me,' Belinda called out, her voice coming out steadier than she felt.

Tia turned, her smile faltering momentarily before she settled back into her playful persona.

'Can I help you?'

Belinda stepped forward.

'I'm Belinda. Richard's wife,' she said, the words tasting bitter on her tongue.

Tia's expression shifted, due to a fleeting recognition, then it held a flicker of something darker.

'Oh', she replied, with no ounce of remorse evident in her tone.

Belinda's heart raced; she had envisioned this moment. The older woman followed at Tia's heels as the girl headed to a small corner table.

'I need to understand why...' Belinda continued, her voice firm. 'Why do you lure men for money?'

Tia settled into a chair and gave a nasty laugh.

'Richard isn't happy, Belinda. I simply offered him what you couldn't, a bit of fun. Don't you think he deserves that?'

Belinda inhaled sharply, outrage bubbling up inside her.

'You are a nasty piece of work young lady and karma is going to get you, that much is certain.'

For a split second, the smirk left Tia's face, revealing a flicker of vulnerability. Then it disappeared as quickly as it came. She looked Belinda over from head to toe in a critical fashion.

'Maybe you should ask him why he looked elsewhere,' she retorted coldly, turning to break away from the conversation that was now boring her.

'Why are you doing this?' Belinda hissed at the girl, desperation threading through her tone.

'You're young. You have your whole life ahead of you. You can still fix this! In any case you can't still blackmail Richard now that I know everything!'

Tia paused, her expression was angry again, her face a hard mask.

'You think this is only about you? This is about him and his upstanding position in the business world. A porno video featuring

Richard and I is hardly going to go down well at the next corporate family event, is it? I don't owe you anything. You should be angry with him, not me.'

The reality of her words struck Belinda hard, as she realised she had come here not to reason with Tia, but rather to blame her, to unleash the fury she felt. Tia was the tangible proof of her husband's infidelity, although the girl was not the sole root of the problem: Richard was. Feeling defeated, Belinda turned to leave, and Tia's voice stopped her in her tracks.

'You know, people like Richard will always seek sex elsewhere if they're unhappy. You probably should take a look in the mirror before you start pointing fingers.'

Belinda kept walking, her face bright red with mortification as her heart pounded in her ears, a mixture of anger and humiliation welling up as she walked out of the café on shaky legs. She hadn't even got around to talking about what she'd found on the mini camera in Richard's pocket. She'd lost her nerve when the confrontation had spiralled into an epiphany that revealed deeper cracks in her marriage. With each step away from Tia, determination began to replace the anger. Belinda needed to confront Richard, not with violence or rage, rather with clarity. She must face him, demand honesty and decide the fate of their relationship with a clear-headed resolve. Much like the women she'd worked alongside who'd survived domestic violence, she'd take control of the situation.

Chapter 17

Ricardo hummed to himself as he followed his cabin cleaning schedule. In a few more weeks he could return to the Philippines to be with his wife and children. He had a nice sum of money saved at this point and was excited to be able to pay for his family's ever-growing needs. He wasn't paid well, but many passengers had given him tips for the most random of favours. Sometimes it was best not to ask why they wanted certain things, such as when they asked him to provide them with chemicals! Now that had been an odd request, although he'd been handsomely paid, so had asked no questions. He was too naïve to give much thought to the purpose of the request in any case. Thinking about his future plans with his family, Ricardo whistled softly to himself as he went about his daily duties.

As he entered cabin 12812, he felt an immediate sense of unease. The energy felt dark and foreboding, and something definitely wasn't right. A gasp gurgled in his throat as his eyes fell on a spray of blood on the wall. His small hand clamped across his mouth in horror as he let out a little gasp. Ricardo willed himself to let his eyes look further into the cabin and then he froze with shock. A battered and bloody body lay on the balcony. Ricardo's stomach heaved horribly as he began to dry retch. It was Tia, her blank eyes glassy, her limbs horribly twisted, and her blonde hair soaked with blood. As Ricardo began to tremble from head to toe, he realised he may be in serious trouble. He'd been bribed with money to give out the deceased's cabin number.

What have I done?

Ricardo's heart thumped painfully in his chest as he pressed the emergency button on the ship's intercom, the dread coiling tighter with every passing second.

'Cabin 12812,' he stammered, battling his rising panic.

'I need security to come… code Operation Rising Star… there's an emergency… it's… there is a dead body on the balcony…'

His voice cracked, and he swallowed hard against the bile in his throat, feeling as though the walls were closing in around him. He gave a furtive glance towards the haunting image of Tia's lifeless body on the balcony, the breeze ruffling her bloodied hair, a cruel reminder of what she had been.

The seconds dragged into eternity, and Ricardo pressed his back against the door of the cabin, desperately trying to think. He knew the *Ocean Breeze* like the back of his hand, having traversed its vast decks and polished its gleaming surfaces for the past year. The familiar surroundings now felt foreign, tainted by blood and death. Who could have killed Tia and why?

Ricardo felt a chill creep up his spine as the weight of his actions bore down on him.

That nice lady… she'd had a seemingly innocent request for him to disclose Tia's cabin number to her. It had seemed harmless at the time, although deep down he'd wondered if the amount of money he was offered in exchange for the information meant it was being requested for a sinister reason. A thought he'd conveniently pushed to one side at the time. Ricardo was afraid, not only of losing his job but also of the implications of his actions. Footsteps thundered down the corridor, and Ricardo's breath caught in his throat. Ricardo peered around the door, trying to assess who was coming. He caught a glimpse of two members of the security team, their expressions serious and focused, their eyes trained on cabin 12812. One of them, a stern-looking woman named Officer Ferrari, approached Ricardo.

'Step aside please, this is now a crime scene. We will have an officer take your statement shortly and you will be treated for shock.'

Ricardo hesitated for only a moment before letting them in, moving clumsily out of the way as they stepped over the threshold. They took in the scene in silence, the splatter of blood, the chaos of the girl's scattered belongings, and finally, Tia's lifeless form on the balcony. Their solemn professionalism was evident, although Ricardo could see the flicker of shock on their faces too. Officer Ferrari quickly radioed in the incident while her partner, a lanky man with sharp eyes, began securing the area.

'Did you see or hear anything unusual?' The female officer turned to the white-faced cabin attendant. Officer Ferrari's voice was sharp, cutting through the fog of fear clouding Ricardo's mind.

Ricardo shook his head slowly as memories of the past few days came rushing back; a blurry haze of familiar faces and forgotten conversations. Then the day of the bribe bubbled to the surface. Ricardo blinked rapidly as he battled with his conscience.

I need to tell the truth! But if I do then I will be found to be guilty also…

'Um, there ugh was a lady who asked me about Tia. She wanted to know her cabin number…' Ricardo confessed, his voice barely above a whisper. The officer's scrutiny felt like a spotlight shining on his guilty conscience.

'What woman? Do you know of her cabin number? Describe her,' Officer Ferrari pressed, her tone urgent.

Ricardo twisted his hands, a tremor creeping into his voice as he willed himself to be truthful.

'She was a middle-aged lady, on the bigger side, with red curly hair, in her 50s I'd say. I don't know her cabin number though.' Ricardo crossed his fingers behind his back as he tripped over his words, feeling the weight of the lie coiling tighter around him. The penetrating stares of the officers turned his insides to liquid, so he quickly changed tack. Ricardo couldn't risk telling them the whole truth, so hopefully the partial truth was enough to appease his conscience.

'The lady offered me cash for the information which naturally I refused, and I did not give her the cabin number.'

Ricardo felt a slick of sweat slide down his back as the weight of another lie weighed heavily on him. His heart raced. The description didn't seem enough; were they going to believe him? If he was partly responsible for the young girl's death, then perhaps he'd unwittingly put his own safety in jeopardy too. Ferrari was weighing him up. She nodded brusquely at her colleague.

'Arrange to get Ricardo's full statement ASAP. We also need to secure this area with crime scene tape and find out exactly who was involved with this young woman. We need her last movements on the ship, where she last dined, who with, and so on. We will find this woman who asked for her cabin number. It will likely be a long process of elimination. It's going to be a long day and night....'

Ricardo looked on miserably. He hadn't admitted that he cleaned the room of the lady in question.

But she was so nice and had such kind eyes. Surely this horrible event had nothing to do with her asking for Tia's cabin number...

As officers processed the scene, Ricardo's thoughts raced. He needed to get out of this mess and find a way to protect not only his life, but also the lives of his family waiting for him back in the Philippines. His heart longed for home even more intensely now, and as fear combined with desperation, he made a silent vow: he'd find a way to free himself. The memories of his family filled him with resolve. Ricardo was not merely a cabin attendant; he was a survivor and he'd do whatever it took to protect those he loved. He'd find a way out.

Chapter 18

Jake took a deep breath, forcing his racing thoughts to settle as the magnitude of the situation hit him. The steady hum of the cruise ship felt suddenly suffocating, stained with the whispers of uncertainty and danger. Jake was good at a lot of things, although dealing with violence wasn't one of them. He felt a little out of his depth. Kayla's wide eyes reflected her fear, and he felt a surge of determination to protect her.

'Kayla,' he said, his voice steady despite his inner thoughts. 'I need you to stay strong for me. I promise you, the ship's protocols for safety are thorough. Vincent will ensure you're safe. I must go now, I will come back to check on you as soon as I can.'

'But Jake…' she started, her voice faltering.

'I'm sorry Kayla,' Jake interrupted gently, his eyes stern yet kind. 'We need to deal with an emergency situation onboard that could put lives at risk. I promise we are going to sort out your situation with Alex. I simply need you to hold on a little longer.'

Jake could see Kayla's resolve weakening as he prepared to leave. As he stepped towards the door, he looked back and gave her a weak smile. Jake was not remotely happy at having to hand Kayla over to Vincent, however he'd been summoned and had no choice. Gathering every ounce of resolve he had, he made his way to the Captain's quarters.

Jake had just received the grim advice that there had been a murder on the ship. He shuddered as a chill settled in his bones. As he hurried through the corridors of the ship, he felt the urgency of the situation tightening in his chest. The thought of a body being found onboard, a life extinguished, only magnified his sense of dread and the responsibility that lay with him as the Cruise Director. The ship was his domain, and he must ensure that the situation was managed appropriately.

Upon reaching the Captain's quarters, he pushed the door open to find Captain Moreno pacing, hands clasped behind his back, his expression grim. The ship's security team stood to the side, their faces hard and unreadable. Jake gave everyone a curt nod as he entered.

'What do we know so far?' Jake asked, his voice steady despite the whirlwind of emotions inside him.

'The body was found on the balcony of cabin 12812,' Captain Moreno replied, his voice low. 'The body of a young woman, Tia Hill, twenty years old from South Australia. Crime scene will commence their work in due course.'

A chill ran down Jake's spine. Fear gripped him as he looked at the copy of the deceased passport photo lying on the table. He recognised the female passenger who'd flirted with all and sundry on the ship including himself. Tia hadn't made any secret of her desire for him. Claire had wanted to scratch her eyes out. Surely Claire wouldn't.... No of course not. Claire could not possibly have anything to do with this. Could she?

Jake considered the possible scenarios and wondered if Tia's death had been as the result of a sexual prank gone wrong. She certainly seemed the type. Although, at this point he had no idea the murder weapon belonged to him.

'She was the sole occupant of the cabin,' stated the head security officer. 'Although we do have further intel on her companion

Tony…we can't disclose the contents until law enforcement arrives. We have been unable to locate Tony as yet and need to keep this information contained for now. We need to seal off that section of the ship with crime scene tape and have security monitoring the exits. We cannot, I repeat, cannot let anyone else into the area until law enforcement arrives.'

Jake ran a hand through his hair, his mind racing. Captain Moreno nodded at him gravely, visibly shaken about the situation yet determined not to let the situation spiral out of control.

Meanwhile, back in Jake's office, Kayla sat in silence. She now felt unsure about reporting Alex, despite her earlier bravado. How had it come to this? She pressed her palms against her forehead, fighting the swell of guilt and shame. Jake's second in command did not appear to be as caring as Jake. Vincent had disappeared and she'd been sitting there in limbo for at least fifteen minutes.

Suddenly, the door creaked open, and Vincent re-entered.

'How are you holding up?' he asked, his voice tinged with insincerity.

'I don't know what to do anymore,' Kayla stammered, her voice barely above a whisper. 'No offence but I don't feel like explaining the whole story again, I had just finished telling Jake. I realise he was called away urgently. Do you think he will be long?'

Vincent hesitated before responding. 'He's with the Captain… There's been a serious incident...' Kayla's eyebrows shot up.

'Do I need to be worried? Does it concern Alex?'

Vincent's expression faltered for a split second, revealing a flicker of uncertainty.

'All I can say is the ship is in a volatile situation. Until we have everything under control, you need to stay put with me. Alex has been detained, you don't need to worry about him.'

Vincent thought he saw a flicker of spite in Kayla's expression.

'Has someone died onboard or something?'

Vincent stared at Kayla. The girl had good intuition, although he'd had his orders so refused to confirm her thoughts.

'I'm unable to tell you anything at this moment, sorry.'

Kayla nodded, as fear gnawed at her insides. She had no idea what the hell was going on and the uncertainty was suffocating. Kayla didn't want to deal with Vincent, and she'd sensed his annoyance when she'd asked when Jake might return. Kayla was fed up with men and their fragile egos. For now, Kayla was trapped in the nightmare of a day that began in the beautiful city of Florence and had since gone horribly wrong.

Chapter 19

Alex was livid. He could not believe he was being held captive on the ship and been questioned about hitting Kayla. He'd vehemently denied everything, outraged that after spending so much money treating his girlfriend to the holiday of a lifetime that she could manipulate him and lie like this. The walls were closing in on him as he struggled to breathe through the mounting layers of fury and disbelief.

'You can't be serious!' he yelled at the imposing officer who stood before him, his arms crossed over a crisp blue uniform, his gaze hard and unyielding.

'It was her who attacked me!'

The officer maintained an unnerving calm, his notepad cradled in one palm.

'Well, I'm afraid your girlfriend claims otherwise.'

Alex shook his head in disbelief. How could Kayla do this to him? Only days ago, they'd been sipping cocktails on the sundeck, laughing under the Mediterranean sun. Now, she was painting him as a monster, and here he was trapped and isolated in this hell hole. Sweat trickled down his back as he wrestled with the uncontrollable swirl of anger and betrayal. The cruise had promised sun-soaked memories, not a nightmare on open waters, and certainly not an accusation that shattered his world.

'Are you sure you don't want to rethink any of this? You could save yourself a lot of trouble,' the officer growled.

Alex glanced at him warily.

'I've told you what happened,' he shot back, a twinge of desperation creeping into his voice. 'I don't know why she's lying! I just wanted to give her the perfect trip and this is how she repays me!' His voice echoed in the small room, as the gravity of his situation finally began to settle upon him. The officer's pen scratched across the notepad, taking notes, and a flicker of impatience flared in Alex's chest.

'Do you honestly think I'm *that* kind of guy?'

'Your girlfriend has indicated a pattern of behaviour that raises serious concerns,' the officer sneered, flipping his gaze from the notepad to Alex. The man held no warmth in his gaze, only a steely resolve. It was clear he'd already made up his mind.

As Alex leaned back in his chair, his mind began to race. He thought back to Florence. The quaint streets, filled with happy tourists. The city had seemed so idyllic only moments before everything turned to shit.

'Look, we had an argument, and I lost my cool for a minute,' Alex grappled to find the words to untangle the mess he was in. 'But it wasn't…'

'Physical violence against women is taken extremely seriously, Alex', the officer interrupted. 'It is fortunate that she was able to get back on the ship and seek help.'

'Help?' Alex looked incredulous. 'What are you talking about? You won't listen to my side at all will you? You have already made up your mind and pigeon-holed me as some kind of woman beater.' His voice rose in pitch. The officer remained unmoved, an unyielding wall against Alex's spiralling panic.

'Witnesses can be compelling,' the officer replied in a no-nonsense tone as he, jabbed a pen onto his notepad a little too forcefully. 'Fights that are overheard and injuries that are sighted by others tend to be pretty good evidence, if you ask me. I'm afraid the lady in the cabin next door claims she heard your fights and saw Kayla's injuries.'

Alex's heart sank. He hadn't counted on the fat old bitch coming forward as a witness.

The officer noted the flicker of fear in Alex's eyes and enjoyed fuelling it further.

'Kayla told us about the shop in Florence where your last assault on her was alleged to have taken place, and police are now looking into the CCTV in the area.'

Alex stared up at the officer glumly.

Fuck I'm up shit creek without a paddle.

The humiliation of that day in Florence played on his mind; a haunting melody he couldn't mute. The beautiful city with cobbled streets had turned into a nightmare with his failed proposal. Had they truly caught something on CCTV? Was it going to show him punching her in the guts? If so, he was finished. For the first time, his arrogance turned into a cold sense of dread. But then he filled his head with self-righteous thoughts: his only coping mechanism.

Surely, they'd also be able to see what a psycho bitch she had been too…

'Let me speak to her,' he pleaded.

The officer stared at him scornfully. 'That is not possible, I'm afraid. Not until the investigation is concluded.'

The finality in his tone left no room for negotiation or appeal. Alex's anger morphed into despair as he slumped down in his chair, the weight of impending doom pulling him down.

'You will be updated in due course,' the officer said in a tone that shattered any hope left inside Alex. As the officer walked out, the door clicked shut behind him and the realisation he had no escape from the situation weighed heavily upon him. He needed to finally face the consequences of his own actions. The hours dragged on as a mixture of self-pity and regret washed over him. He gave a slow outwards breath, and for the first time he began to face the reality of who he truly was. The memories of Kayla began to blend with the bitterness and the gnawing guilt he'd tried to ignore. Alex remembered their passion in the bedroom and groaned aloud. He'd had such strong feelings for her…now he was slowly realising they were toxic together. He remembered the fun they'd had in the lead up to their last fight, her soft hand in his while they walked through the streets of Florence. The same hand he'd punched her with.

I can't keep blaming my childhood for my actions. I know I need help. We both do…

Chapter 20

Vincent tossed and turned. He sighed as he rolled over and saw on his mobile display that it was 3.15am. He calculated that he'd only get a couple of hours sleep even if he did manage to doze off and conceded he may as well give up. He was going to struggle with the non-stop itinerary of activities lined up for the passengers who were not disembarking in Rome. He'd asked Jake for more responsibility and now that Maisie had blabbed to him, the prick had not only given him a verbal warning but also more tasks than he could reasonably handle.

Vincent sat up on the edge of his bed, still groggy from the minimal rest he'd managed to get out of the night. The cabin felt stifling, despite the low hum of the air conditioning. He closed his eyes for a moment, wishing fervently that the chaos of the past few days would simply dissolve into thin air. He stretched and splashed cold water on his face.

The team were still acting cold towards him, and it was pissing him right off. Now to make matters worse, the unthinkable had occurred: the body of that flirty young Tia had been found battered to death. It was the last thing the crew needed. There were always deaths aplenty on cruises, the passengers didn't know the half of it. The onboard morgue already had six pensioners lying on cold slabs. Murder was in a whole different league, though. Passengers needed to be interrogated and an investigation would hamper their fun. The decision making around such a crime was so much more complicated while at sea. For starters they must establish which jurisdiction was responsible and the legalities were a nightmare.

Most passengers are clueless about the sinister side of cruises.

For a fleeting moment, Vincent was glad not to have Jake's level of responsibility.

Every cloud has a silver lining after all.

Vincent began to fantasise about Jake being arrested for the murder. It'd put him right in his place! The more he thought about it, the more his wicked mind ticked over. Maybe he could plant a few more seeds there.

On top of Jake being a power tripping jerk, he'd also left Vincent to deal with Kayla following the domestic violence situation with her boyfriend Alex. The authorities were now the main ones dealing with that issue thankfully, and he'd been lumbered with checking in on her wellbeing given that she'd chosen to remain onboard for the rest of the cruise. The perpetrator had been questioned, although Alex was yet to hear anything further about his fate. Alex was currently detained in a lockup facility on the ship referred to as the brig.

I bet he isn't so cocky now.

Vincent didn't envy the Captain; he'd been forced to make the decision whether to dock early and report the crime or continue on course. The Captain had opted for the latter after discussing it with Kayla.

The number of competing issues on Vincent's mind was overwhelming to say the least. His life was one big fuck up and he did not know what to work through first. Vincent had not told anyone the real reason he had separated from his wife Jane. He'd hoped that being far from home might somehow make the nightmare go away, however it wasn't that simple. That was a battle for another day.

When the sun came up over Rome and the hustle and bustle of the day finally began, Vincent received confirmation from Jake that the passengers were going to be delayed from disembarking due to the requirement that they wait yet again for officials to arrive.

Great just what I need, irate passengers who might miss their pre-booked excursions.

At 10.30am, two vehicles arrived at the Port, one with "Polizia" on the side and the other with "Polizia Mortuaria" on it. It was a sobering sight, and the passengers began spreading rumours like wildfire. Vincent's mobile buzzed, jolting him back to stark reality. He opened the text from Jake.

You are required to attend the Captain's quarters at 11.00am prompt for an update.

Vincent scowled as he mimicked Jake while reading the text aloud. Why did he need to act so pompous! Vincent felt his thoughts spiralling. The murder had certainly sent shock waves through the crew and strained what was already a fraught atmosphere. He typed the briefest message he could think of.

Roger that.

Vincent tossed the phone onto the bed. His face darkened at the thought of facing Jake, whose smugness grew with every ounce of power he wielded. No way he could let Jake know exactly how much pressure he felt. Vincent took a deep breath, steeling himself for the day ahead. As he stepped out of his cabin, he braced himself for the blazing sun as he walked along the outdoor deck.

Inside the Captain's quarters, the atmosphere was thick with tension. Vincent noticed the cold stares of his colleagues as he pulled up a seat. The silence was palpable. Only a few days ago, they all seemed willing to joke and laugh between shifts; now they were distant, their camaraderie frayed by the grip of what had transpired. Jake's eyes surveyed the room as he spoke.

'We've got a lot to cover. The police are here again, and they'll want to interview more of the crew and passengers. We need to be ready to face a bunch of uncomfortable questions and be clear on what we can and cannot say.'

As the officials discussed the logistics and next steps, Vincent found himself drifting in and out of the conversation. He couldn't help glancing at Jake, a loathsome idea creeping in again. What if he were to plant a few doubts about Jake's involvement in the murder, even if only in jest? The thought made him chortle, but he swallowed it down. He must focus.

'Right,' Vincent said curtly, brushing aside the chaos in his mind. 'Let's start delegating who does what and when.'

Later that afternoon, the passengers were crammed into the grand atrium, murmuring anxiously as they awaited news. Vincent stood on the stage at the front, his arms crossed tightly over his chest. The passengers' stares picked him apart. He felt like an imposter in an atmosphere rife with confusion, anxiety and anger.

Just as things began to escalate as questions were fired at him about missed excursions, a voice cut through the crowd.

'You won't believe what I heard!' Rhonda, an older passenger with a tendency to embellish stories was calling out in her foghorn voice. 'The Italian mortuary people are onboard doing their thing and that's why we haven't been able to get off!'

Gasps echoed, followed by whispers and gradually the passengers became more heightened. Vincent's heart sank. He forced a reassuring smile, attempting to quiet the crowd, it was too late. The atmosphere was electric with fear.

'Now, now, folks,' he attempted, his voice strained yet authoritative over the microphone.

'Please try to remain calm, folks. The authorities are handling the situation, and while there has been a crime committed, we don't yet have the full facts. You will be able to disembark shortly for your excursions, but for now, we simply must cooperate with the officers and follow their instructions, okay?'

Although Jake had asked Vincent to address the passengers, Vincent noted with disgust that he still felt the need to butt in so he could say his bit too. Jake couldn't just delegate to his second in command for once, could he? Jake's eyes darted around the sea of faces as he spoke.

'I assure you, your safety is our top priority,' Jake said, doing his best to appear confident, while doubt crept like a shadow along his spine. No one appeared convinced.

Finally, when the never-ending day was over, Vincent lay in his cabin once more. He squeezed his eyes shut and as sleep evaded him. His mind took him back to that fateful day two months ago; the day his life had unexpectedly changed course.

Vincent and Jane had been eating lunch at the kitchen table when they heard the chime of the doorbell. Jane had rolled her eyes, 'Shall we ignore it? It's likely to be Jehovah's Witnesses or someone selling something...'

Vincent shrugged, 'I'm not curious enough to care who it is. If it is important, then they will soon let us know.'

They sat in silence hoping they'd hear the person walk back down the gravel; however, the caller became insistent, ringing the bell multiple times.

Jane frowned, 'What do you have to do to enjoy a bite of lunch in peace around here? I better see who it is, maybe it's to do with old Joe across the road. He doesn't have anyone looking out for him.'

Vincent nodded disinterestedly. When Jane opened the door and Vincent heard the gravelly voice of his cousin Susan Blaikie on the other side, his face froze in fear; the ham and cheese sandwich in his hand suspended between the plate and his mouth.

Chapter 21

Belinda was relieved to hear that Alex was now detained on the ship. She was proud of Kayla for making the brave decision to complete the cruise with Belinda's support. While one problem was sorted, she had another much bigger one that was becoming harder to ignore. Her marriage was in tatters and, to make matters worse, widespread panic was spreading through the passengers due to the young woman's death that had resulted in the presence of police onboard. The Chinese whispers about the ongoing investigation were becoming more elaborate by the minute. At breakfast, Belinda overheard two women in the main dining room discussing rumours that the girl had been beheaded. Belinda shuddered, although she noted that the woman doing most of the talking obviously enjoyed embellishing her stories. Belinda highly doubted she had any evidence to back up her sorry tale.

Feeling exasperated, Belinda rolled her eyes, the gossip was becoming next level crazy. The crew appeared extremely reluctant to discuss the matter in great detail with the passengers who probed, so instead they made up their own theories and the increasingly bizarre rumours were spreading like wildfire. The authorities were systematically interviewing as many passengers as they could, however they also needed to allow the cruise to carry on as normally as possible to avoid mass hysteria. The staff had to try and give people the experience they'd paid copious amounts of money for.

Today Richard was helping the authorities with their enquiries. Belinda was permitted to still go on the expensive excursion they'd already paid for, therefore she was taking Kayla in his place. As Belinda got ready for the day, she stared at herself in the mirror. Her hands shook as she applied factor 50 sunscreen. Belinda tried to convince herself that Richard's interview was purely routine. But she was afraid. Somehow, she'd managed to avoid telling Richard of her discovery; she convinced herself she was merely biding her time. Belinda had a sickening gut feeling that the girl who'd been killed was Tia, although she didn't have the facts at this point. Somehow, she was managing to live out the cruise in a constant state of denial: first about Richard's secrets and now she had her own secrets to add to the mix.

Belinda checked in with Kayla as the two women disembarked from the ship and boarded the coach that was taking them to Pompei for the day.

'How are you feeling today, love?'

Kayla glanced at her older companion, 'Not great, if I'm honest. I'm so grateful for your support and for letting me take your husband's place today. I must confess I don't know much about Pompei though.'

Belinda smiled, 'You are in for a treat. It's a city of the Roman Empire. It was destroyed in the first century due to Mount Vesuvius erupting.'

'Oh, it sounds like a cool site to visit,' replied Kayla. She was glad to be out of her head for a while.

'So, what we are seeing is the ruins that are left, I take it?'

'That's right, love.' Belinda smiled as she fiddled with the air conditioner above her head.

'Jeez it's stuffy on this coach!'

As the coach trundled towards the meeting point at Pompei, Kayla noticed Belinda was off in her own world.

'Belinda if you don't mind me asking, is everything okay? I mean I know it's probably routine, but with Richard being questioned today and you know…you alluding to him acting weird since you got on the cruise. I'm not suggesting he… Oh, I don't really know what I'm trying to say here. I only hope all is well. The focus of our chats has always been about me dealing with Alex. I feel bad as it's obvious you have stuff going on too. If I'm overstepping by asking, then I'm sorry, just tell me to butt out.'

Kayla knew she was babbling and couldn't seem to stop herself. Belinda turned to her younger companion, a reassuring smile on her face.

'I'm honestly fine love. Don't you worry your pretty little head about me. Who said anything about Richard being questioned? He is merely helping with enquiries, it's a routine thing. I will have to take my turn too, it's likely everyone on the same deck as the victim will.'

Kayla nodded; she was unconvinced with Belinda's explanation.

As the coach continued its bumpy journey through the Italian countryside, Belinda couldn't shake the growing unease in her gut. The whispers about the tragic death of the girl haunted her thoughts. Her imagination went into overdrive. Did Richard's moody temperament and unpredictable behaviour of the last few days mean he'd been holding something even more sinister back? Something more than the infidelity? The more she thought about it, the harder it became to maintain the façade of reassurance. Belinda had secretly monitored him a bit more carefully and had even done a bit more digging of her own. For some god forsaken reason she was simply unable to confront him. Every time she went to do so, her mouth opened then nothing came out. As Belinda's throat tightened, she shook her head; she mustn't think about that today.

She turned to Kayla, 'It's just… you know, being here, in such a beautiful place, with everything that's happened, it feels surreal knowing that a young girl has died on the ship. It feels wrong that some of us are still having fun. At the same time, what good does it do anyone to sit moping around? It doesn't change what happened does it?' Belinda's voice trailed off as she stared out the window.

Kayla turned her head slightly, offering a sympathetic nod. 'It's okay to feel that way Belinda. We're all on edge after what happened. I can't help but think it could have been me if I hadn't reported Alex's violence. I even wondered if he'd killed that girl before I found out he was detained. I can't believe only a few days ago I thought I was with the man of my dreams and now I'm talking about him as though he is capable of murder! The whole thing is just so unbelievable. Alex will be fuming that he is being held captive on the ship and I'm terrified that I won't be protected from the aftermath of that once we disembark at the end of the cruise.'

Belinda nodded sympathetically, placing her hand over Kayla's. 'The authorities will make sure you are protected, try not to worry. Let's change the subject now love. While we're here, we need to make the best of it eh? Let's make sure we enjoy Pompei.'

Kayla gave a glum nod, blinking away her tears. For some reason this journey felt never ending. When they finally arrived and stepped off the coach, the sun was beating down mercilessly on the ancient stones of the ruined city. The air was rich with history and Belinda tried to focus on the magnificence surrounding her. They wandered through the meandering streets, guided by an enthusiastic female Italian tour guide whose voice somehow cut through the dense atmosphere via their headsets. Every so often, Belinda caught snippets of conversations behind her; their increasing speculation kept reminding her of the very thing she was trying to escape. Belinda sighed in annoyance as she overheard a loud American man boom, 'You hear about the girl who was killed onboard? They say her body was found all bashed up on her balcony.'

His companion drawled, 'Yeah, I heard it was her boyfriend who did it. He must've been a real psycho.'

Belinda's stomach twisted. She exchanged glances with Kayla, who seemed as cool as a cucumber.

'Shouldn't we be able to simply enjoy this without listening to this shit all the time?' Kayla asked quietly to herself.

Suddenly, a loud commotion broke out nearby. A group of tourists were gathered around a statue, and at first, it seemed innocuous enough. As Belinda approached, she saw that police officers were present. 'Stay close to me,' she hissed at Kayla, sensing her apprehension as she trailed behind the older woman.

As they merged into the huddled crowd, the tension sizzled in the air. In that moment, something clicked in Kayla's mind. There must be more to Belinda than met the eye, she was acting shady for some reason.

She suspects her husband killed that girl and she is protecting him.

The police were heading in their direction as onlookers stared. All the breath left Belinda's body as panic rose within her.

Are they coming to ask me if I was the one who paid Ricardo in exchange for Tia's cabin number?

She spun to face Kayla, her face drained of colour.

'We must go back to the ship now,' Belinda stated firmly, her heart racing. She grabbed Kayla's arm in a bid to move away quickly. The two women moved against the swarm of the crowd, and when the police did not catch up with them after all, Belinda visibly sagged with relief. The officers had clearly been there for an unrelated matter.

The coach ride back to the cruise terminal was filled with an ominous silence as the weight of unanswered questions weighed heavily upon them both. Kayla stared intently at Belinda's profile.

Why did Belinda overreact that way? Why did she think the police were there for her? Why was she protecting her husband?

The return to the ship was full of stifled breaths and furtive glances. Both women were fearful and doing their best to mask it, and they both knew it.

Chapter 22

The *Ocean Breeze* cruise ship swayed gently at its port side. The vessel, a floating city of leisure and distraction, was now a scene of chaos and fear; an unsettling juxtaposition to its sunny exterior. Lead investigator Francesco Rossi stood at the foot of the gangway, surveying the passengers milling about in confusion; their jovial vacation spirits shattered by the recent and abrupt news.

Rossi was fully briefed and was aware the victim was Tia Davidson. She'd been found murdered in her cabin under heinous circumstances. Rossi had seen his fair share of crime scenes, although murder on a cruise ship added a whole new layer of complexity. The jurisdiction was murky, this floating paradise traversed international waters, and the myriad of passengers and crew members from all corners of the globe only added to the complications.

Through gritted teeth, Rossi groaned inwardly. It was never a good time for a murder investigation, and the timing of this one was particularly inconvenient for him. His mind drifted to Elena, the woman who had recently burst into his life igniting a passion he hadn't known could exist. Rossi's obsession with Elena was not only due to her beauty, but also her intellect and wit. Elena had the all-round winning combination. The two of them had been inseparable and constantly in bed together when he was summoned to the ship.

'Francesco!' a voice broke through his reverie. It was detective Maria Sullivan, his partner in this chaotic endeavour. The female detective was the only colleague who called him by his first name. Maria was tall, with fiery red hair that matched her fierce demeanour. She approached him, a notebook in her hand, her sharp eyes sweeping her surroundings.

'You ready to start interviewing witnesses?'

'Si, let's get this over with,' Rossi replied, forcing a smile despite his inner turmoil. The Captain greeted them with a pale face and sunken eyes, a stark reminder of what lay ahead: a tedious web of testimonies woven into the fabric of a luxury vacation gone wrong. As they began conducting their interviews, Rossi found himself becoming a magnet for the passengers' stories. Some stated they'd witnessed an argument between Tia and Claire, and others reported various men lurking around the victim's door at different times. As the tales began to intertwine, Rossi felt the weight of each account, the pressure mounting as he grappled with a multitude of narratives.

Rossi tried to shelve his thoughts about Elena. Due to the urgency of the investigation, they'd cancelled their plans, including a romantic getaway. The idea now felt more like a distant dream than a reality. Rossi couldn't get enough of Elena, yet here he was, forced to navigate the complexities of betrayal and jealousy that had led to murder. Rossi was expected to figure out the connections between the ship's passengers and any motives. Rossi yawned. He was tired of dealing with stupid tourists. Rossi decided he'd deal with them the Italian way, whether they liked it or not. As Rossi delved deeper, he began to notice patterns take shape. Motives clashed: jealousy amongst performers and passengers, and whispers of hidden affairs. Looking at his watch, Rossi brought his thoughts back to the present as he prepared for his next interview.

Richard's heart raced as he waited his turn in the interrogation room, while watching Rossi pace with growing frustration. The air was thick with tension, each tick of the old school clock amplifying his anxiety. Richard found himself desperately wishing for a way out; he simply must prove his innocence. He was sweating profusely and knew it was not a good look. Richard was in too deep and had completely lost his cool at this point.

'Tell me', boomed Rossi, 'why did my officers find your mobile phone in the victim's cabin? It had been kicked under the bed?'

Richard wiped his face with the back of his hand. His mouth was horribly dry, and a sour taste coated his tongue.

'Now that sir, I honestly can't explain. I suspect Tia's side kick Tony set me up by planting it there. Tony and I had words, we had a scuffle and then he took off with my phone. I swear I was not anywhere near her cabin when she was killed. Although I do want to confess my whole sorry tale to you about my unfortunate experience with this girl because it's all going to come out now anyway.'

Rossi gave an abrupt nod and waved a hand. 'So, tell me!' he barked. His patience was running thin with the morons on this ship.

Richard leaned forward, desperation etched into his features. 'You must believe me. I can't begin to imagine who'd be capable of… of killing a young girl like this...'

Richard's eyes darted around the room then rested on Rossi's face. He was searching for a semblance of understanding in the officer's hard gaze, however the man did not even blink.

By the time Richard finished explaining how he had been lured into bed by Tia and then blackmailed, his head was hanging down in shame. Rossi weighed up the man in front of him. The man presented as sincere, decent even, although it was evident he had a motive for killing Tia. Rossi gave him a weary stare. It had been a long day and he wasn't even done interviewing suspects yet.

'You see the thing that is not adding up Richard, is the fact that you claim to have filmed this girl more or less admitting her crimes in the library, yet the camera you used has gone missing, this is a little convenient, no?'

Richard started bouncing his right leg up and down, a sure sign he was agitated. 'As I said, I've been set up. My phone has been stolen and planted, and my camera has been taken. I'm telling you it's her side kick you need to find, not me! Have you even interviewed this Tony character?'

Rossi began to pace the room. 'That is not of your concern,' he barked. Rossi was not going to admit that no one had been able to locate Tony since Tia's body had been found. Security confirmed he had not swiped his identity card to disembark the ship, which meant he was still onboard presumably in hiding and was possibly armed and dangerous. With over 4000 passengers onboard, it was going to be a huge task to locate him. Despite looking through extensive footage, he had not been spotted yet.

Rossi was becoming desperate to interrogate Tony. He knew Tony was Tia's business partner and no doubt he had been intimate with the girl himself, given the nature of their joint venture. A partner in crime was notoriously the number one suspect in a brutal murder such as this one, so locating him was a priority.

Rossi stopped pacing and turned to face Richard, his arms crossed in a defensive stance. 'You're telling me a convenient story, Richard, yet I see red flags everywhere. You're an intelligent man; I can tell. Yet, somehow, you've gotten tangled up with the wrong people. What kind of smart man puts himself in that position?'

Richard sighed, running a hand through his hair. 'Tia played me, she was convincing, and my inflated ego let me believe she was into me.' A red flush crept up his face. 'I'm simply an old fool who wanted a moment's escape, and then it all turned to shit.'

'Escape?' Rossi repeated, pulling a chair across the room and dropping into it with a thud. 'That's a dangerous word here. It implies intention, desire to break free…from what Richard? Did it end up making you want to take Tia's life? Because that's what blackmail does to people Richard. It captures you. It winds the ropes tighter until the only choice left is to submit or retaliate.'

Richard's breath caught as Rossi's words lingered in the air. The detective's analytical demeanour unnerved him; it was as if he could see right through his fraught exterior and into the murky depths of his mind where fear and guilt intertwined.

'I didn't kill her, I swear,' Richard blurted out.

Rossi leaned back in his chair, tapping his fingers on the desk, his eyes narrowing.

'Then help me understand how your phone ended up in her cabin. Help yourself, Richard, because right now, I'm starting to think you're more involved than you're letting on.'

Richard clenched his hands into fists, fighting back the urge to scream. His voice cracked, 'I didn't leave it there! As I said, I was on my way to the lounge when I got Tia's messages. She wanted to meet up again to sort out this whole payment mess. I haven't had contact with her since. I promise you, I only met with her once in the library as you already know. I offered Tia a way out, to escape from Tony's control. So to reiterate, I then had words with Tony and he…'

Rossi stood up abruptly, his face thunderous, 'If you were truly innocent, why didn't you go straight to the security team the moment you realised you were being blackmailed?'

Richard was annoyed, it was pretty obvious why a man would keep it quiet. 'Because I was ashamed!' Richard shouted, desperation creeping back into his voice. 'I thought I could handle it, that I could make it go away without involving the authorities. I didn't want anyone to know about my stupidity, that I'd had sex with her. I thought I could talk to her, convince her to stop this madness. Instead, I walked into a trap.'

Rossi leaned forward, his gaze piercing. 'So, this Tony, where does he fit into all this? You're painting him as the mastermind, yet he's nowhere to be found.'

'I don't know!' Richard yelled, the frustration of his situation bubbling over.

'From what I could see it was obvious the girl needed help, deep down I think she wanted to protect herself from him… I could never have imagined he'd go so far as to kill her. It's possible Tony forced Tia to admit she was thinking of leaving their arrangement… he could have killed her in a rage!'

Rossi squinted, his brow furrowing. 'So now you are clutching at straws saying Tony killed her, is that it? I can see that you are becoming very heightened, Richard. I'd say you are more afraid than you want me to think you are. Do you honestly expect me to believe this tall story of yours?' he challenged, his voice low.

Richard hesitated desperately trying to appear calmer than he felt.

'I know how it seems officer, but I can't change what happened. I've told you the truth. It's Tony you need to interview, not me.'

Rossi's intense scrutiny faltered briefly, and for a moment Richard thought he saw a flicker of empathy in the officer's eyes.

'Let's say I believe you,' Rossi said, leaning back, his arms crossed across his broad chest once more.

'I'm going to ask you once again, how do you explain your phone being found in Tia's cabin?'

Rossi was deliberately asking the same questions over and over in an attempt to break him and it was grating on Richard's nerves big time. The detective was obviously trying to get him to reach snapping point, to make him admit to something that hadn't even happened.

'I… I don't know!' Richard spat. 'I had no idea she was dead until I came here to help with your enquiries, alright?'

Rossi watched him for a moment, weighing up each word. 'The truth is a slippery thing, Richard. You have paid the ultimate price for your stupidity. Tia was a mistake, a weak and irresistible temptation that pulled you in deeper than you could ever have imagined.'

Richard clenched his jaw, understanding washing over him as the detective's words rang true. A bitter defeat surged through him. He'd already admitted that his time with Tia was a big mistake. It was obvious Rossi wanted to completely break him.

'Yes,' he said, his tone resigned. 'My involvement with Tia was a big mistake. But I never laid a hand on her.'

Just your cock, Rossi thought.

Richard finally met Rossi's sharp gaze. The hard reality of the situation gripped him; he'd been well and truly played, and now he was a cornered rat. If he wanted to walk out of this room with his reputation intact, he'd need to start playing the game smarter. When Rossi finally dismissed Richard for the day, Richard was emotionally drained. Richard feigned feeling ill to Belinda. All he wanted to do was crawl into bed and never come out.

Rossi moved on to the next interview. He observed Vincent as he sat in the cramped, dimly lit office of the investigative team. The flickering overhead light cast stark shadows across the room as the Assistant Cruise Director weighed up how to project an air of concern towards his boss, Jake. Yet Vincent was secretly relishing the chaos that had erupted due to Tia's death. Rossi noted with interest that Vincent took his time before replying to his questions with carefully crafted replies. Rossi was a highly experienced investigator and could tell Vincent hoped to come across as someone who was tentatively sharing information rather than presenting his true scheming self.

As Vincent pondered his replies, the thought of Jake's escalating discomfort only fuelled his eagerness. If Jake was implicated, it'd mean Vincent could finally step into the brilliance of the spotlight that had always eluded him beneath Jake's commanding presence.

Vincent cocked his head to one side, feigning a concerned expression as he looked into Rossi's eyes. 'Well, something that does concern me is that Jake's lover Claire was extremely threatened by Tia. As you know there are a few witnesses that saw them having a vicious argument the other night. While that implicates Claire, I have also wondered whether Jake had given into temptation and you know, perhaps become physical with Tia. Having chatted to Tia myself, she joked to me after a few drinks that her sights were firmly set on Jake. Tia also admitted she uses men for financial gain. So, she could easily have been after Jake's money – after all he is on an extremely high salary. I hate to say it, but Jake could have a motive for getting rid of Tia if she threatened to reveal something unsavoury about him that might impact his job.'

Rossi stopped writing and stared at Vincent intently for a few seconds, as though processing his words carefully. Vincent couldn't be sure if this was due to the shock at the suggestion that Jake the *highly* respected Cruise Director could be involved, or whether it was merely because he thought he was onto something.

Vincent thought he saw a flicker of contempt in the dark-skinned man's eyes, however, it was lost when the detective commenced writing furiously in his notebook. Rossi asked Vincent the remaining standard questions that were required and then dismissed him. As he watched Vincent swagger out of the room, his eyes narrowed. The Assistant Cruise Director was not a sincere man, that much was evident. Vincent's contrived act was all an attempt to drop Jake in the shit and unfortunately Rossi could not divulge to Jake that his second in charge had just tried to throw him under the bus as it might jeopardise the investigation if it had any truth to it. Jake would find out soon enough.

As Rossi stretched, he considered that perhaps Vincent had made a valid point, so all of the presented information would be carefully examined. However, it was obvious the man reeked of insincerity. When they'd looked each other in the eyes, they were both aware of their mutual dislike of each other. In Vincent's mind he'd been presented with the perfect opportunity to mastermind a cunning plan to frame Jake. His envy was morphing into a chilling, cold-blooded plot, fuelled by the belief that only by removing Jake could he seize the position he craved.

After a quick croissant and a Starbucks coffee courtesy of one of the crew members, Rossi met with Claire. Rossi observed the jumpy young woman who fiddled with her hair and clothes incessantly. Rossi wished he could slap Claire's hands away from the necklace around her throat as her mannerisms were beginning to grate on his nerves. Rossi spoke in an authoritative tone, and Claire couldn't help but think that in any other circumstances, she'd find his Italian accent incredibly sexy. The way Rossi rolled the letter "r" and elongated his vowels would ordinarily turn her on. Claire got the feeling Rossi was well aware he made most red-blooded females hot around the collar with his dark brooding eyes, chiselled physique and sharp jawline. Claire fixated on his fleshy lips as he spoke, the confidence in his tone giving him an undeniable charm. However, the fact that Rossi was investigating a murder and she might be a suspect was a sobering thought. So, shifting her thoughts, she braced herself for what was to follow.

Rossi flipped through the pages of Claire's statement, his brow furrowing slightly. He didn't look like the kind of man who was easily fooled, and that only made her more wary of how precarious her situation was.

'Claire,' he said, pulling her from her thoughts. His voice was a rich timbre, smoky and deep, yet strained by the weight of his work.

'There are several witnesses who attest to you having a jealous outburst towards the deceased that resulted in a verbal and physical fight. I also have further information to suggest that you were jealous of Tia's attempts to talk with Jake. Others claim you were openly hostile towards Tia on more than one occasion. What can you tell me about that?'

Claire's stomach twisted. She'd avoided eye contact for most of their conversation; now she met his gaze, wanting desperately to see compassion instead of suspicion.

Rossi leaned back, scratching his chin; the stubble rasping against his fingertips as he considered the tightness around Claire's mouth and her inability to sit still. Despite her obvious discomfort, his gaze remained fixed on her, his eyes boring into her as he crossed his arms over his solid chest.

Claire's left eye began to twitch. She knew she'd caused trouble by bitching about Tia to anyone who'd listen, including her new friend Kayla. She felt uneasy about this now although she doubted that this had influenced whoever the murderer was. That was an absurd idea and was bordering on paranoia.

I must get a grip and simply answer the bloody questions so I can get the hell out of here!

In the back of Claire's mind, the memory of Tia's smirk lingered, taunting her as Jake's eyes flitted over her with intrigue. It played on a loop, igniting her jealousy once more. Claire smoothed down the front of her dress in a bid to dry her sweating palms as she recalled the fiery confrontation she'd exchanged with Tia.

Claire's words tumbled out in a stutter, 'I know how awful our fight sounds, and I'm not going to deny I intensely disliked the way this girl presented herself or the fact that she made several obvious beelines for my boyfriend Jake, but Jesus Christ, I could never murder someone!'

Rossi winced at Claire's shrill voice; she was becoming hysterical despite her pleas of innocence. Rossi asked further questions as per the standard procedure and noticed Claire's voice increased in pitch with every query, and at times she closed her eyes in distress or looked away from him. By the end she was a babbling mess. Going by Claire's body language and overall presentation, something was troubling her. Rossi scratched his chin thoughtfully as he weighed up his findings. Claire had avoided eye contact for most of the interview. She was definitely up to something. The ship continued to sail through the tranquil waters, yet the atmosphere onboard grew increasingly strained.

Vincent, fuelled by his bitterness, was subtly trying to sabotage Jake's credibility while Claire's neurotic traits are becoming more annoying by the minute. Were either of these two guilty of murder?

Chapter 23

Three months before the cruise.

The unwelcome guest barged into the kitchen, her wild eyes full of fury. Jane trotted behind her; confusion etched on her face. Who was this mad woman named Susan claiming to be her husband's cousin? Susan pointed an accusing finger at Vincent, whose face was becoming paler by the second.

'I bet you thought I'd never track you down, that your past would never catch up with you? Well, here I am! You are a scumbag of the highest order; do you know that?'

Suddenly Jane's lunch was no longer appealing as her stomach churned at the woman's words. Vincent remained silent, a stricken look on his face.

Susan shook her head savagely in disgust, 'Are you going to fill your lovely wife in, or shall I?'

Jane looked between Vincent and Susan, her eyes wide with fear, her jaw tense. Her voice came out in a squeak, 'Is someone going to tell me what the hell is going on around here?'

Vincent decided he was not going to make it easy for Susan, so he continued to stare at his cousin blankly, willing her to disappear back through the door she'd just stormed through.

Susan's voice shook with emotion as she turned to face Jane, 'Your lovely husband my dear, is a pathetic excuse of a man who fled from London after his children Caleb and Mila were removed from the care of his ex-partner Tracey, who is a drug addict. The children were placed with me as I was the only relative willing to take them on. Vincent was nowhere to be found and completely denied paternity!'

Susan waved an arm wildly in Vincent's direction. 'Vincent fucked off as far as possible to start a new life, met you, and no doubt spun you a pack of lies! I'm sorry but when I found you on social media, and I saw you guys had a kid together, I had no choice but to warn you about my charming cousin, who incidentally does not ever ask about his first two children or contribute anything meaningful to their lives! It's taken me a while to find out where you lived. Now here, I am, reunited with Vincent at last!'

Jane's face twisted in confusion, as she spat, 'Vincent what the hell is this woman talking about?'

She could hear the tinge of hysteria in her voice, and she didn't like it one bit. Jane had a dreadful feeling in the pit of her stomach that this woman was telling the truth and deep down she did not particularly want to hear Vincent's response.

Vincent stood up and clapped.

'Great delivery Susan, why not make sure yet another family falls apart?'

Vincent's lack of ownership made Susan's blood boil, and she lunged at him, scratching his face with her long pink nails in the process. Vincent smirked and Susan knew right away she'd been goaded into attacking him so he could use it against her. He truly was a nasty piece of work.

'Tracey neglected those poor kids Vincent. All she cared about was her next fix.' Susan looked pointedly at Jane, 'Vincent didn't even consider taking the kids on himself, he simply fucked off to the other side of the country and met you! Well, I'm not letting him do this to another child! For god's sake woman, how much do you even know about the man you married? Clearly not a lot!' Susan paused, she suddenly felt bad for the poor woman in front of her who was clearly grief stricken.

Jane's voice was a whisper. 'If he denied being the father, then how do you know they truly are his kids?'

It was a desperately lame question, and they all knew it. Susan looked Jane straight in the eyes. 'Because they are his absolute double and I'm sorry to tell you that refusing DNA testing doesn't let him off the hook. The children have a rare genetic heart condition that runs on our side of the family. Vincent and I have it too. I was the only family member willing to take them on and my own DNA test proves the children and I are related.'

Jane promptly ran from the room and threw up in the toilet next-door. Her mind was racing as her limbs shook uncontrollably. This Susan woman was right, she could not deny that she did not know much about Vincent at all. When they met on a dating site, she'd respected his explanation that he came from a dysfunctional family in London who were too painful to talk about, thus he had distanced himself from them. Jane admired Vincent's bravery and never pushed him to talk about his past for fear of opening old wounds. Now she felt like a complete idiot. She'd married this man not knowing who he truly was or what he was capable of. The truth was that when Jane reached 35 years of age, she'd become desperate to marry and have a child. Admittedly, she'd taken whoever she could get her claws into without thinking it through. Vincent had come across as a decent catch, and he was certainly smart enough; he'd even recently won the role as Assistant Cruise Director with a posh cruise line. Surely, he wasn't the type of person who'd ignore two children that he'd fathered? How could he possibly have offspring she did not know about? Their own child Braydon had just had his first birthday. Was he going to end up with an absent father too?

Thankfully Jane's mother had taken Braydon out for the day. Jane dry wretched again before splashing her face with cold water as she tried to steady her shaking hands. Whether she liked it or not, she must get back in there and face the truth.

Vincent and Susan were still bickering, and Jane's voice trembled as she walked back into the kitchen raising her hand to attempt to diffuse the situation. Jane fought against the dizziness. Susan noted the other woman might pass out at any minute going by her pallor.

Jane stood with her hands on her hips. 'Vincent you better start talking, I want the truth, and I want it right now.'

Susan hovered, unsure whether to stay or not. She'd said what she'd come to say, and wasn't feeling so good about it now despite Jane's right to know the truth. Jane watched the thoughts play out on the woman's face.

When Vincent remained silent, Jane turned to Susan instead.

'Where are Vincent's children at the moment… and how old are they?' Jane stammered.

Vincent blanched at her words, wondering how he was going to talk his way out of this one. He'd kept up the pretence successfully with Jane up to now and concealed his untreated personality disorder well too.

Susan spoke softly, noting the pained expression on Jane's face. She knew that hearing they were so young would be a fresh blow to Jane.

'Caleb is five and he just started school, and Mila is three, she goes to childcare.'

Jane's face flushed a dull red as spittle formed in the corners of her mouth, she'd finally lost control.

'What do you have to say for yourself Vincent?' she screamed the words, his nonchalant attitude finally making her lose all composure.

'It's all true,' Vincent replied simply, without emotion.

Jane marched over to him and slapped him hard across the face. Then she punched him repeatably until she fell into a sobbing mess on the floor. Vincent remained perfectly still, he was a statue, and oddly aware he was becoming detached.

Feeling strangely unsatisfied with her mission, Susan turned on her heel and left. Maybe now the bastard might pay towards the children's upkeep at the very least. She'd be damned if he was going to live in suburbia with his new family and not help her and the children out somehow.

Susan slammed the door behind her, leaving a deafening silence that enveloped the kitchen. Jane lay on the cold tiled floor, her breaths coming in ragged gasps as tears streamed down her face. The kitchen, once a space of leisurely lunches and laughter, now felt foreign and dark.

'Jane…' Vincent's voice piped up, he hesitated, knowing his tone lacked the remorse she desperately needed to hear.

'How could you do this to me?' she finally managed between sobs. The question echoed in the air. 'You never ever mentioned them. You lied to me and worse of all you denied their existence. I feel ill at the thought.'

'Lied? No. I just didn't speak about them. I thought it was for the best.'

'Best for who?' Jane interrupted. 'You? You thought it was best for you to erase your own son and daughter from your past? To pretend they didn't exist? To pretend you didn't destroy their lives? Who even are you?'

'I was trying to protect you from my past!' he shot back, his frustration bubbling to the surface. 'I'm not that person anymore! I've built a new life with you and Braydon!'

Jane shot up from the floor, anger surging through her, overpowering the fear that had gripped her moments before. His lack of remorse infuriated her further.

'Built a new life? By abandoning your children? By hiding from the consequences of your actions?' Her voice cracked with disbelief.

'They went to live with Susan. It's not as though I left them in a care home. They are with a family member.'

'But they should be with you!' Jane's words pierced the air. 'You're their father! You're supposed to care. You're supposed to be part of their lives! They are not Susan's responsibility!'

Vincent shrugged, a gesture so dismissive it was a kick in the guts. The man she thought she knew, the one who was an ambitious family man and eager to provide, was crumbling before her eyes, revealing a narcissist she never imagined existed.

'I'm not sure what this means for Braydon,' she cried, as sadness crept into her tone.

Vincent grabbed her arm. 'I want to do the right thing by him, to get it right this time. I used to be on the gear too Jane, that's why I'd have made a shit father to those kids. I swear I'm not that guy anymore, you must believe me. I needed to escape from Tracey and the old crowd and sadly that included the kids. I moved as far away as possible to remove myself from all our cronies so I could become the version of me that you see now!'

'Is that supposed to make me feel better?' she challenged as she leapt to her feet, her fists clenched at her sides. 'You think that I'm simply going to accept this, ignore it? What about Caleb and Mila?' The names felt foreign on her tongue, achingly real in the context of their unspoken past.

'Look,' he said, running a hand through his dark curls, 'I didn't want any of this to happen. But Susan found us and now we must deal with the truth. I didn't want you to find out this way. I was going to tell you one day, I swear!'

'Oh, sure Vincent, like when? When they were all grown up?' Her voice became a whiplash of accusation. 'What exactly were you going to say? "Oh, by the way, I have two kids I don't talk about that grew up without me being around because I'm a selfish piece of shit?" Is that how you intended to break it to me?'

His eyes flickered, revealing a glimpse of vulnerability. 'I didn't know how to bring it up.'

'Apparently, you don't know much at all,' Jane fired back, her heart racing.

The room felt stifling, the walls felt like they were closing in around them. Vincent dropped his head, his hands falling to his sides as she pushed them off her shoulders.

'I thought if I distanced myself from them, from my old life, I could make a fresh start. I did it for us, for my new family. You must believe me.'

'Believe you? You're asking for my trust right now? After this? I'm not sure we still have a future…' The disbelief dripped from her words.

'Don't do this,' Vincent urged, stepping closer. Jane took an instinctive step back, the chasm between them widening. 'Please Jane… is destroying our family the right answer?'

'Your self-centred actions destroyed our family!' she yelled, the realisation crashing down upon her with a brutal force. She thought she'd left behind her scattered dreams and insecurities when she married him. Now, they rose again increasing her sense of panic.

'We'll find a way to figure this out,' Vincent pleaded, trying to close the distance. Jane shook her head, as fresh tears shimmered in her eyes.

'Figure out what? How to erase the past? You can't rewrite the pain you've caused your children. I had an absent father myself and I wouldn't wish the pain that void caused to anyone.'

Jane's heart felt weary at the thought of becoming a single mother and giving up the security of all they'd built together. The weight of his silence enveloped them both, as the acknowledgment of their fractured trust was laid bare.

'Do you ever think about those kids, Vincent?'

His shoulders sagged, his usual arrogant stance replaced with the look of a lost boy.

'Not really,' he admitted quietly. Knowing his answer only made things worse between them, he moved away from her. Jane felt a wave of despondency wash over her.

'I need time,' she whispered hoarsely. 'I need to think about everything. About us…'

As she turned away, making her way to the door, she stopped, glancing back at the man she thought she knew.

'Don't come looking for me Vincent, I need space,' she said quietly. Jane stepped outside, the crisp air biting at her flushed cheeks. She thought of poor Caleb and Mila, and then of the life she had built so lovingly for Vincent and their son, and felt the world shifting beneath her feet. So much needed to be unpacked, so many truths obscured beneath layers of heartache. For now, all she could do was keep walking.

Chapter 24

Rossi leaned back in his chair, the dim light from his desk lamp casting a warm glow, but doing little to alleviate the chill creeping into his heart. He had spent the last few hours reviewing the evidence gathered so far. Each thread of the investigation was winding tighter and tighter, creating a knot that refused to unravel. Tia's death, while tragic, had unfolded like a tightly scripted drama, complete with a cast of characters that were both compelling and suspicious. Tia's body had been battered in an utterly brutal manner, but by whom and why? Rossi's mind wandered once more as he considered the people involved with Tia, each one bearing a potential motive.

First, he considered Jake, the fun-loving Cruise Director; clearly a man used to the spotlight being trained on him. In his world full of showbiz and entertainment, he commanded attention and admiration. Rossi had learned that Jake owned the sleek bronze statue that had served as the murder weapon. It had held a place of honour on his desk, a gift from Claire, the theatre performer whose affection for Jake was reportedly somewhat obsessive. Rossi looked at Tia's passport photo once again. She had been a striking young woman who'd clearly caused a lot of trouble among the passengers and the crew. But what drove someone to strike her down in such a brutal fashion?

Rossi's mind drifted back to Vincent, the Assistant Cruise Director. Rossi accurately summed him up as someone who had a temper that could ignite at the slightest provocation. Rossi recalled the unsettling report suggesting that Vincent had threatened Jake with the same statue. A weighty silence filled the air when this information was dropped during the interrogation. Jake sheepishly acknowledged that he should have divulged this information when it occurred and took full ownership of his mistake. Still, it caused Rossi to become agitated as it was a rookie error to ignore such behaviour from a senior staff member. Jake would be lucky if he kept his newly appointed role of the Cruise Director at this rate. The man was making dumb decisions.

Rossi sighed, rising from his chair to pace the small confines of his office. The bronze statue was more than merely a piece of art; it had become a common denominator linking these suspects together. Was it a mere coincidence that the weapon used to kill Tia belonged to Jake? Was it a token of passion turned deadly?

Rossi decided to bring Claire back in for further questioning.

'Can you tell me about the bronze statue? Why did you give it to Jake as a gift?'

Claire murmured, 'I bought it while we were in Cannes. It was supposed to represent strength. I wanted him to remember he could withstand anything, even from Vincent. They don't see eye to eye you see. Jake told me they had a few disagreements. He assured me it was nothing to worry about. He didn't go into any details.'

Rossi considered her response as he scribbled notes. Something murkier was lurking beneath the surface of Claire's relationship with Jake, and the stakes were rising.

Returning to his desk, he reviewed the timeline. Tia had been seen lurking near Jake's office that day, supposedly waiting for a private word with him. The ship had been buzzing with activity as it prepared for the next big event and Jake claimed he did not have time to speak with her. His alibi was watertight. Was someone covering for him?

After a few more basic questions, Rossi reluctantly let Claire go. The investigation was at a junction. One path veered toward jealousy and passion, and the other leaned towards toward vengeance and rage. Rossi needed more than simply inquiries. He needed to uncover the secrets being kept that had cost Tia her life. As he closed his notebook with a snap, determination burned in his chest. Rossi had collected several pieces of vital information. Now it was time to fit them together before any more foul play occurred. As he dozed off with his head on the desk his thoughts whirled incessantly about the suspects.

Jake owns the statue that is the murder weapon. It was kept on his desk in his office.

Claire was the one who bought the statue as a gift for Jake, as a token of her love.

Vincent allegedly threatened Jake with the statue, although Jake failed to divulge this at the time.

Richard was being blackmailed by Tia, so he had a motive. His wife might be seeking revenge…

Collectively what does all of this mean, if anything?

Chapter 25

Vincent disembarked at Cagliari, feeling the heat as he stepped onto the Italian soil. He was grateful for the chance to explore the beautiful capital of Sardinia alone. Yet beneath his need for solitude lay a heaviness, a reminder that the team hadn't included him in their plans for the day. Instead of camaraderie, he felt an unwelcome sense of isolation, as if he were a mere apparition among a team who had long since decided he was best left unseen.

As he ambled through the quaint narrow streets lined with pink and lemon facades, Vincent took in his surroundings. The buildings leaned towards one another. He imagined them whispering secrets of the past, their weathered stones telling tales of lovers' quarrels and traders' exchanges. Laundry hung from wrought-iron balconies like banners of local domestic life. Vincent was mesmerised by the garments swaying gently in the warm breeze. He tried to imagine who lived inside the small apartment block.

'Maybe this is what I need,' Vincent muttered to himself, feeling the sun's rays wrap around him. 'A simple life in a Mediterranean climate. Away from everyone and everything.'

Vincent strolled along and paused at a small café boasting a collection of tables spilling into the street. He guessed the food must be good as he observed locals talking in Italian while sipping steaming cappuccinos. The aroma of freshly baked cornetti, dusted lightly with powdered sugar, floated toward him.

Ah Italy's version of the croissant. I've always wanted to try one!

As if possessing a will of its own, his feet led him to the outdoor seating area. It felt good to sit and soak in the ambiance, far from the prying eyes of the team who had made him feel so small.

'Una cornetto, per favore,' he said to the barista, a woman with warm brown eyes and a wide smile. The barista nodded, as she reached for a pastry with a pair of tongs. Vincent gave a rare smile back, sensing kindness in this foreign land. It was as if Cagliari itself was embracing him.

As Vincent savoured the first mouthful, memories of recent encounters with Jake and the others bubbled up in his mind. He thought of all the sideways glances that spoke louder than words. They had written him off, convinced he was a trouble maker.

Maybe I am.

After leaving the café, Vincent continued to wander, his heart lighter with each step as he forgot about work for a while. He went further afield and found a fish market pulsating with life; vendors shouting about their freshest catches, children laughing, and the rhythmic crash of waves against the harbour in the background. For a moment, Vincent allowed himself to enjoy the beauty of it all.

Vincent found a bench by the harbour, where fishermen mended their nets, and sat to watch the sun's glare on the water's surface. The vibrant blues and greens reflected in his mind, washing away the clutches of insecurity and doubt. He closed his eyes and let the lapping waves tease his ears, the call of seagulls mingling with his thoughts.

'If this is what isolation feels like,' he murmured softly. 'Maybe I should seek it more often.'

Then a shadow fell across his face as a figure approached. He knew instinctively it was Jake, chasing away the sun's glow with his shadow.

'Vincent!' Jake exclaimed, clapping a hand on his shoulder. 'There you are! We thought you'd got lost. Are you okay?'

Vincent opened his eyes, annoyance bubbling within him. 'I'm fine,' he replied curtly, trying to dismiss the weight of the past few days. He stood up, readjusting his posture, determined not to let Jake loom over him any longer.

For a moment, an uneasy silence settled between them, both men grappling with the reality of their working relationship and the trouble that festered between them. Vincent closed his eyes once more, this time in contemplation.

'Did you want to join us?' Jake pointed to Maisie and the rest of the events team. It was obviously said out of obligation and they both knew it.

'No, I don't,' snapped Vincent.

'Well, if you change your mind…' Jake started. Vincent cut him off, his tone abrupt.

'I won't,' he said firmly.

Vincent turned and walked away, leaving Jake gaping after him. He walked along the harbour; a sole figure enjoying the vibrant colours of Cagliari. He needed to get away from Jake and from the judgments, the need for validation, and the constraints of working with a team that enraged him more than comforted him. As he walked along, Vincent was suddenly haunted by his cousin Susan's words.

You are a selfish bastard, do you realise that? Zero emotional intelligence whatsoever. You're simply a narcissist who does what he wants, when he wants and to hell with everyone else. You are a father for god's sake! Just because your dad abandoned you, it doesn't mean you need to be that guy too! Why do you think you can't get on with others, eh? Have you ever truly taken a good hard look at yourself? Always the victim but never the one at fault…

Vincent's jaw tightened. He hated his cousin Susan. What did that stupid bitch know about anything? She'd even taken over with his kids. She'd muscled in as though she was their mum!

After a while Vincent became weary with walking and thinking and he slowly headed back towards the ship. He needed a stiff drink.

Later that afternoon, after answering more of Rossi's questions, Vincent leaned against the polished mahogany bar, swirling the ice in his single malt absentmindedly as he surveyed the vibrant crowd in the lounge. The ambient clink of glasses and laughter around him felt distant, as if a bubble of tension had cocooned him in solitude. In his mind, the murder investigation was all part of an elaborate game; one that he hoped to win.

Vincent's thoughts drifted back to the earlier conversation with Rossi. The man had an imposing presence; his sharp eyes pierced through him when he spoke. Vincent had felt the weight of Rossi's suspicion hanging in the air after he tentatively threw Jake under the bus. It had been an instinctive move, the kind of self-preservation he had practiced countless times. Would it pay off? The uncertainty gnawed at him.

Vincent glanced toward the lounge entrance as Claire walked in with the other performers. Her demeanour was still fraught with the nervous energy from her earlier interview with Rossi. Claire scanned the crowd, her fingers twisting the ends of her hair. The spectre of Tia's death hovered over them all like a dark cloud.

'Hi, Vincent,' Claire said, her voice a blend of anxiety and feigned cheerfulness as she approached. 'You look like you have the world on your shoulders.'

Vincent turned to Claire, forcing a smile. 'Just contemplating the wonders of the universe,' he replied lightly, pushing aside his dark thoughts. 'How about you? Survive the interrogation?'

Claire forced out a laugh, aware it sounded hollow. 'Just about. Rossi is relentless. He has a way of making me feel as though I'm the only suspect.'

Claire immediately regretted the remark. She was clearly on edge. Vincent stepped closer, lowering his voice.

'He's only doing his job, Claire. Everyone gets scrutinised after something like this. You know they'll look at everyone connected to Tia.'

Claire's eyes widened. 'I can't help but feel that he thinks I'm hiding something. I didn't want her dead, Vincent. I simply hated how she hunted Jake all the time.'

Claire was annoyed that her voice was trembling slightly.

'Maybe you should focus on getting your story straight,' Vincent advised, trying to appear helpful when they both knew he was being a touch sadistic.

'Very funny Vincent! Stop being a dick. I know you are trying to freak me out! How come you are so calm about all of this anyway?' Claire snapped suddenly, her eyes bright with frustration. 'It's as though you don't get affected by anything.'

Vincent shrugged, masking his amusement with a cloud of indifference.

'Would you rather I panic? It's not my style.'

'Not caring about anything or anybody isn't normal!' she shot back, anger sparking in her eyes. 'What if they truly think I did it?'

The tension remained between them and Vincent stared at her thoughtfully.

'Well, I'm not being funny Claire, you have been a bit of a psycho while around Tia. Everyone knows you were jealous of her, and you did have a fight with her in the ladies, so…'

Claire stared at Vincent with unbridled fury in her eyes then promptly stormed out of the bar. Vincent downed his drink with a smirk; it was time to call it a night.

Back in his cabin, Vincent stared down at his mobile phone screen; the weight of Jane's words a tight band around his chest. He'd been so hopeful when he noticed his wife's missed call. He thought that maybe she'd been ready to sort things out between them. Now that he'd returned her call, the flicker of hope had been well and truly snuffed out leaving the bitter taste of disappointment in its place. Jane's voice still rang in his ears.

I want a divorce ASAP, Vincent. I won't be changing my mind.

Vincent tossed the phone down on the vanity, where a cold cup of coffee sat waiting for him, having long lost its warmth. Only minutes ago, he had filled his head with hopeful thoughts of getting back together with Jane. Now, the silence felt heavier than ever.

Vincent slowly unbuttoned his shirt and walked outside. The muggy air on the balcony was doing nothing to help with the heat of the rage building inside him.

Susan, his bitch of a cousin, was responsible for driving a wedge between him and Jane. His cousin would pay for this. Vincent had foolishly believed he could solve everything with long conversations and heartfelt apologies. Instead, Jane had pulled back and retreated into her shell. Now all this divorce talk felt final, and he was only sorry at being found out, not for his actions. He was still smarting at Jane's cold tone, and the way she'd delivered the news of her decision with such finality.

Suddenly, Vincent felt suffocated and, against his better judgment, he buttoned his shirt back up and headed back out to the ship's busiest bar. He ordered a drink and watched the interactions around him. There were couples sharing quiet moments, friends from all over the globe catching up, and the twenty somethings whose shrieks of glee echoed all around him. It all felt so far removed from his reality that it made his anger intensify. Vincent sipped his drink slowly, letting the alcohol soften the sharp edges of his pain. As the time passed and the bar grew more crowded, Vincent continued to wallow in self-pity as the vibrancy of the people around him continued to contrast with his own despair. He failed to consider that he hadn't given any of his children a second thought while feeling sorry for himself about his crumbling marriage. Vincent was a carbon copy of his own father by all accounts, although he still couldn't recognise the fact.

Chapter 26

Rossi tried to shake off the persistent fog of fatigue that clung to him like the remnants of a bad dream. He leaned against his desk, the cool metal providing a momentary distraction as he gazed at the wall cluttered with case photos, timelines and suspects. It was a puzzle that was still missing its final piece. Tia's smiling photo contrasted starkly with the chaos surrounding her demise; it was a reminder of the young life that was lost and the secrets that swirled, a storm in the aftermath.

Rossi enjoyed entertaining his dramatic thoughts; he was quite poetic in nature. He compared the current investigation to walking through a hall of mirrors, reflecting nothing but distorted images and fleeting truths. Rossi knew he was enveloped in a web of emotions, including jealousy, rage and passion. Somehow they were all woven together, yet he was no closer to nailing Tia's killer. Because of the complexity of the crime scene being onboard a cruise ship, it was taking longer to get the fingerprints back from the murder weapon. In addition, Tia's companion Tony was still at large on the ship. Rossi's team of officers had searched every corner of the ship to no avail.

Rossi leaned forward, taking a deep breath as he considered the information at hand once again. Jake, the suave Cruise Director, was known for his charm, but also rumoured to have a darker side when it came to matters of the heart. The statue with a likeness of a mythical figure was not merely an innocent ornament. It was the murder weapon and had gone missing from Jake's desk. *But why and who took it?* Rossi rubbed at his eyes.

Once again, Rossi studied the information gathered on Claire, whose sweet demeanour shielded a fierce loyalty. Claire bought the statue for Jake not only as a gift, but it was also a symbol of the love she apparently had for him despite their brief affair. Claire's eyes held a glimmer when she spoke about it, and Rossi couldn't shake the look of anguish that flickered behind them.

Rossi thought about Vincent next; a man whose temper was as notorious as his talent for stirring trouble. Rossi had learned how confrontational Vincent could be. The kitchen staff were quick to fill him in about the rivalry between Jake and Vincent, and they spoke of the nasty gossip Vincent spread about Jake at every opportunity.

Finally, Rossi's thoughts shifted to the middle-aged couple Richard and Belinda. Tia had blackmailed Richard, and it was unclear at this point just how much his wife knew about it. Both could potentially have a motive. Belinda had been spoken to, but was yet to have her formal interview, having been allowed to get off the ship for an expensive prepaid excursion.

Rossi pinched the bridge of his nose, willing himself to focus. The murder of Tia had shaken the entire community aboard the luxury cruise ship. He was yet to fully make sense of it all. Rossi sighed, he only had a few more days left to piece together the clues before the ship docked back at Barcelona. His mind returned for the hundredth time to the statue. A beautiful, intricate piece, forged in bronze and marred with sharp edges, stunning and deadly.

A gift from Claire to Jake. The perfect display of love turned into a weapon.

Rossi considered that several witnesses had recounted Claire's demeanour; the way her smile faded whenever she spotted Tia trying to talk to Jake. There had been a spark of jealousy, and a consequent bathroom brawl between the two young women.

With each detail, Rossi felt his uncertainty grow. Jealousy could drive someone to murder, yet so could rage. He leaned back in his chair, trying once again to connect the dots. Suddenly, the tension in the room shifted. Rossi snapped his notebook shut with a decisive thwack. He must dig deeper. Gathering his resolve, he thought of the most prominent individuals in the investigation once more. Each possessed a motive based on retribution, thus each may be capable of creating a plan that led to murder.

Feeling restless, Rossi rocked his chair backwards, the wood creaking beneath him as he mulled over the details before him for the hundredth time. Rossi rolled up the sleeves of his linen shirt, showing impressive muscular tanned forearms. His mouth was set in a grim line. Even if it killed him, he would piece together the timeline of Tia's last days.

Rossi decided to go and see Jake, who was nursing his pride in the Cruise Director's office. The statue's absence from its usual spot on the desk was jarring. Rossi noted the way the light hit the dust where it used to sit.

'Jake,' Rossi began, his tone casual yet probing, 'I'm still wondering why you didn't mention Vincent trying to discredit you straight away? Your staff have spoken a lot about this, and you played it down.'

Jake's face paled, his mouth opening and closing as he searched for words. The crew had obviously been talking.

'I knew Vincent was causing trouble. I gave him the benefit of the doubt because frankly I needed the extra manpower to get things done… As I said before, I realise it was a grave error on my part. I still can't believe he threatened me with the statue! Luckily, I was able to calm him down at the time. All I can say in Vincent's defence is that he is going through a messy divorce, and his mental health isn't good at the moment. I stupidly estimated that I could support him through this cruise and then have him seek therapy at the end. Once again, I acknowledge it was a poor decision on my part. I hope for his sake that he hasn't done anything stupid...'

Rossi sighed as he leaned back in his chair. He hoped he'd finally grasped a thread that could tie the loose ends together.

'Jake, is it possible that Vincent took your statue and used it as a weapon for real this time?'

Jake's expression was grave as he addressed Rossi. 'While I'm trying to give Vincent the benefit of the doubt, I must admit, that's where my thoughts have been going too…'

Chapter 27

Tony had often wondered if Tia would end up dead. He recalled learning in his youth worker training that young people who had been severely abused in their early years may present with risk taking behaviours that led to their early demise. Tony should know; he'd worked with many young people and come to understand that kids with Tia's level of trauma history often remained vulnerable into adulthood. Tony went into youth work for all the wrong reasons and now he felt a semblance of shame that he'd manipulated Tia for his own gain.

Tony knew they couldn't blackmail and threaten men and keep getting away with it. He'd figured that someday, between them they'd pick the wrong victim, and the man would snap under the pressure, putting Tia's life at risk. Yet Tony had been willing to take the chance. Tony had selfishly figured that by the time something went badly wrong, he'd have made plenty of money out of it.

Tony had used Tia as everyone else in her life had. The girl had been physically, emotionally and sexually abused as a young child. As her youth worker, he'd taken full advantage of her vulnerability and even had a bit of action for himself. Tony had talked Tia into this way of life, and the lure of money and power meant she'd loved every minute of it. Tia had been as power hungry as he was. They were two sides of the same tarnished coin, drawn together by desperation and a need to feel needed that could never be satisfied.

Now she was dead and he was in hiding on the ship. Tony knew the Italian police were swarming all over the place looking for him. Clearly, they weren't that smart as he'd lost track of how long he'd been hiding down here for.

Tony reflected about how he'd watched Tia transform from a fragile young girl into a force of nature. Tia had learned quickly how to manipulate the world that had treated her as an afterthought. Blackmailing men who thought they were untouchable, threatening them into submission with a ferocity that came from years of surviving abuse. She was so good at it, that at times it scared him. Tony was not a man to turn down easy money, and he had made a fair amount from exploiting Tia. In the end, the same thing that made their partnership lucrative had also cemented her inevitable demise.

Tia's laughter echoed in his mind, high-pitched and manic, reminiscent of a child who had never learned to care about the consequences of her actions. The irony of it all made his stomach churn. Tia had welcomed danger like an old friend, she had loved the risky games they played. They had both tasted power. While he'd been content to sit back and watch her put on a show, she was always clawing for more. Now she was gone forever, her body lying cold and lifeless. It was hard to believe.

Tia had been willing to barter the only currency she had: her body and her charm. She was a moth drawn to a flame, using her sexuality to gain power and control in a world that had stripped her of both. For Tony, familiarity bred contempt, and with each successful con, he had come to see Tia not as a tragic soul but as a tool, a wild card in a game much larger than either of them. Tony was convinced Tia had relished the thrill, thriving on the danger, like a dying plant soaking up a final kiss of sunlight.

As Tony crouched low behind a stack of crates, the ship rocked gently with the tide; a soft lullaby that contrasted starkly with the chaos in his head. Could he somehow slip away to a new life somewhere far away? He had set up countless accounts and hidden money in places that only he knew about. He may have the chance to disappear entirely, although he'd then carry the weight of Tia's death forever.

Suddenly, a shadow moved overhead; a torch's glow lit up the side of the ship. Tony held his breath, the thud of heavy boots were coming closer now. Had the police finally arrived in his dark little corner? Tony glimpsed a police badge as it crossed the narrow beam of light, and his heartbeat quickened. Tony suddenly felt like a hunted animal, he realised he'd gambled and lost, and Tia had paid the ultimate price. He'd mistakenly thought he could escape and outrun the consequences, but it wasn't to be. The ship began to creak ominously around him. Tony realised with a creeping dread that a hiding place did not exist which was safe from the choices he had made.

In that moment, as silence filled the air, Tony understood the truth. It was not possible to escape from Tia, despite her death. He had an overpowering sense that she was there with him, in the shadows. She was in every corner of his mind, howling for justice in a world where he had only offered her betrayal. As the officers stormed around, he felt her presence pressing down; he was no longer the one in control. Not anymore. Tony couldn't be sure if Tia's spirit was truly nearby or whether it was merely paranoia and fear coming to bite him on the arse.

Tony's breath hitched as he pressed himself deeper into the shadows, every nerve ending screaming in protest. This was it; the police had finally found him.

The footsteps grew closer, and his heart raced as a beam of light swept over him, illuminating the scattered debris of his failed escape.

'Tony come out and make yourself seen,' one of the officers bellowed, his tone dripping with hostility.

The silence spread thick around him, the damp air punctuated only by the cries of seagulls.

'Now!' the imperious voice boomed out, demanding his submission. 'Come out, Tony! We don't want to make this any harder than it has to be.'

'Okay, okay,' Tony addressed the looming shadows, resigned to the fact it was time to surrender to the inevitable. Each step toward the light of the officer's flashlight was heavy with regret yet also ripe with a need for atonement. Emerging from his hiding place, he launched himself into the beam of light.

The officer spoke into his radio, 'Suspect Tony Bishop located, over.' The officer sagged with relief; it had been a stressful long-drawn-out search.

'I'm ready to talk,' Tony announced, his voice steady despite the turmoil inside. Tia must not go unavenged. He decided it was the only way to redeem himself. The officers advanced, surrounding him in a pack, each determined to call an end to the never-ending shift. The men were ready to take Tony down if he tried to take off.

Tony spoke again, 'If you want to know why I've been missing in action, then hear me out. I admit did the wrong thing by Tia, but I didn't kill her.' He was astutely aware of the desperation edging his words.

The officers' demeanour shifted from sceptical to intrigued, and they gathered closer, listening intently even though Tony was a prime suspect.

'Let's hear it then, hot shot?' the burly officer who'd located him shot back.

Tony shook his head. 'Not here, not now. I desperately need a drink of water. I've lost track of how long I've been down here.'

The officer remained motionless, weighing up Tony's intent. The tension in the air crackled as the sea lapped at the ship's hull. All Tony could think of was Tia's wicked smile, her belief in him when she was a youngster, and how he had shattered that belief.

'Okay, we will get you a bottle of water, and then you will talk,' the officer said, nodding slowly. 'No tricks, Tony. One wrong move and you will regret it.'

Tony hoped he'd taken a step toward redemption. As the police surrounded him tightly, it felt for the first time that he was embracing the chance to save the remnants of Tia's memory and, in doing so, perhaps save himself too.

As soon as Tony was interrogated by Rossi, he broke down, gulping back sobs as he stumbled over his words.

'I was Tia's youth worker when she was in care. I'm not proud to say I took advantage of my position and when she was old enough, we uh, we um, together we started scamming men for money. Luring them in to have sex with Tia. We'd film them and then blackmail them for large sums. But I swear on my life, I did not kill her.'

Tony willed the ground to swallow him up; he couldn't meet the eyes of the authoritative investigator. Saying the truth out loud in front of someone as imposing as Rossi made him feel sick with shame. Tony thought things over when he'd been in hiding. He'd initially wanted to run, to deny everything. He knew they'd have found Richard's phone by now and he himself may have been implicated during the filmed exchange with Tia in the library if what Richard told him was true. If he confessed all now, there might be more leniency with his sentence.

Rossi's voice dripped with venom. 'You are a sick bastard, Tony. You are unfit to walk this earth. Like a cornered rat, you only confess now because you know we have you by the balls.'

Tony quivered, 'You are correct officer. I can't argue with you. I was in a position of trust, and I breached it in the worst possible way.'

Rossi gave a disgusted snort. 'People like you should be eradicated! But for now, I want to know every detail about the men on this ship that you and Tia scammed; starting with Richard Henderson. No bullshit. Only facts, okay?'

Tony decided to be truthful, no doubt Rossi knew what had occurred anyway. He gave a small sniff.

'So, Richard was one of the men Tia lured into her bed on this cruise. After the deed, I turned up at her cabin and we let the sucker know he'd been filmed having sex with her. Then we put the hard word on him to come up with the money. Tia kept in contact through a burner phone and Richard saved the number under "Frank". On the day of Tia's death, I happened to see Richard at the atrium. He was super agitated when he spotted me. He came up to me and started poking me in the chest, so I talked him into going out on the deck for a bit of fresh air to calm down and get away from prying eyes. Richard told me he'd managed to persuade Tia to meet him in the library to make a deal behind my back. I was shocked and angry that she'd agree to that. I didn't want to believe him... he doesn't seem like the kind of guy who'd make it up though. Richard said he'd tried to talk her out of the lifestyle she was accustomed to under my regime, and Tia supposedly broke down, telling him about her childhood and how I was meant to be her saviour, and it turned out I wasn't.' Tony paused looking suitably ashamed.

Rossi pressed his hands together under his chin as if in prayer. 'Continue!' he barked.

Tony sighed. 'Richard didn't mince his words about what he thought of me, but in the end, he said Tia didn't back down. She wouldn't agree to do a deal with him and instead she continued to demand the money. He obviously didn't get anywhere with Tia, so he became desperate and decided to turn on me instead. Then Richard told me he'd secretly filmed this conversation with Tia and captured her confession about extorting money from men. He said I was implicated in this footage and demanded that I drop the blackmail, or he'd use it against me. He had his phone in his hand at this point, and he was waving it around like a mad man while he was ranting and raving. So, I took the opportunity to snatch it from him. I bolted as fast as I could to Tia's cabin to ask her what the hell was going on. I have a swipe card for her room, so I stormed in there ready to confront her about meeting Richard behind my back. Then I saw her battered and bruised body on the balcony and flew into a wild panic. I knew she was gone. At some point I must've dropped Richard's phone from my hand in my shocked state. I panicked and went into hiding until I could figure out what to do next. Once I calmed down, I realised I'd probably dropped the phone in her cabin… and in that case if Richard had truly filmed the exchange with Tia on it as he said, then I was fucked.'

Rossi nodded slowly; it was all adding up. 'It was futile grabbing Richard's phone from him though wasn't it, Tony? You have just made a confession based on the evidence you believe is on Richard's phone. He obviously didn't tell you that the device he filmed Tia with was a micro camera and not his mobile phone: a camera which is currently missing.' Rossi gave a satisfied smirk as he watched the blood drain from Tony's face as he realised he'd unwittingly dropped himself in it.

Now that's karma for you.

Chapter 28

What Kayla had not divulged to the authorities or to Belinda was that every day in life she made a concerted effort to hide her shadow self: the part that she hid so well, the part that housed her trauma, her abandonment issues and her many negative impulses that were rooted in her early childhood.

Deep down she was equally as jealous and possessive as Alex was. She was simply better at hiding it. Kayla knew how to talk the talk and play the deep wounded innocent girlfriend. Alex was still the scum of the earth for hitting her, but was he the only one who should be locked up in the brig? She cackled out a nasty laugh. Her strange feelings of late had given her violent thoughts that shocked her. Maybe she truly was worse than Alex.

Belinda had been beyond sweet and protective. She had insisted on reporting Alex to the authorities, dismissing Kayla's feeble attempts at downplaying the situation.

'You need to get out of this toxic relationship,' Belinda had said, her hazel eyes full of concern as she'd taken Kayla's hand. 'You deserve better love.'

Kayla had nodded obediently. Part of her wanted to agree with Belinda completely, to revel in the self-righteous indignation that came with being the victim, yet another part of her shied away from the reality. She'd done a stellar job playing the part of the kind-hearted girl who'd showed empathy towards Alex's tumultuous past. Now the mask she wore felt heavy. It was definitely time to remove it once and for all.

In the dark corners of her mind, she'd felt shadows flickering where jealousy and rage intertwined. Where had that twisted urge to possess another come from? It gnawed at her, whispering vile thoughts that were hiding beneath her carefully constructed exterior. Not wanting anyone to see the dark void she felt inside, she'd forced herself to smile at Belinda when she offered comfort. She shifted uncomfortably as her thoughts only amplified her inner turmoil, as she attempted to drown out the shrill voice warning her that she, too, was a monster.

The truth was that Kayla had become suspicious of Alex when he'd insisted on having lengthy gym sessions every day on his own, citing it as his 'me time'. He did not know that Kayla had spied on him and Tia flirting at the onboard gym. Kayla had watched them from the adjacent RPM cycle studio, which had tinted windows. Those in the open gym area remained unaware they were being watched by whoever was inside. There were no classes on, therefore Kayla left the studio door ajar and watched Alex and Tia together. The irony was that Tia was not even out to blackmail Alex; she simply genuinely fancied him for a bit of quick dirty sex. The fact he had a girlfriend was irrelevant.

Kayla glanced at the gym mirror. Her reflection was a mask of calm, but beneath the surface swirled a tempest of fury. She adjusted her hair, the careful flick of her wrist betraying the rage brewing inside her. The gym echoed with the thud of weights being dropped on the floor, and all she could hear was Tia's flirtatious giggle; it was slicing through her like a serrated knife. Kayla bided her time and when Alex left to take a shower, adrenaline surged through her, igniting a fierce determination. Kayla stormed over to confront Tia, her eyes ablaze with a dangerous intensity that sent a shiver down the other girl's spine. Tia felt Kayla's grip tighten around the fabric of her gym top.

'Stay away from, Alex, you little slut,' Kayla hissed, her voice low and lethal, the words dripping with venom.

Tia's smirk faltered for a heartbeat, before she caught herself; the power of the confrontation feeding her twisted sense of superiority. Tia was used to women reacting this way and she loved the power it gave her. A rush of adrenaline surged through her; it was intoxicating and terrifying all at once. Tia noticed something was a little unnerving about the other girl's mesmerising amber eyes, they were such a rare colour, almost gold.

Composing herself, Tia revelled in the power of the moment feeding her ego. She had witnessed this kind of jealousy before; welcomed it, even.

'Maybe I've already had Alex,' Tia smirked defiantly.

Kayla drew back her right fist, then a nearby gasp from an onlooker brought her to her senses. Their confrontation was beginning to attract an audience, and Kayla, feeling the weight of others staring at her, released Tia; her heart racing as she backed away, leaving Tia to gloat over her victory.

'Are you alright?' Kayla recognised Claire, one of the ship's performers. She approached Kayla cautiously. Claire had been at the gym spying on Tia herself. Kayla quickly filled Claire in about her suspicions regarding Alex and Tia. Claire's weary response twisted the knot in Kayla's gut even more.

'She's after my Jake too; we've already had words. She is a nasty piece of work that one. She only wants men who are off limits. Look I'm sorry to tell you but from what I'm hearing about her, it's pretty likely she has already had sex with your boyfriend.' Claire scowled, her brows knitted together. 'She seems to be wreaking havoc everywhere she goes.'

The comment fuelled something dark within Kayla. Instead of seeking comfort from the other girl, she was drawn deeper into a web of anger. The two young women slipped into Jake's nearby empty office, forbidden territory unless you were meeting with him. Kayla was intrigued with what else Claire might share with her. Looking at the intricate statue on Jake's desk, Kayla felt an urge to smash it over Tia's skull. The thought of Alex with Tia twisted the knot in her stomach.

When Kayla had rejected Alex's proposal in Florence, she'd conveniently blanked out the part where he told her in a moment of spite afterwards that he'd succumbed to the temptations of Tia, the sexy blonde he'd met at the ship's gym. The truth was that Kayla had struck Alex first with a blow to the side of his head before he retaliated and punched her in the guts. Kayla had omitted this information when giving her version of events to Rossi, knowing that playing the weaker sex card would win over the powers that be. Kayla told the authorities she'd gone straight to the buffet when she returned to the ship after their altercation and sought Jake's help. The reality was that she'd swung past Jake's office first, knowing he'd be mingling with passengers at lunch. She'd seized the statue and placed it in her oversized beach bag before hiding it in her cabin.

Claire told her new friend she'd been following the blonde slut all over the ship and therefore she knew all about Tia's movements. Apparently, Tia liked to order room service at lunch time. Kayla nodded, her eyes like slits as she took mental notes.

That information has come in handy.

Claire showed Kayla where Tia's cabin was when the two of them thought about paying her a visit to teach her a lesson, then they thought better of it at the last minute. Later when Kayla cut three holes in Alex's black woollen beanie hat to make a balaclava, she felt a strange sensation of empowerment mingled with fear wash over her. It had not been difficult to grab the cabin attendant's swipe card left carelessly on top of his cleaning cart. The cleaners storeroom had been ajar, and she was able to bribe the gormless looking cabin attendant who was rummaging around in there to give her access to a tub of strong chemicals in exchange for easy cash. He hadn't even asked many questions; he'd been too busy staring at the wad of cash in disbelief.

At that moment Kayla had felt something dark twist within her; a hunger for retribution that was both thrilling and horrifying. Standing behind Tia's cabin door, hesitation gripped her, then it was drowned out by the intoxicating rush of revenge. Kayla's adoptive parents had long worried about her mental state, however she'd covered it up perfectly: she could play the unassuming innocent girl extremely well. Beneath the veneer, darkness churned, waiting for its moment to rise. The thought of Alex with Tia wrapped around her heart like a vice, squeezing until it hurt. With a swift breath, she steeled herself. This was not only about love or pain; it was about power. Kayla intended to reclaim it, one way or another. The door loomed before her, the threshold between the person she claimed to be and the real Kayla who was finally ready to break free. She was no longer merely a pawn in someone else's game, she was ready to become the queen. She giggled softly.

My life has Gone Girl vibes, I've managed to outsmart them all...

Kayla felt nothing as she smashed the statue over Tia's head. It was fascinating to watch Tia's blonde hair turn red. Once she was sure the bitch was no longer fighting back, Kayla calmly wiped down the murder weapon and wrapped it up in the spare blanket on the top shelf of the cabin wardrobe. She had thought about disposing of it elsewhere, but she could hardly let herself be seen walking around with it on the ship. Kayla had known for a long time that she was capable of killing someone and it felt weird but exhilarating to know she had finally done it.

As Kayla sauntered back to her cabin, she laughed inwardly. Alex was being held captive, while she was running free. The sad thing was that her passion for Alex was genuine: the sexual chemistry could never be matched by another man. But Alex had raised his hands to her and that was not acceptable. Alex had failed to realise he had unwittingly attracted a partner who deliberately goaded him; someone cold and manipulative: a carbon copy of his dear mother. Of course, Kayla had flirted with the men he accused her of cock teasing. She had enjoyed every minute of his jealousy and anger. She'd loved denying it and pleading her innocence even more...

As for Belinda, she was a nice lady, and her advice regarding domestic violence would be spot on if she delivered it to a normal level-headed woman. No one in the current political climate ever stopped to consider that there were a minority of women who were master manipulators. Kayla was one of the rare ones who enjoyed seeing how far she could push a man. Did it excuse domestic violence perpetrated by men onto women? No, it absolutely did not. However, it gave Kayla the perfect cover for her mental state. She deserved an Oscar for her performance. She had the doe eyed vulnerable act down to a tee; she'd perfected widening her brown eyes to look fearful. Kayla presented as the perfect victim. She'd done this many times before. But committing murder was a first...

Kayla had researched personality disorders, pouring over studies and anecdotal evidence until she finally identified with the traits. She considered she might have an antisocial personality disorder.

Or perhaps I'm merely a psychopath.

The idea lingered in her mind, providing a strange comfort. From a young age, her adoptive parents had whispered in dark corners, concerned about the little girl they had taken on who could easily discard others in order to save herself. Empathy was a skill she never learned, however it was a mask she could wear when it suited her. With a smirk curling at the corners of her lips, Kayla stood and took a long, deliberate breath as she thought about the delicate balance she had maintained; one moment she was the sweet girl-next-door, the next, a cold-hearted predator.

Chapter 29

Rossi leaned back in his chair and rubbed the back of his neck. As the lead investigator on Tia's murder, he'd been feeling the pressure intensifying each passing day.

The conclusion was finally drawing closer now that he had the CCTV footage back from outside the shop in Florence where Alex had struck his girlfriend Kayla. A separate matter altogether, yet now he was wondering about a possible connection. Obviously, Kayla had not considered that an old-fashioned city such as Florence had cameras in the little cobbled laneways. She had inadvertently dropped herself right in it by mentioning exactly where the altercation took place.

Rossi now had video evidence of Kayla striking Alex first. What the recording revealed was shocking. It showed Kayla, her eyes flashing with an intensity that was palpable, even through the grainy imagery. The footage revealed that Kayla approached Alex first. The young woman's demeanour was aggressive, her fist clenched, like a boxer ready to strike. Kayla's teeth were bared as her lip curled back. Rossi felt a knot tightening in his stomach as he watched Kayla deliver a solid blow to the left side of Alex's head. Alex staggered backwards clearly stunned. Alex then retaliated by punching Kayla in the stomach. It was abundantly clear that both of them were caught in an unhealthy dance of domestic violence, and on this occasion, Kayla had instigated it.

Alex had not been given the time of day by his officers, yet now Rossi could see they had all made assumptions when in fact this couple were simply as bad as each other. Rossi had been led to believe that Alex was the sole perpetrator, yet now he was faced with the undeniable truth: Kayla was equally culpable. Rossi leaned forward, his elbows resting on his desk. His instinct told him from the start that there was more to Kayla than met the eye, yet he hadn't been able to put his finger on it. Rossi, with his eye for details, decided to look into the young couple's relationship a bit more closely. Rossi had been intrigued by the information provided by Claire about Alex reportedly cheating with Tia. If this was true, he must consider whether Kayla was capable of the level of revenge that he thought she might be.

With renewed determination, Rossi summoned Kayla to sit in one of the hard chairs in his office. Kayla arrived all smiles, clearly thinking it was to do with the charges against Alex.

'We have a lot to discuss,' Rossi snapped, as he began playing the footage that laid bare the true sequence of events.

Rossi watched Kayla's face morph from defiance into a steely grimace. Kayla flared her nostrils; indignation seeping through her erect spine as if she were desperate not to collapse under the weight of the moment.

'You think I wanted any of this?' Kayla snapped, her voice rising in pitch. 'You think I was asking for trouble?'

Rossi noted that Kayla's appearance was strikingly different from the earlier version she presented during the initial stages of the domestic violence report. Formerly doe eyed and timid, she now sat hunched over, her face a mask of undisguised rage. The seat, usually a mere chair, had transformed into a confessional. Rossi leaned back slightly, studying her, trying to decipher the layers beneath Kayla's initial façade.

'I know Alex is a violent man, I do not dispute that at all,' Rossi replied steadily. 'But you instigated the violence in this instance, and you lied about it. Therefore, you both participated in the dysfunctional relationship.'

Rossi watched as the gold flecks in her amber eyes dimmed, revealing a smouldering anger bubbling under the surface. Rossi continued. 'You both engaged in toxic behaviour. There's a fine line here, and you crossed it.'

Kayla remained silent, her fingers digging into the fabric of her dress. Rossi leaned forward.

'Now to change direction. Let's revisit the day of the young woman's murder and check if there is anything you want to tell me about your movements that day. I have just heard from Claire that you had an unusual interest in the young woman's movements given her interest in Alex. I knew Claire was hiding something…' Rossi paused as he saw Kayla's eyebrows shoot up.

Rossi continued, 'Claire didn't drop you in it easily if it makes you feel any better. I have a way of probing until someone cracks. Now on that note, I suggest you start talking…'

Kayla slumped in her chair with a defeated breath, her expression remaining cold and hard. The case was slowly becoming untangled. She assumed the investigating team had gathered all their evidence; she hadn't exactly hidden it well.

Kayla spoke calmly. 'I killed Tia with Jake's statue. She had it coming.'

Rossi inhaled sharply at her words.

'I killed her,' Kayla repeated, her voice steady, devoid of remorse, her eyes blank.

The confession permeated the air as Rossi leaned forward; his expression a mixture of disgust and palpable relief. Finally, after hours of probing and piecing together fragmented narratives, they had a breakthrough.

'Let's talk about the statue,' Rossi prodded gently, his voice lowering to a conspiratorial whisper. 'Jake's statue. How did it come to be the murder weapon?'

Rossi observed Kayla closely. Her cold stare flickered for a brief moment, as if she were considering his question. The light from the single overhead bulb caught her amber eyes again, revealing a glimmer of something; he couldn't tell if it was anger or fear. Perhaps it was simply the weight of the truth pressing heavily upon her.

'It simply felt right,' Kayla finally replied, her voice still calm, yet with an edge that suggested deeper feelings.

Rossi stared at Kayla intently. 'Can you elaborate?'

Kayla nodded wearily. 'Tia was fucking around with several men, including mine, and I wanted to put an end to it. When I was young, my dad took off with another woman you see… with a girl just like Tia. I guess it triggered me; she was one of those homewrecker bitches that destroys couples' lives. Well not on my watch! So, when I spotted the statue in Jake's office, I felt it was calling to me.'

Rossi felt his jaw tighten. 'Talk me through exactly what happened that day. Can you do that?' he asked, forcing his voice to remain neutral.

Kayla paused and tried to collect her thoughts. 'I don't remember all of it… I tend to lose time a lot.'

Rossi shifted in his seat, 'You mean you often disassociate, an out of body experience, that type of thing? Did you realise what you were doing?'

'I wanted her to understand,' Kayla answered, her gaze unyielding. 'To see the pain she caused others. But maybe I wanted more than that.'

'Maybe you wanted to feel something different?' Rossi suggested, trying to get behind her hardened façade. 'Maybe you wanted to stop feeling powerless?'

Kayla looked away. 'I've always known I'd reach breaking point one day and that I'd probably take someone's life.'

'Is there a part of you that wants forgiveness, Kayla?'

Kayla scoffed, a bitter laugh escaping her lips. 'Forgiveness? Do you honestly think I care about that? I know what I did. Tia was toxic, she needed to be stopped. In my own way, I did the world a favour.'

The air in the room was suffocating. As Kayla's resolve withered, it metamorphosised into a twisted sense of pride. It was true, she'd seen herself as a warrior, striking down the young woman who tormented others. Then she realised a warrior often stood alone to bear their scars.

'I can't make excuses for you, Kayla, and neither can you,' Rossi said, his voice firm now. 'You need to face the consequences of your actions, regardless of how you think you can justify them.'

'I'll face whatever I need to,' Kayla replied, a hint of steel returning to her tone. 'But don't assume for a second that I regret it.'

Rossi nodded slowly, knowing that the case may take many more dark turns before reaching its resolution. Rossi finally felt the weight of the case shift. The truth had unfurled, raw and unrestrained, and perhaps, the image of justice would mirror the statue's ferocity, both beautiful and terrible.

Chapter 30

The flickering light overhead cast long shadows on the cold, stark walls of the small room where Alex found himself pacing. His footsteps echoed in the cramped space and moved in time with the thoughts racing through his mind. The metallic smell of the room exacerbated his nerves as he paced back and forth. His fingers brushed against the rough, cold walls, grounding him as he thought of the events leading up to this point. Rossi had been to see him. Alex felt a rush of relief flood through him as the news that there was evidence of Kayla punching him first sunk in. It was poetic justice; a flicker of hope in a situation that had spiralled way beyond his control. With a renewed confidence, Alex began telling his side of things, explaining that following his failed marriage proposal, he'd had a lot of time to think while detained in the brig. Alex had started to suspect Kayla's mental state was rather dangerous.

The marriage proposal was supposed to be a new beginning. Instead, it had turned into a harsh revelation of the level of toxicity within their relationship. Alex acknowledged to Rossi that he'd been the main perpetrator of the violence that marred his relationship with Kayla. Alex explained he'd realised this was due to his own insecurities translating into rage and hurt. Yet, deep down, he felt a desperate need for Kayla to be held accountable too. Kayla had clearly enjoyed winding him up and messing with his sense of reality. Kayla badly needed help, Alex could see with clarity that she had gaslit him on many occasions.

As Rossi explained that Kayla intended to drop the charges of assault against him after watching the CCTV footage, Alex sighed loudly with relief.

For the first time, Alex felt the tiniest spark of hope that he might emerge from the darkness. In that moment, as he pushed away from the wall, he resolved that this time, whatever came next, he was going to work on his issues, go to therapy and become a better person. He'd realised with resounding clarity that Kayla thoroughly enjoyed poking the bear. Alex kept ruminating over how he hadn't been able to see it before now. Not that this revelation could ever excuse his violence; he was willing to take ownership of that much.

I've been thinking with my cock and not my head.

Alex turned his thoughts back to Rossi. Thank god the man had connected the dots. Rossi had found out about his quick fuck with Tia, which showed him for the bastard he truly was. Alex couldn't deny that. But he'd been utterly sickened to hear from the gossiping officer minding him that Kayla's fingerprints were being taken. Apparently, she was being questioned in relation to Tia's murder. Perhaps the truth about their entwined toxicity might see the light of day, forcing both of them to confront their shared demons. Alex finally felt a flicker of resilience within the cocoon of hopelessness.

As the hours passed, Alex began pacing again. Rossi hadn't explained whether he was to be released or what the next steps were. Alex was struggling with being confined to a small area. He began to wrestle with the thoughts spiralling around in his head about the good times with Kayla. Alex recalled the moments of love and kindness that were overshadowed by increasing outbursts and arguments. Each was more explosive than the last. They had both ruined something that could have been so beautiful.

'I should've seen it sooner,' Alex muttered to himself, his voice tinged with regret. He realised he'd let his insecurities morph into anger, throwing him into a cycle of violence that only spiralled deeper when fuelled by Kayla's own unpredictability.

Alex felt like he was going crazy. His thoughts kept returning to Kayla's penchant for provocation. Kayla had taunted him, revelling in getting under his skin; perhaps testing the limits of what he could endure. The realisation dawned on him with great clarity that he'd often played into her hands, letting her goad him until he flew into a rage. Together they had been toxic.

Chapter 31

Belinda passed Ricardo in the corridor, and he frantically pulled her into the cleaners storeroom, panic etched on his young face. Ricardo spoke in a low hiss, 'Why did you ask me for that girl's cabin number? I told the officers that a lady asked me for this, but I did not identify you.'

Belinda's eyes widened, her voice sharp. 'I just needed to give her back a borrowed item…Did you say anything about being offered money for this information?'

Ricardo nodded, 'I did…then I said I did not take it. I protected you.'

Belinda snorted, 'You protected yourself more to the point… but okay I believe you. I've already been questioned because I fit the description of the lady you mentioned. Thankfully, I seem to have a few clones in the vicinity so I'm not the only one who fit the bill. I denied it was me and there is obviously nothing on the ship's cameras to prove otherwise, so I think it's safe to say we are off the hook.'

Relief flooded Ricardo's face as he exhaled loudly. 'I've been so worried. I have learned a valuable lesson and will never take money from passengers again.'

Belinda was curious. 'Have other passengers offered you money other than me?'

Ricardo nodded solemnly. 'I was greedy and took the bribe, I will never do this again. You already know this right? I'm guessing so because the girl who paid me in exchange for chemicals was your cabin neighbour, your friend…'

Belinda's mouth dropped open in shock and Ricardo realised his mistake. He stammered. 'I… I thought you were both up to something together. I have been praying I was wrong. I was first to find the girl who was killed. I found a strong smell of chemicals throughout the cabin. Please tell me her death has nothing to do with your friend?'

Belinda stared at Ricardo as a chill ran over her.

'I barely know that girl,' she replied stiffly as she promptly turned on her heel and left.

Ricardo stood for a long time staring down the corridor. He was no detective, yet even he could tell there was something was rather odd about the passengers on this ship. The sooner it returned to Barcelona the better. He was not getting involved any further; he must protect himself and was keeping quiet. As far as he was concerned his questioning was over and done with.

Belinda went outside to sit on a lounger, reeling with the information she'd just received about Kayla.

What the hell?

The sun was low in the afternoon sky, casting elongated shadows across the sparkling pool deck. Sunbathers were sprawled out on deckchairs and Belinda noticed a group of women sipping brightly coloured cocktails while they chattered with abandon. Belinda suddenly felt the weight of the world press down on her as she looked on at their carefree manner. Belinda stepped into the cool water hoping to feel refreshed, however her anxiety only intensified as the jovial laughter around her clashed with the chaos swirling in her mind. Shaking her head, she changed her mind and returned to her sun lounger where she fixated on the droplets of water glistening on her wet skin.

I don't really know who Kayla is at all. Maybe I don't really know Richard either. Do we ever truly know anyone?

Belinda's phone vibrated on the slick surface of the table beside her, pulling her from her thoughts. She glanced down to read that Richard was on the walking deck *again*. Belinda hesitated for a moment, then tapped out her message:

It's time to talk, I know everything, and I have your secret camera.

With a pounding heart, she pressed send. The thought of confronting Richard sent chills racing up her spine. Her husband's response was instantaneous.

Meet me at the café by the bow. I will tell you everything.

Belinda's stomach knotted as she rose from her spot; her mind whirling with trepidation at the thought of finally confronting Richard about his act of betrayal. As much as she wanted to get this over with, she also felt herself stalling. She knew it was make or break time and whatever was said between her and Richard at this point could never be unsaid. Belinda made a point of carefully folding her beach towel, hovering by the sun lounger as she built up the courage to move.

Slowly Belinda made her way to the café; her senses alert as she navigated through the seemingly blissful couples and families. All the passengers she passed by seemed ominous somehow, every snippet of cheery conversation a reminder of her horrible predicament. As Belinda approached the doorway of the cafe, she spotted Richard seated at a table near the window. He looked up, a flash of relief in his eyes that swiftly morphed into apprehension as he noticed the tension etched across her face.

'Hi,' Richard said softly, his voice surprisingly calm.

Belinda slid into the chair opposite him, folding her arms as she stared him down. She noticed he'd ordered scones with jam and cream for them both. Something that they often enjoyed together. She swallowed a lump in her throat.

'Cut the pleasantries, Richard.' Belinda's voice trembled, and he was aware it was fuelled by betrayal and fear.

'Listen,' Richard leaned forward, his voice urgent. 'The last thing I wanted was for you to get hurt. I've been a bloody moron… I…I well I don't really need to tell you the details, do I? You've obviously seen the texts and footage.' Richard lowered his head for a few seconds. When he lifted it again, he met his wife's gaze with sorrow in his eyes.

'No more lies or secrecy, okay? I will just come out with it and own up. It's the decent thing to do… I'm disgusted to say that I had sex with a girl who blackmailed me for money… her and her sidekick were into extorting money from men and evidently business is good on cruises as they are full of middle-aged men going through a midlife crisis, such as yours truly. The girl... she ugh, she is the one who was found dead…

I'm fairly sure she must have died at the hands of a bloke who doesn't appreciate being blackmailed. Her death has definitely got nothing to do with me.'

Belinda's heart thumped as the weight of Richard's admission settled in. She glared ominously at her husband. 'I could happily kill you right now you stupid bastard.'

Belinda turned her head away as her anger turned into hot salty tears. Richard grabbed his wife's hand from across the table.

'Belinda, you have every right to kick me out and tell me I've lost everything. If you do, it will be my own stupid fault. Strangely though, this experience has given me the kick up the butt that I needed. It made me realise how much I love and value you, and don't want to lose you. I realised that being with a good woman is the most important thing of all. But we had lost each other love, can you admit that? We haven't been near each other in god knows how long and I stupidly gave into the urge. I'm honestly so ashamed. Can you ever forgive me?'

Belinda blinked away her rapidly falling tears and dabbed at her eyes with a paper napkin. 'I honestly don't know, Richard. I'm still processing it all. You have hurt me deeply.'

Richard's shoulders sagged, and for a moment, he aged right before her eyes; the weight of his guilt pressing down on him.

'I was a stupid old fool and now I will have to deal with the consequences whatever they might be.'

Richard seemed so incredibly sad and sincere that Belinda's heart constricted in confusion. Their marriage was on a new ground, a place where anger would now coexist with vulnerability. Whether they liked it or not, their story was being rewritten. Whether it ended up as a tragedy or a tale of redemption, they were yet to find out.

Richard felt hopeful that perhaps they might rediscover the parts of each other they thought were long gone. With a final squeeze of his hand, Belinda stood up; her heart heavy, yet at the same time lighter somehow. She knew that the road ahead might be difficult to navigate, yet deep down she knew she still loved her husband. As much as he had hurt her beyond measure and broken her trust, she was wise enough to see that this one act was not the sum total of who he was. Not that she was going to make it easy for her errant husband; he could damn well grovel. Richard looked at his wife with renewed gratitude. He could see deep in her eyes that she still loved him. Richard felt a surge of hope that they might just make it after all.

'Take all the time you need, Belinda. But if you took that mini camera from my blazer pocket, you must give it to officer Rossi as soon as possible. It's crucial evidence.'

Belinda nodded. 'That much I will do. I kept it because I was initially worried you had something to do with that girl being killed…'

Richard interrupted, 'What the fuck? Are you serious?' His earlier smile turned to a look of outrage.

Belinda was quick to clarify. 'I don't mean that I believe you are capable of murder, Richard. I was worried it had occurred in an accidental way, in a scuffle or something, you know? But I've just heard something pretty alarming from our cabin attendant.

I think I might just know who the responsible culprit is for that girl's death…'

Chapter 32

Being at sea had been the catalyst for Kayla to grapple with the conflicting concepts of imagination and reality. Somehow floating in the ocean meant that her true character was free to emerge, and she no longer felt the need to be the sweet innocent Kayla she presented to the world. Kayla had played the part of the gentle, compliant girl to a tee. She was the perfect girlfriend, at least to begin with. Kayla wore the mask so well that she sometimes forgot the ugly version existed beneath the surface. It was easier to smile and nod, to take on the role assigned to her, than to admit her true depraved identity. She thought about her favourite quote from Psychologist Noam Shpancer.

Mental health is not a destination but a process. It's about how you drive, not where you are going.

Kayla's lip curled spitefully; *I enjoy using the helpless woman card to get away with the terrible things I do.*

Kayla had been detained following her confession and her prints had been matched to the murder weapon. She felt strangely calm. Now that the truth was out, Kayla could be free. She'd been looking for the perfect excuse to murder someone and, here at sea, she had lived out her fantasy. Kayla knew she'd be put away for a long time and she'd finally be among her own kind. She was honestly okay with it. It had been exhausting playing the game in the real world.

The moment Kayla had smashed the statue onto Tia's head, it had not felt at all like an evil crime. Rather it had been a wonderful release. It was cleansing, in a way; a purging of all the resentment that festered within her. As Kayla's eyes traced the outline of the dark room she was detained in, thoughts of Alex flooded her mind. Both of them had experienced the sharp sting of emotional abuse, physical abuse and neglect as children; although she'd never shared her story, instead allowing him to take centre stage in the victim role. Together, they'd been feeding off each other and somehow it had morphed into something electrifying and terrifying. Kayla thought back to what she'd learned from her psychology books.

We attracted each other as we have similar emotional wounds. We are bound by a trauma bond. We were stuck in a cycle of reactive abuse, and deep down we both knew it and got off on it.

Kayla became aroused as she thought of the chemistry she shared with Alex. They'd had mind-blowing sex and she'd definitely miss that. Their powerful animal magnetism had been intoxicating, and the explosive passion that followed had been like a drug. Now Kayla found a certain comfort in knowing she'd be among others who understood her depravity, her anguish; others who could reconcile the exhilaration she felt when she crossed lines that others dared not approach. Kayla would finally meet those who had also danced with their demons and come out the other side bruised, but ultimately liberated.

In Kayla's daydream, she imagined Alex standing at the entrance of the prison; a look of intrigue and yearning on his face as he stepped inside to embrace her. Perhaps they'd ignite a new kind of passion there, one that thrived amidst the confinement of their realities. She'd forgive him for his infidelity and violence, as he'd forgive her sins also. Kayla smiled, feeling exhilarated by the darkness that had enveloped her. She was exactly where she was meant to be. As she awaited her fate, she fell into a deep sleep, her subconscious mind returning to her childhood…

Seven-year-old Kayla was locked in her room again. It was cold and dark, and she had wet the bed. She looked at the cracked wardrobe mirror. Her bones were sticking out, and she knew people whispered about how skinny she was. Kayla peered at her pasty white skin, and the dark circles under her eyes. She couldn't remember the last time she ate. Kayla sat on her bed, a glum expression on her face. Her daddy worked away for long periods of time. When he came back, life was much better. When he was away, her mummy became depressed and drunk vodka until she passed out. Kayla's stomach rumbled. She stood up and banged her tiny fists against her bedroom door.

'Please mummy, let me out. I'm hungry and cold and I'm scared!'

The desperation in her voice reverberated around the room. It was met with only the stillness of the house, the intermittent creaking of the floorboards and the soft whisper of the wind outside. Kayla's mummy lay passed out on the sofa, an empty vodka bottle on the floor, oblivious to her daughter's pleas. Kayla huddled on the bed, her knees pulled tightly to her chest. The darkness of her bedroom pressed in around her, suffocating the little girl, as if the walls shared in her sense of despair.

When her daddy was home, Kayla's world was a bit better; she was the apple of his eye. Kayla's mummy made more effort to look after her to keep up the pretence. Those days were faraway dreams now. Her daddy's lengthy work trips often left Kayla feeling abandoned and unloved.

Kayla's breath caught in her throat as she thought about her mummy. It was painful to watch her transform into someone who barely spoke, lost within the depths of her drunken mind. Suddenly, a thought flickered in Kayla's mind. She shuffled over to the window, hope stirring faintly within her. Perhaps if she could pry it open; she could escape into the cool evening air or even call for help. Kayla tugged at the window latch with all her might, it wouldn't budge. Tears pooled in her eyes as frustration bubbled up inside her. What could she do?

Defeated, Kayla turned back towards her bed. As her gaze landed on her favourite soft toy dog named Mac, she gave a small smile. Mac was tattered and worn from years of hugs, but he had been her friend through it all. The little girl clasped him tightly, feeling the familiar softness against her cheek, wishing for the strength to overcome her fears.

As Kayla lay down on her bed, her stomach rumbled again, louder this time, a reminder that her mummy didn't care about her.

The next morning, Kayla heard her mummy moving around.

'Mummy?' she called hopefully. The footsteps paused, and for an agonising moment, silence fell again. Then came a muffled voice, thick and weary.

'Go back to sleep Kayla. Stop being a fucking pain in the arse or I'll smash you.'

The words stung like a slap, cold and harsh. Kayla hugged Mac tighter, his worn fabric bringing her a semblance of comfort amidst the chaos of her emotions. She lay there, staring at the ceiling as if it might magically transform into a ceiling dotted with stars, lighting up her darkened room with hope. The reality around her was suffocating, weighing heavily; a thick fog that wouldn't lift.

The hours passed, stretching into a hazy blend of longing and desperation. Kayla could hear her mummy clattering around in the kitchen, as cabinet doors slammed, and dishes rattled. Part of her wanted to stay in her room, hidden from the world, while another part of her yearned for connection, for her mummy's touch, even if it was only a light brush against her hair.

The rumbles of her stomach grew louder, and despite the weight of the day pressing down on her, she couldn't lie there anymore.

With wobbly legs, she pushed herself off the bed, feeling the chill of the floor beneath her bare feet. She crept toward the door, listening intently. The scuffling noises continued, a sign that her mummy was still up and about.

Taking a deep breath, she knocked lightly on the door.

'Mummy?' she called again, this time letting a tremor of hope seep into her voice. 'Can I come out? I'm really hungry…'

Silence met her again, but this time it was shorter. The footsteps quickened, and Kayla could hear her mumbling something incoherent. The moment stretched infinitely as she hovered at the door, unsure if she'd be met with kindness or anger.

Finally, the door was flung open. Kayla squinted at the light that poured in, temporarily blinding her. When her eyes adjusted, she saw her mummy standing there, dishevelled, her hair tangled, her eyes droopy with fatigue.

'What do you want?' Her mummy's voice was sharp and irritated, not the soothing tone Kayla desperately longed for.

'I'm hungry…' she ventured softly, her small hands fidgeting against each other. 'Can I please have something to eat?'

A flicker of irritation crossed her mummy's face before the shadows of guilt began to settle in.

'Fine, but stay out of my way or you will get a slap.'

Her mummy turned away, stumbling slightly as she walked back into the kitchen. As Kayla followed hopefully, her mummy rummaged through the cupboards. Kayla watched as she poured herself a glass of vodka before grabbing a mouldy loaf of bread.

'Mummy, can I have a bit of bread and butter please?' Kayla asked meekly.

Her mummy paused, and for a moment, Kayla thought she'd refuse. Then, mechanically, her mummy smeared the putrid butter on a slice of mouldy bread and handed it over.

'Here. That's all you get.'

With a swift movement, her mummy went to take another swig from her glass. Then she banged her glass down on the counter and it made Kayla jump, although she didn't care. The bread was hard, yet the butter melted on her tongue as she took her first bite of food in what felt like forever.

As she chewed slowly, she watched her mummy from the corner of her eye. The glass was emptying too quickly; she knew it wasn't a good sign.

'Mummy, can we go out somewhere today?' The question slipped from her lips before she could stop it.

Her mummy looked at her, the light in her eyes flickering dimly, similar to a candle on the verge of extinguishing.

'Maybe,' she muttered absently, lost in her thoughts.

Kayla took another small bite, while her eyes filled with fresh tears. As her mummy poured another drink, Kayla clung to Mac, feeling the familiar softness. She so wished he was a real black cocker spaniel and not a toy one.

'I'll be okay,' Kayla whispered softly to him, even as the heaviness in her heart remained.

'Do you love me, mummy?'

Kayla whispered the question timidly. She didn't expect a reply therefore she was startled when her mummy opened one eye and slurred her words.

'I wish you had never been fucking born. It was your daddy who wanted you, not me. Well guess what? Daddy dearest aint coming back this time! He has a bit on the side and now he has fucked off for good! Daddy doesn't give a shit about you anymore! As for me, I wish you'd fucking died at birth; you are the devil in disguise, do you know that? I've decided to put you into care, but first I'm gonna teach you a lesson you won't forget!'

Her mummy's fist connected with the side of the little girl's head and sent her flying across the room. Kayla lay on the floor, terrified, a searing pain shooting through her skull. Her mummy marched over and leant over Kayla, grabbing a fistful of her hair, her teeth bared with rage. Kayla's trembling only served to make her mummy angrier and she began laying punches into the little girl, watching her skinny body writhing in agony as the blows rained down on her. Kayla's raised hands did nothing to protect her.

'Get out of my sight and go back to your room!' her mummy roared.

Kayla staggered to her feet, as great gulping sobs shuddered through her tiny body. She grabbed at the coffee table to steady herself. As Kayla used her hands along the wall in the hallway to help fight the dizziness, she felt the hot sting of urine running down her legs. The dim light flickering above her barely masked the reality of her situation as her mummy's words echoed in her mind, twisting like a knife.

I wish you'd fucking died at birth.

The sting of those words was sharper than the pain radiating from her head. Kayla knew no one was able to help her or comfort her. This was her world, and it felt dark and suffocating; where there should be love, there was only hatred and fear.

Kayla hesitated at the threshold of her room. She was alone, surrounded by the faint scent of old, rotting memories of her daddy. He wasn't coming back. Kayla forced herself to move forward; the floor creaking beneath her as she shuffled towards the bed, her mind whirling in a cacophony of confusion and sorrow.

As Kayla crawled under the thin blanket, fear mingled with a flicker of hope. Maybe she'd wake up and find this was all a bad dream. She pressed her face into the pillow, stifling her sobs, wishing she could disappear altogether. Her small body shivered as the pain of what had happened washed over her.

After a while, she raised her head and peeked out cautiously. Her mummy was snoring, an empty bottle beside her as usual.

The world outside her room seemed eerily quiet, as though the house was holding its breath. Kayla's heart raced as she listened, straining to catch any noises that suggested her mummy might wake up. She clutched the thin blanket, feeling the harsh fabric against her skin.

No yell came. No footsteps thundered down the hall. With a sense of trepidation, she swung her legs out of bed and into the cold floor. The living room remained still, the remnants of the earlier chaos casting long shadows across the space. Kayla's heartbeat, a drum in her chest as she darted to the front door, her desire to escape overwhelming.

Kayla stepped outside, the cool night air washing over her like a soothing balm. The moon was high, casting gentle silver rays across the barren lawn. For a moment, she felt free from her mummy's fury, and she imagined she was floating above the ground like a leaf on the wind. The sense of liberation was fleeting, as the memories of the abuse she'd suffered anchored her feet to reality.

Faint laughter escaped from the neighbouring houses; young voices filled with the innocence she had long forgotten. A hollow pit formed in her stomach. Kayla knew she was different to them. While other children played without fear, she tiptoed around life, constantly looking over her shoulder.

Kayla knew she could not stay out much longer. She turned to go back, her stomach churning with apprehension as she recalled her mummy's threat.

I'm gonna teach you a lesson you won't forget, echoed in her mind. The thought of another beating made her heart race as she slipped back inside, the door creaking ominously behind her.

Back in her bedroom, Kayla sank to the floor and willed herself to find strength in the pain. She hated her daddy for going off with another woman. He had loved her and now he was gone forever. He left because her mummy was a nasty witch. In that moment, Kayla wished with all her heart that she could kill her mummy, and if she couldn't kill her then one day she'd kill someone just like her, so the world became a better place. Kayla wanted to kill someone who didn't care how much they hurt others. One day she might just do it.

Epilogue

Jake took a deep breath, steeling himself before stepping onto the deck where the crew gathered. Everyone immediately noticed Vincent's absence. The tension in the air was palpable, and the general vibe of uncertainty served as a reminder of the fear Vincent had fostered. As Jake walked toward them, he felt a mix of trepidation and resolve. This was not just about him anymore; it was about the crew and the toxic environment that had manifested under Vincent's influence.

'Listen up, everyone!' Jake's voice cut through the hushed conversations, drawing the crew's attention. The murmurs subsided, and the eyes of his colleagues were upon him; a mix of concern and curiosity mirrored in their faces.

'I want to be clear about something,' Jake continued, 'I've become aware of the rumours circulating about me and more importantly I know they've been spread intentionally. I also know who is behind them.'

Jake paused, watching as whispers erupted among the crew. Miranda stood to the side, her heart racing. She had initially made a choice to protect herself, but the burden of guilt weighed heavily on her. Miranda had helped Vincent to spread lies about Jake, yet she now saw the devastating consequences their actions had brought. She wondered if she'd already been implicated, if so, it was best to confess now.

With a glance at Jake, Miranda felt the tide of her conscience turn. It was time to speak up. 'Jake, I… I need to tell you something,' Miranda stammered, her voice rising above the murmurs. The crew turned, eyes widening as they anticipated her revelation.

'Vincent has been behind all of this. He's been spreading lies to manipulate the crew into turning against you. I'm ashamed to say that I got caught up in it too and want to confess I was also involved in the gossip.'

Jake's gaze bore into hers, a mixture of surprise and dismay. 'I can't lie about how disappointing that is to hear Miranda, although I appreciate your honesty and ownership.' Jake locked eyes with her, and she struggled to not look away.

Jake softened slightly, 'I will talk to you alone later and we can figure out between us what the consequences for this debacle should be.'

Miranda finally dropped her eyes. She felt awful, yet was glad she'd confessed her part in it all. She felt lighter despite the sense of shame.

Noticing the way the crew exchanged concerned glances, Jake continued, 'I will be pressing charges against Vincent for threatening to assault me and for the slander he has thrown my way. I want every single one of you to know that truth, honesty and respect are what we will cultivate in this crew from now on. You all deserve an environment free from fear and manipulation.'

Murmurs of agreement rippled through the group as they clapped in agreement. Maisie stepped forward, her posture straightening with newfound strength.

'As the Events Manager, I want to role model this too. I will give my statement about Vincent's slander. We cannot allow this type of behaviour to continue. It's time for a reform of our team culture.'

With Maisie's support, Jake felt a surge of confidence. He had allies: people who wanted to reclaim the spirit of their team. Setting an example was imperative, and he'd ensure that the future they built together was bright, free from manipulation and fear.

Claire stood beside her fellow performers, still clad in their sequined outfits from the final show.

'Come on, Claire! What's with the sourpuss face?' Joel nudged her playfully. 'You look as though you're sucking on a lemon!'

Claire forced a smile, yet it felt mighty thin. A lump of bitterness remained lodged in her throat, twisting her stomach into knots. Jake had been the highlight of her cruise experience, yet he'd also shattered her hopes of a long-term relationship with him. He had given her the old "let's stay friends" line, and the rejection still cut deep.

'Maybe she's processing too many feelings,' Joel quipped, winking at Claire.

The other performers all joined in a chorus of laughter, however the quip struck her. It was a low blow and their echoes of mirth only amplified her sense of isolation. Against Claire's will, memories of their last late-night conversation flooded her mind. The way Jake had leaned against the bar, casual and playful, with a smile that made her heart melt. Then when she had gathered the courage to lay her feelings bare, she had been met with a polite refusal. Jake's words danced mockingly in her thoughts.

I'm simply not in the head space for a serious relationship right now, Claire.

In her haze of disappointment and drunken bravado, Claire had confided too much to a group of passengers, sharing whispers of Jake not being as nice behind the scenes as his public persona suggested. It was a harmless bit of gossip, she had thought at the time, and now guilt gnawed at her insides. What had possessed her to say such a thing? Was she becoming a gossip like Vincent? Maybe it had been the wine coursing through her veins, or more likely it was the need to make herself feel better about Jake's casual indifference. Being intoxicated certainly felt better than the hurt simmering beneath the surface. Claire had seen the way most of the passengers looked up to Jake, his glowing reputation shining like a beacon in the night. A reputation she was now staining. Jake didn't deserve that, and she needed to put things right.

'Everything okay, Claire?' Joel asked, glancing at her with concern. The laughter faded, replaced by an unexpected silence carried on the wind. Claire sighed, fully aware of how her plummeting spirits contrasted with the lively atmosphere around her.

'Yeah, I'm fine. Just a bit tired.'

'Tired of what? The gorgeous ocean views?'

Joel raised an eyebrow and gestured at the horizon, trying to pull her back into their camaraderie.

'Come on, it's a beautiful day!'

'Beautiful day or not, I don't feel like putting on an act, okay?' Claire snapped back, her voice sharper than she intended. 'I'm done pretending everything's fine.'

An awkward silence lingered. The other performers exchanged glances, unsure of how to comfort her. Claire's heart ached as she realised she was letting a single rejection twist her into someone bitter and vindictive. Suddenly, from the edge of the crowd, she saw Jake stepping off the gangway. The sight of him sent a jolt of conflicting emotions spiralling through her: a mixture of hurt, anger and an undeniable longing. Jake waved at a group of passengers, the picture of charm with his easy grin and relaxed demeanour, completely unaware of the storm brewing in her heart only a few feet away.

Suddenly, something inside Claire clicked. She didn't want to be this spiteful version of herself who gossiped and revelled in the downfall of others. She'd be no better than Tia and Kayla, both of whom had turned out to be real pieces of work. If she'd learned one thing as a performer, it was the importance of authenticity. Jake's decision might have hurt her, yet lashing out wasn't going to heal her wounds. Instead, it would only deepen them. Taking a deep breath, she stepped away from her friends, a newfound resolve guiding her steps. She approached Jake, suddenly feeling strong. As he turned and met her gaze, his smile faltered slightly.

'Hey, Claire,' he said, his voice softening. 'Everything all right?'

With a shaking exhale, Claire nodded, pushing past the residual bitterness.

'Well, no. I'm not really okay but I wanted to say no hard feelings… and after reflection, I realise you were upfront all along about not wanting anything serious. I just chose not to hear it.'

Jake frowned, genuine concern etched across his features.

'I didn't mean to hurt you, Claire. I do feel shit about it. I'm glad to hear you are being so mature about it now.'

'Thanks, Jake,' Claire replied, her voice steadier. 'Can we stay in touch?'

Jake hesitated, then nodded. 'Sure.'

As they made their way down the quieter side of the ship, Claire felt a weight lift. She wasn't sure what might happen next, yet she felt a glimmer of hope for a friendship worth nurturing; one rooted in honesty instead of resentment.

Jake felt bad about the way he'd ended his fling with Claire. He grimaced as he recalled how she'd sobbed messily on his shoulder; his new beige suit covered in rivers of black mascara and patches of orange foundation. He was relieved that she'd finally accepted that they weren't a couple.

As the cruise finally came to an end, Jake grinned widely. Despite the stress and the drama this particular cruise had caused him, he knew he could not resist the excitement of doing it all again.

There was something about plunging into the unknown, stuck at sea with droves of strangers, people with murky pasts. Jake craved the thrill, the uncertainty, the joy of connections that could lead anywhere. Much like the ocean, life was unpredictable, sometimes it was beautiful, sometimes chaotic, yet always full of mysteries waiting to be uncovered. For Jake, life was about the thrill of the unknown, the allure of the open sea filled with strangers, each with their own tangled stories and unfinished tales. Though he had hoped for an easier sail, part of him craved the fast-paced drama that only life onboard could surely bring. There would be new passengers, new narratives, and certainly more challenges ahead.

Vincent was stood down from his role as the Assistant Cruise Director for multiple breaches of the code of conduct, including defamation. Only days earlier, Vincent had strutted around the ship with a misplaced sense of power, yet today he found himself completely isolated. It was a stark reminder of his downfall. The call from HR had been expected, yet the gravity of it struck him hard. Multiple breaches of his contract had painted him as the villain in a story he had long spun to paint himself as the hero. The rumblings of discontent among the crew had grown louder, with whispers circulating about his unethical manoeuvres to undermine Jake. Vincent languished in his own bitterness, as building resentment cut across his thoughts.

He characterised his life as a series of betrayals, dismissing the glaring reality that he had driven everyone in his life away through his own actions. His family had distanced themselves, his colleagues had disappeared and now he was left alone to deal with his choices. Vincent had no job and no family to return to. Instead, he decided to stay on the "poor me" train, and never get off.

Vincent frowned, rubbing his temples as the weight of isolation enveloped him. The crew, once willing to follow his lead, had grown wary of the man who stirred trouble and manipulated circumstances. He had stupidly orchestrated gossip campaigns against Jake, the rising star of the entertainment team, believing he could snuff out the competition by tarnishing Jake's reputation.

After packing up his belongings, Vincent stood, gripping the edge of his desk with white-knuckled fists. In his mind, he was still crafting elaborate stories that depicted him as a poor misunderstood genius surrounded by envious fools. The truth was stark and unyielding. He had sabotaged his marriage and friendships, severed bonds with his kids, and now, he was left grappling with the consequences of his actions.

His family had fallen away; they were tired of his excuses and dismissive behaviour.

You're always the victim, Vincent, his cousin Susan's words echoed in his mind. He had chosen his path, and now it was a lonely one, darkened further by the bitterness that clouded his heart. His kids were better off without him; he had nothing to offer them, especially now.

It was easier to keep wallowing in his perceived grievances that only deepened his despair. It was a comfortable position, one that required no action, no accountability. After all, it was easier to find solace in self-pity than to confront the wreckage of his own making.

Tony accepted his fate. He'd be up for a number of charges in relation to blackmail, extortion and sexual exploitation. He was in over his head at this point. All he could do to redeem himself was to help the police with their enquiries as much as possible. Tony sat on the cold, metal bench of the holding cell, his heart pounding in his chest as he stared at the stark, bare walls. The lights buzzed overhead, casting a harsh glow on his weary face.

Tony explained how it had begun on a small scale with Tia. It was a little side hustle to supplement his youth worker role; only a few gullible men on the side. It had fascinated him how easy it was to suck men in with Tia's looks and charm. Men found it hard to refuse her, and prominent men were both rich and afraid to be exposed.

Tony had thought he was so clever by outsmarting the system. After years of poorly paid youth work and mounting debt, he'd craved moving up in the world, to break free from his mundane existence. The deeper Tony got into it, the more entangled he became, until he was clawing his way up a ladder that only led downward in the end.

Now, Tony faced a number of charges; each one more serious than the last.

As the hours dragged on, a police officer finally approached the cell. Officer Delgado was a seasoned investigator, sharp-eyed and hardened from years of dealing with the underbelly. He looked at Tony, his expression unreadable.

'How are we going to play this, Tony?'

Tony took a deep breath, feeling the gravity of his decision settling on his shoulders like a shroud.

'I can help you,' Tony said, his voice steady despite the whirlwind of emotions within.

'I know things about people in high places…I'm not the only one who has taken advantage of kids in care. There's a network. It's much bigger than me. It's bigger than the care system itself… if you show me a bit of leniency, I can tell you more.'

Delgado raised an eyebrow, sceptical, 'Why should we trust you? You're a criminal much like the rest of them.'

'Because I can admit that what we do is fucked up,' Tony replied, his tone earnest. 'These guys, they're ruthless. A few of the kids are very young.'

The officer studied him, contemplating for a moment. The dim light caught his ID badge and, for a brief second, Tony felt the desperation weigh him down.

'All right,' Delgado finally said, his voice low. 'But understand that this is a one-way street. Cooperation will help with your case, yet you're still facing serious time. If I had my way you'd be castrated. You are scum do you hear me?'

The thought of prison horrified Tony. He imagined with terror the big overpowering men who might sexually assault him in the showers and beat him up. He knew all about power and control and using it to make smaller weaker victims complaint. Tony experienced an epiphany too little too late.

I think it's called karma.

Alex was still shaken at the events of the last few days. Kayla had dropped the charges against him. This was agreed to on the provision that he attend a men's behaviour change program. Alex couldn't help but shake his head at the irony given that Kayla was the one who'd turned out to be a cold-blooded murderer. Alex shuddered, he still could not understand how he could have read her so wrong. He was usually the abusive one. With Kayla he had met his match and more. Alex read the program outline and sighed. He was to attend an intensive 18-week program to learn to make better choices and develop safe and respectful relationships with women. He genuinely wanted it to work.

I'm sick of this cycle. It's time to man up and face my demons.

Alex was incredibly relieved to finally be off the ship and back at home. He decided to go for a drive and after a while he stopped near a lush green park to gather his thoughts before attending his first session. Alex leaned back against the worn leather of the driver's seat, his fingers gripping the steering wheel as he read through the program outline again, trying to focus. He muttered to himself hoping no one was watching him.

'I have eighteen weeks to learn how to be a better man.'

It felt hollow to think about it after everything that had happened, yet deep down, Alex knew it was a necessary step if he was to have any sort of future in the dating world.

Alex wanted to make meaningful change. He knew he was someone who lashed out in anger, who struggled with the demons within him. With Kayla, he had been blindsided; he hadn't seen her as a predator until it was too late. Alex had encountered his demons and wrestled with them alone. Now he must confront them publicly with a group of strangers: other men like him who were seeking help in order to change.

The first session was in a dull room filled with plastic chairs arranged in a circle. The walls were decorated with motivational posters that seemed like hollow platitudes. Alex felt a tinge of embarrassment wash over him as he took a seat beside a few other men who also wore expressions of uncertainty. The facilitator, a middle-aged man with salt-and-pepper hair, introduced himself as Gerry and welcomed them into the program.

'You're here because you want to change,' Gerry said, his voice warm yet firm. 'Together, we will explore the choices we make and how to create respectful relationships.'

As the introductions began, Alex listened to the stories that poured out around the circle. Grown men grappled with their pasts, tearing at the seams of their troubled lives. A few men spoke openly about their violent outbursts, while others recounted emotional manipulation that had left deep scars on their partners. Each story was a thread weaving into the shared narrative of hurt and recovery.

The group delved deeper into discussions about respect, empathy and accountability. Alex surprised himself with how much he learned, not only about women, but about himself. Alex began to recognise the cycles of rage and blame that had characterised his own relationships. Slowly, he acknowledged the fear that lay beneath his anger.

Alex realised how deeply his own insecurities had shaped not only his interactions with Kayla but his entire understanding of love. Their insane chemistry hadn't been enough; it had always been fuelled by fear and control.

Alex recalled moments with Kayla when he had felt powerful, how he had revelled in the control he believed he had. Then he remembered her smile so warm, even when it was illuminated by the cold light of betrayal. The memories haunted him, yet this time, he didn't push them aside. He embraced them, allowing himself to feel the truth of his actions.

As time went on, Alex noticed a shift within himself. He was truly beginning to take responsibility for the way he had treated women. It was a long road, yet he was committed to changing, to breaking the cycle that had consumed both him and Kayla. He shared his insights with the group.

'I used to think I had power when I lashed out at my girlfriend,' he said, standing at the centre of the circle. 'I thought I needed to overpower my partner to feel strong. But I was wrong. I've learned from Gerry that it's in vulnerability that we find connection.'

There were nods of understanding around him as an unspoken bond formed with his classmates. They were all working towards a hope that had felt elusive not long ago.

As he walked out of the room, a strange sense of lightness filled the air around him. The demons hadn't vanished, but they felt more like companions now, whispering lessons instead of threats. Alex was ready to embrace whatever came next with a renewed sense of self in a future yet unwritten.

The investigation concluded and Ricardo the cabin attendant miraculously came out of it unscathed. While he had not been implicated, his guilty conscience remained. Ricardo returned to his family in the Philippines and spent sleepless nights praying and lighting candles at the small shrine he had kept at home. 'Forgive me for my sins,' he whispered, staring at the flickering flame. 'I promise I will do better.'

Days turned into weeks, and yet he still felt the weight of giving out Tia's cabin number to Belinda and the chemicals he gave to Kayla in exchange for cash. The money was dirty, yet he had still kept it and gave it to his wife. Ricardo kept imagining officers bursting through his door at any minute, ripping apart his integrity and exposing the lies he had spun to keep his family safe and fed. When Ricardo found out later that Kayla had confessed to Tia's murder, he'd nearly passed out with shock and fear. She had appeared to be such a lovely young woman.

To date Kayla had not disclosed how she managed to access the chemicals used at the crime scene and the fear that she might decide to change her mind weighed on Ricardo heavily. Ricardo and his team had been told off for leaving the cleaning supply cupboards unlocked on many occasions, therefore it was fair to assume everyone thought Kayla had accessed them due to careless cleaning staff. As for Belinda, her saving grace had been that coincidently there happened to be a number of women fitting her description and every woman who was interviewed had denied asking to exchange money for Tia's cabin number. This had included Belinda who'd obviously been a convincing liar.

The fear of being caught lying about it all felt insurmountable, and yet, with each passing day that he remained untouched, Ricardo felt a flicker of hope. He still prayed every day, and when it was finally time to return to the cruise ship, he was filled with gratitude and a promise he felt he could keep. Ricardo shuddered at the thought of cleaning cabin number 12812 again. He wondered if it was haunted now. All Ricardo could do was his best every day. From now on he'd choose honesty over temptation. In the light of newfound hope and purpose, Ricardo stepped into his cabin attendant uniform and resolved to shape a legacy defined by compassion, service and resilience.

Rossi sat at the table set for two, the gentle glow of candlelight flickering against the walls. The air was thick with the aromatic scent of Cacio e pepe, a simple yet indulgent pasta dish that his girlfriend Elena had expertly crafted for him. Ricardo took a moment to appreciate the scene before him: the beautifully set table, soft jazz playing in the background, and the woman who had finally turned his haphazard life into something filled with warmth and romance. Rossi knew he was an attractive man; he'd seduced many women. Now it was time to find something more meaningful in his life and Elena fit the bill. She was beautiful, sophisticated and ridiculously sexy.

Elena's long, dark hair cascaded over her shoulders, and tonight, she had chosen a fitted black dress that accentuated her curves. As she bent over to retrieve the garlic bread from the oven, Rossi found his eyes lingering on her silhouette. He licked his thick lips, savouring not only the delicious home cooked meal but also the anticipation of taking her to bed later.

'Elena, you outdid yourself tonight,' Rossi said, raising his glass of Pinot Grigio in a toast. She turned, her radiant smile lighting up the room.

Elena ran her tongue over her top lip. 'I thought you could use a good meal after everything that happened on the cruise.'

Elena's eyes sparkled with mischief, and Rossi could sense the unspoken agreement between them. Now was the time for distractions and comfort after the chaos of the murder investigation he had been so hellishly caught up in.

Rossi nodded in agreement, recalling the events that had unfolded during the ill-fated cruise. Now, with the perpetrator locked up, it was time for them to refocus on each other. As the glamorous couple tucked into the rich pasta, Rossi turned the conversation toward lighter topics, reminiscing about their first date: a picnic in the park, where they had both nervously picked at their food between bursts of laughter. He found himself navigating the boundaries of their relationship, weaving through his feelings, and affirming their connection. It felt so easy with her. Elena's laughter fuelled his confidence, and he savoured every moment spent in her magnetic presence.

Elena took Rossi in as he ate his meal. The man simply oozed sex appeal without even trying. Everything about him set her nerve endings on edge. Elena's eyes lingered on his strong tanned forearms as he ate his dinner. She felt a tingling in her groin as she ran her eyes lazily over her boyfriend's sharp jawline and dark brooding eyes. She watched him place a forkful of pasta into his mouth and wished it was her tongue.

As the meal came to an end, Elena poured them each another glass of wine; the evening drawing into a comfortable lull. She leaned back in her chair, her eyes glistening with curiosity.

'So, do you think we can get back to normal now that the investigation is over?'

Rossi felt a grin spread across his face. 'With my luck? Probably not.' He raised his glass and clinked it against hers.

Rossi laughed, 'I wouldn't have it any other way though, it's my job after all. As long as you are still here ready to pick up where we left off then it works for me.'

Elena blushed, her cheeks slightly tinged with pink as she bit her lip, clearly pleased with his response. They finished their drinks, and Rossi felt a warm sense of contentment wash over him. Outside, the moonlight spilled through the window, casting a silver glow and he suddenly felt the urge to close the distance between them.

Without thinking, Rossi moved to Elana's side of the table, lifting her from her seat and pulling her into his arms. 'You know,' he said softly, 'I'm glad I met you. I don't care to chase other women anymore.'

Elena looked up at him, sincerity shining in her eyes. 'I feel the same way. Just you and me, right? We can deal with whatever comes next together.'

Rossi nodded as he crushed his fleshy lips onto hers. He finally knew what being in love was all about.

As Richard disembarked the ship, he felt lighter; the burden of blackmail lifted. He had faced the storm and emerged on the other side, ready to return to the life he had forged with Belinda: a life of honesty and trust. The cruise ship, once a symbol of his downfall, now represented a hard-won victory. Richard returned home with his wife, the weight of his secret lifted, ready to face the consequences of his actions, determined to rebuild the life he could have lost, one step at a time.

Back home in Sydney, Belinda stood in the kitchen, staring out of the window at the blooming garden that surrounded their home. It was a sun-drenched afternoon and the vibrant colours seemed in sharp contrast to the turmoil that clouded her mind. Richard had let her down. The pain of betrayal was still fresh and the weight of their shared life pressed heavily on her shoulders. After a few sleepless nights spent wrestling with her emotions, she decided it was time to confront the situation head-on.

'Richard,' she said, her voice steady yet quiet, as he entered the room. Her husband turned to face her, his expressions a mixture of hope and trepidation.

'I've been thinking,' Belinda continued, 'I'm willing to forgive you…only if you commit to marriage counselling.'

Richard's response was immediate. The flicker of relief was evident in his eyes, yet Belinda noticed the tension still remained. He nodded slowly, acknowledging the challenge ahead.

'I'll do whatever it takes, Belinda. I love you and I don't want to lose you.'

As the weeks went by, the couple attended marriage counselling sessions that peeled back the layers of their relationship. With every shared thought, and every tear shed, they began to rediscover the bond that had drawn them together all those years ago. It was an arduous journey, filled with uncomfortable truths and raw emotions, but it was one they chose to take together. During their sessions, they explored the dreams they had built as a couple: dreams of holidays, careers, and the bright-eyed children who'd filled their home with laughter that were now grown up.

'What do you want our future to look like?' Belinda asked one evening after a particularly intense counselling session. They were sharing a bottle of chilled rose wine, the remnants of dinner still on the table.

Richard took a deep breath as he considered his response thoughtfully. 'I just want us to be happy again. I want to see our kids getting married and hopefully giving us grandchildren one day. I want to watch them play in this garden.'

Richard gestured toward the window, where the sun began to set, casting a warm glow over the peaceful yard. The couple began to remember why they had fallen in love in the first place. Richard reminded his wife of stories from their early days and Belinda recounted the moments of support during the challenging times when they had stood by each other. They were partners in every sense of the word.

As the weeks turned into months, Belinda felt the resurgence of love within her. The betrayal still stung, yet Richard's commitment to change, coupled with their efforts in counselling, had begun to heal the wounds. One evening, sitting together on the porch, the crickets serenading them, Belinda reached for Richard's hand. She looked into his eyes and smiled, feeling lighter than she had in months.

'I think we're on the right path. It feels good. I feel good.'

Richard squeezed her hand, his own eyes glistening with unshed tears.

'I promise to cherish what we have from now on. You and our family mean everything to me.'

The couple resumed building their life, stronger than ever, taking baby steps towards a new chapter. The shadows of the past were still there, however they had transformed into lessons learned, a foundation to build upon rather than a weight to suppress them.

Together, Belinda and Richard had weathered the storm within, and now, a new dawn awaited them.

Gill D Anderson's first novel *Hidden from View* caused a sensation when it was first published as it threw readers head first into the seedy side of Adelaide in South Australia. Derived from Gill's child protection social work experience, this domestic drama showcases Gill's talent for writing hard hitting narratives with bold 'in your face' writing that doesn't hold back when it comes to depicting true to life depravity. Gill's clever use of six degrees of separation allows the reader to follow various deviant characters who have no awareness of their connection. *Trigger warning contains themes of violence, sex/ erotica and refers to child abuse (non-graphic).*

Gill went on to write 3 more novels as follows:

The Chosen Seven

Readers Favorite Gold medal winner in 2020 for in the category Fiction Drama

https://www.amazon.com/dp/B0821X35FB

Farzad Abed is an unhinged Iranian immigrant living in Australia. His sociopathic tendencies coupled with his political views make him extremely dangerous. Farzad wants the world to sit up and take notice of him and thus he randomly selects six bystanders to hold hostage at a city restaurant. Follow the roller coaster ride of emotions as these strangers find themselves embroiled in a terrifying siege orchestrated by a madman. The authorities scramble to put together a definitive plan of action to contain the situation quickly. But not everyone will come out alive…

Melita

Readers Favorite Gold Medal winner in 2021 in the category Fiction Women's

https://www.amazon.com/dp/B08D66WSBF

Melita is a novel about a mother and daughter who become estranged, depicting how family patterns can be repeated unless reflection and repair work takes place. If Emily and her mother can't break the cycle, the future generation will be compromised. As the only child of a single parent, and with little knowledge of her father or her paternal relatives, Emily struggles with identity issues throughout her childhood. Her mother's past and family history are shrouded in secrecy. Moving from Scotland to Vancouver, Emily unintentionally becomes estranged from her mother, Melita. The tension between Melita and her daughter finally comes to the surface and slowly, the truth about Melita's harsh childhood growing up in Malta unravels, revealing the inevitable impact it had on Emily's upbringing. Will the dysfunctional familial patterns remain entrenched forever? Or can Melita and Emily find a way to reconcile with the past?

Primed for Vengeance

Readers Favorite Silver Medal winner in 2022 in the category Fiction Social Issues

https://www.amazon.com/dp/B09BPS8W9R

Butch is a young man who plans to seek revenge towards those responsible for his suffering and he intends to punish them in the worst possible way. Butch harbours intense feelings of anger and self-loathing and blames his upbringing in state care for this. Will he ever find a way to reconcile his past to make peace with the present?

Sarah puts her heart and soul into her role managing young people living in state care. Her intentions are good, however out of the blue, her life starts to unravel in the most horrific way. Sarah finds herself in the middle of a terrible dilemma whereby the choices she makes have a much bigger impact on those she cares about than she could ever have imagined. Jock is a youth worker who brings the light into the darkest days of the young people he works with. Jock steps up to tackle the most challenging situation he has ever faced and does not waver. But will he succeed in his attempt to talk a troubled youth out of committing yet another heinous crime?

Acknowledgements

Thank you to all the readers who have taken a chance on me thus far and continued to follow my author journey up to now. It's surreal to believe that *The Storm Within* is my fifth novel! Like many other authors, I have days when I feel I can achieve anything and others where I feel like the biggest fraud! Thankfully the numerous writer friends I've accumulated along the way continue to remind me how unique and vulnerable we are to fly solo and put our imaginations out into the world for all to critique. Please do leave reviews if you can on Amazon and Goodreads and tag me on social media with photos of your books if you are that way inclined, I love it!

Thankyou to Jacki F for the manuscript appraisal and on point advice. I'd also like to thank the team at InHouse Publishing for helping me to perfect my book. My novels can be purchased from their bookstore in Queensland using the following link:
https://inhousebookstore.com.au/search?q=gill+d+anderson

Manufactured by Amazon.ca
Acheson, AB

16917339R00143